Raspberry Jam

By Carolyn Wells

Originally published in 1920

Raspberry Jam

© 2011 Resurrected Press
www.ResurrectedPress.com

Published by Resurrected Press

This classic book was handcrafted by Resurrected Press. Resurrected Press is dedicated to bringing high quality classic books back to the readers who enjoy them. These are not scanned versions of the originals, but, rather, quality checked and edited books meant to be enjoyed!

Please visit ResurrectedPress.com to view our entire catalogue!

ISBN 13: 978-1-937022-11-2

Printed in the United States of America

OTHER RESURRECTED PRESS MYSTERIES

By Carolyn Wells
The Man Who Fell Through the Earth
In the Onyx Lobby
Vicky Van

By J. S. Fletcher
The Orange-Yellow Diamond
The Middle Temple Murder
Scarhaven Keep
Ravensdene Court

By A. A. Milne
The Red House Mystery

By Agatha Christie
The Mysterious Affair at Styles

By Arthur Griffiths
The Passenger from Calais
The Rome Express

From the Dr. John Thorndyke Series
By R. Austin Freeman
The Red Thumb Mark
The Eye of Osiris
The Mystery of 31 New Inn
John Thorndyke's Cases
A Silent Witness
The Cat's Eye

By Arthur J. Rees
The Hampstead Mystery
The Mystery of the Downs
The Shrieking Pit
The Hand in The Dark
The Moon Rock

Visit RessurectedPress.com to see our entire catalog.

FOREWORD

In Carolyn Wells' 1920 *Raspberry Jam* the author presents her take on the classic locked room mystery. A wealthy businessman is found dead in the locked bedroom suite of his tenth floor Park Avenue apartment. The deceased had been in perfect health, there is no visible cause of death, nor are there any means that someone could have entered the bedroom. Only the wife and her elderly aunt shared the suite with the dead man. When it is discovered that the victim had been poisoned, the wife is the obvious and perhaps only suspect.

The setting for *Raspberry Jam* is New York City at the dawn of the Roaring Twenties. Showmen and charlatans abound. The book opens with a publicity stunt by a "psychic," the kind of public spectacle made popular by the numerous escape artists, wing walkers, flag-pole sitters and human flys that entertained the masses. The old, stuffy pre-war world is quickly changing under the influence of movies, women's suffrage, and new money, and the characters in the book, though they come from the top level of society, are uncertain of their place in the new order.

One of the sub-themes of the book is the supernatural. The character "The Great Hanlon" gives his performances as a man open to mental influences, though in private he admits that it is all a trick. Aunt Abby is a true believer. She believes in telepathy, mediums, and the spirits of the departed. Even the skeptics have their doubts. These attitudes mirror those of the public at the time, and Wells uses both the belief and the skepticism to good use in building and resolving the mystery.

Wells' favorite detective, Fleming Stone, makes an appearance. Stone is somewhat unusual as a detective.

He never seems to do that much, and most of the actual detecting ends up being done by others, in this case his assistant Fibsy. Still, his cases always end up being solved, and he is always there at the end to explain it all and tie up the loose ends.

While *Raspberry Jam* is an interesting mystery and the ultimate solution depends on one of the most unusual clues ever, the best thing about Carolyn Wells is her insight into the society and times she writes about. Resurrected Press is happy to bring this edition of Raspberry Jam to its readers.

About the Author

Carolyn Wells, June 18, 1862 - March 26, 1942 was an American writer and poet. She was best known for her books of poetry and humor until around 1910 she read one of Anna Katherine Green's mysteries and took up the genre. Many of her mysteries featured the detective Fleming Stone. She was married to Hadwin Houghton, heir to the Houghton-Mifflin publishing company. She was a collector of poetry by other authors, and, upon her death, she bequeathed her collection of the works of Walt Witman to the Library of Congress.

Greg Fowlkes
Editor-In-Chief
Resurrected Press
www.ResurrectedPress.com

TABLE OF CONTENTS

CHAPTER 1: THE GREAT HANLON

"You may contradict me as flat as a flounder, Eunice, but that won't alter the facts. There is something in telepathy—there is something in mind-reading—"

"If you could read my mind, Aunt Abby, you'd drop that subject. For if you keep on, I may say what I think, and—"

"Oh, that won't bother me in the least. I know what you think, but your thoughts are so chaotic—so ignorant of the whole matter—that they are worthless. Now, listen to this from the paper: 'Hanlon will walk blindfolded—blindfolded, mind you —through the streets of Newark, and will find an article hidden by a representative of The Free Press.' Of course, you know, Eunice, the newspaper people are on the square—why, there'd be no sense to the whole thing otherwise! I saw an exhibition once, you were a little girl then; I remember you flew into such a rage because you couldn't go. Well, where was I? Let me see—oh, yes—'Hanlon—' H'm— h'm—why, my goodness! it's to-morrow! How I do want to go! Do you suppose Sanford would take us?"

"I do not, unless he loses his mind first. Aunt Abby, you're crazy! What is the thing, anyway? Some common street show?"

"If you'd listen, Eunice, and pay a little attention, you might know what I'm talking about. But as soon as I say telepathy you begin to laugh and make fun of it all!"

"I haven't heard anything yet to make fun of. What's it all about?"

But as she spoke, Eunice Embury was moving about the room, the big living-room of their Park Avenue apartment, and in a preoccupied way was patting her

household gods on their shoulders. A readjustment of the
pink carnations in a tall glass vase, a turning round of a
long-stemmed rose in a silver holder, a punch here and
there to the pillows of the davenport and at last dropping
down on her desk chair as a hovering butterfly settles on
a chosen flower.

A moment more and she was engrossed in some
letters, and Aunt Abby sighed resignedly, quite hopeless
now of interesting her niece in her project.

"All the same, I'm going," she remarked, nodding her
head at the back of the graceful figure sitting at the desk.
"Newark isn't so far away; I could go alone—or maybe
take Maggie—she'd love it—'Start from the Oberon
Theatre—at 2 P.M.—' 'Him, I could have an early lunch
and—'hidden in any part of the city—only mentally
directed—not a word spoken—' Just think of that,
Eunice! It doesn't seem credible that—oh, my goodness!
tomorrow is Red Cross day! Well, I can't help it; such a
chance as this doesn't happen twice. I wish I could coax
Sanford—"

"You can't," murmured Eunice, without looking up
from her writing.

"Then I'll go alone!" Aunt Abby spoke with spirit, and
her bright black eyes snapped with determination as she
nodded her white head. "You can't monopolize the
willpower of the whole family, Eunice Embury!"

"I don't want to! But I can have a voice in the matters
of my own house and family yes, and guests! I can't spare
Maggie to-morrow. You well know Sanford won't go on
any such wild goose chase with you, and I'm sure I won't.
You can't go alone —and anyway, the whole thing is bosh
and nonsense. Let me hear no more of it!"

Eunice picked up her pen, but she cast a sidelong
glance at her aunt to see if she accepted the situation.

She did not. Miss Abby Ames was a lady of decision,
and she had one hobby, for the pursuit of which she
would attempt to overcome any obstacle.

"You needn't hear any more of it, Eunice," she said, curtly. "I am not a child to be allowed out or kept at home! I shall go to Newark to-morrow to see this performance, and I shall go alone, and—"

"You'll do nothing of the sort! You'd look nice starting off alone on a railroad trip! Why, I don't believe you've ever been to Newark in your life! Nobody has! It isn't done!"

Eunice was half whimsical, half angry, but her stormy eyes presaged combat and her rising color indicated decided annoyance.

"Done!" cried her aunt. "Conventions mean nothing to me! Abby Ames makes social laws—she does not obey those made by others!"

"You can't do that in New York, Aunt Abby. In your old Boston, perhaps you had a certain dictatorship, but it won't do here. Moreover, I have rights as your hostess, and I forbid you to go skylarking about by yourself."

"You amuse me, Eunice!"

"I had no intention of being funny, I assure you."

"While not distinctly humorous, the idea of your forbidding me is, well—oh, my gracious, Eunice, listen to this: 'The man chosen for Hanlon's "guide" is the Hon. James L. Mortimer—' —h'm—'High Street—' Why, Eunice, I've heard of Mortimer —he's—"

"I don't care who he is, Aunt Abby, and I wish you'd drop the subject."

"I won't drop it—it's too interesting! Oh, my! I wish we could go out there in the big car—then we could follow him round—"

"Hush! Go out to Newark in the car! Trail round the streets and alleys after a fool mountebank! With a horde of gamins and low, horrid men crowding about—"

"They won't be allowed to crowd about!"

"And yelling—"

"I admit the yelling—"

"Aunt Abby, you're impossible!" Eunice rose, and scowled irately at her aunt. Her temper, always quick, was at times ungovernable, and was oftenest roused at the suggestion of any topic or proceeding that jarred on her taste. Exclusive to the point of absurdity, fastidious in all her ways, Mrs. Embury was, so far as possible, in the world but not of it.

Both she and her husband rejoiced in the smallness of their friendly circle, and shrank from any unnecessary association with hoi polloi.

And Aunt Abby Ames, their not entirely welcome guest, was of a different nature, and possessed of another scale of standards. Secure in her New England aristocracy, calmly conscious of her innate refinement, she permitted herself any lapses from conventional laws that recommended themselves to her inclination.

And it cannot be denied that the investigation of her pet subject, the satisfaction of her curiosity concerning occult matters and her diligent inquiries into the mysteries of the supernatural did lead her into places and scenes not at all in harmony with Eunice's ideas of propriety.

"Not another word of that rubbish, Auntie; the subject is taboo," and Eunice waved her hand with the air of one who dismisses a matter completely.

"Don't you think you can come any of your high and mighty airs on me!" retorted the elder lady. "It doesn't seem so very many years ago that I spanked you and shut you in the closet for impudence. The fact that you are now Mrs. Sanford Embury instead of little Eunice Ames hasn't changed my attitude toward you!"

"Oh, Auntie, you are too ridiculous!" and Eunice laughed outright. "But the tables are turned, and I am not only Mrs. Sanford Embury but your hostess, and, as such, entitled to your polite regard for my wishes."

"Tomfoolery talk, my dear; I'll give you all the polite regard you are entitled to, but I shall carry out my own wishes, even though they run contrary to yours. And to-morrow I prance out to Newark, N.J., your orders to the contrary notwithstanding!"

The aristocratic old head went up and the aristocratic old nose sniffed disdainfully, for though Eunice Embury was strong-willed, her aunt was equally so, and in a clash of opinions Miss Ames not infrequently won out.

Eunice didn't sulk, that was not her nature; she turned back to her writing desk with an offended air, but with a smile as of one who tolerates the vagaries of an inferior. This, she knew, would irritate her aunt more than further words could do.

And yet, Eunice Embury was neither mean nor spiteful of disposition. She had a furious temper, but she tried hard to control it, and when it did break loose, the spasm was but of short duration and she was sorry for it afterward. Her husband declared he had tamed her, and that since her marriage, about two years ago, his wise, calm influence had curbed her tendency to fly into a rage and had made her far more equable and placid of disposition.

His methods had been drastic—somewhat like those of Petruchio toward Katherine. When his wife grew angry, Sanford Embury grew more so and by harder words and more scathing sarcasms he—as he expressed it—took the wind out of her sails and rendered her helplessly vanquished.

And yet they were a congenial pair. Their tastes were similar; they liked the same people, the same books, the same plays. Eunice approved of Sanford's correct ways and perfect intuitions and he admired her beauty and dainty grace.

Neither of them loved Aunt Abby—the sister of Eunice's father —but her annual visit was customary and unavoidable.

The city apartment of the Sanfords had no guestroom, and therefore the visitor must needs occupy Eunice's charming boudoir and dressing-room as a bedroom. This inconvenienced the Emburys, but they put up with it perforce.

Nor would they have so disliked to entertain the old lady had it not been for her predilection for occult matters. Her visit to their home coincided with her course of Clairvoyant Sittings and her class of Psychic Development.

These took place at houses in undesirable, sometimes unsavory localities and only Aunt Abby's immovable determination made it possible for her to attend.

A large text-book, "The Voice of the Future," was her inseparable companion, and one of her chief, though, as yet, unfulfilled, desires was to have a Reading given at the Embury home by the Swami Ramananda.

Eunice, by dint of stern disapproval, and Sanford, by his good-natured chaffing and ridicule had so far prevented this calamity, but both feared that Aunt Abby might yet outwit them and have her coveted seance after all.

Outside of this phase of her character, Miss Ames was not an undesirable guest. She had a good sense of humor, a kind and generous heart and was both perceptive and responsive in matters of household interest.

Owing to the early death of Eunice's mother, Aunt Abby had brought up the child, and had done her duty by her as she saw it.

It was after Eunice had married that Miss Ames became interested in mystics and with a few of her friends in Boston had formed a circle for the pursuance of the cult.

Her life had otherwise been empty, indeed, for the girl had given her occupation a-plenty, and that removed, Miss Abby felt a vague want of interest.

Eunice Ames had not been easy to manage. Nor was Miss Abby Ames the best one to be her manager.

The girl was headstrong and wilful, yet possessed of such winsome, persuasive wiles that she twisted her aunt round her finger.

Then, too, her quick temper served as a rod and many times Miss Ames indulged the girl against her better judgment lest an unpleasant explosion of wrath should occur and shake her nervous system to its foundation. So Eunice grew up, an uncurbed, untamed, self-willed and self-reliant girl, making up her quarrels as fast as she picked them and winning friends everywhere in spite of her sharp tongue.

And so, on this occasion, neither of the combatants held rancor more than a few minutes. Eunice went on writing letters and Miss Abby went on reading her paper, until at five o'clock, Ferdinand the butler brought in the tea-things.

"Goody!" cried Eunice, jumping up. "I do want some tea, don't you, Aunty?"

"Yes," and Miss Ames crossed the room to sit beside her. "And I've an idea, Eunice; I'll take Ferdinand with me to-morrow!"

The butler, who was also Embury's valet and a general household steward, looked up quickly. He had been in Miss Ames' employ for many years before Eunice's marriage, and now, in the Embury's city home was the indispensable major-domo of the establishment.

"Yes," went on Aunt Abby, "that will make it all quite circumspect and correct. Ferdinand, tomorrow you accompany me to Newark, New Jersey."

"I think not," said Eunice quietly, and dismissing Ferdinand with a nod, she began serenely to make the tea.

"Don't be silly, Aunt Abby," she said; "you can't go that way. It would be all right to go with Ferdinand, of course, but what could you do when you, reached Newark? Race about on foot, following up this clown, or whoever is performing?"

"We could take a taxicab—"

"You might get one and you might not. Now, you will wait till San comes home, and see if he'll let you have the big car."

"Will you go then, Eunice?"

"No; of course not. I don't go to such fool shows! There's the door! Sanford's coming."

A step was heard in the hall, a cheery voice spoke to Ferdinand as he took his master's coat and hat and then a big man entered the living-room.

"Hello, girls," he said, gaily; "how's things?"

He kissed Eunice, shook Aunt Abby's hand and dropped into an easy chair.

"Things are whizzing," he said, as he took the cup Eunice poured for him. "I've just come from the Club, and our outlook is rosy-posy. Old Hendricks is going to get, badly left."

"It's all safe for you, then, is it?" and Eunice smiled radiantly at her husband.

"Right as rain! The prize-fights did it! They upset old Hendrick's apple-cart and spilled his beans. Lots of them object to the fights because of the expense—fighters are a high-priced bunch—but I'm down on them because I think it bad form—"

"I should say so!" put in Eunice, emphatically.

"Bad form for an Athletic Club of gentlemen to have brutal exhibitions for their entertainment."

"And what about the Motion-Picture Theatre?"

"The same there! Frightful expense,—and also rotten taste! No, the Metropolitan Athletic Club can't stoop to such entertainments. If it were a worth-while little playhouse, now, and if they had a high class of performances, that would be another story. Hey, Aunt Abby? What do you think?"

"I don't know, Sanford, you know I'm ignorant on such matters. But I want to ask you something. Have you read the paper to-day?"

"Why, yes, being a normal American citizen, I did run through the Battle-Ax of Freedom. Why?"

"Did you read about Hanlon—the great Hanlon?"

"Musician, statesman or criminal? I can't seem to place a really great Hanlon. By the way, Eunice, if Hendricks blows in, ask him to stay to dinner, will you? I want to talk to him, but I don't want to seem unduly anxious for his company."

"Very well," and Eunice smiled; "if I can persuade him, I will."

"If you can!" exclaimed Miss Abby, her sarcasm entirely unveiled. "Alvord Hendricks would walk the plank if you invited him to do so!"

"Who wouldn't?" laughed Embury. "I have the same confidence in my wife's powers of persuasion that you seem to have, Aunt Abby; and though I may impose on her, I do want her to use them upon me deadly r-rival!"

"You mean rival in your club election," returned Miss Ames, "but he is also your rival in another way."

"Don't speak so cryptically, Aunt, dear. We all know of his infatuation for Eunice, but he's only one of many. Think you he is more dangerous than, say, friend Elliott?"

"Mason Elliott? Oh, of course, he has been an admirer of Eunice since they made mud-pies together."

"That's two, then," Embury laughed lightly. "And Jim Craft is three and Halliwell James is four and Guy Little—"

"Oh, don't include him, I beg of you!" cried Eunice; "he flats when he sings!"

"Well, I could round up a round dozen, who would willingly cast sheeps' eyes at my wife, but—well, they don't!"

"They'd better not," laughed Eunice, and Embury added, "Not if I see them first!"

"Isn't it funny," said Aunt Abby, reminiscently, "that Eunice did choose you out of that Cambridge bunch."

"I chose her," corrected Embury, "and don't take that wrong! I mean that I swooped down and carried her off under their very noses! Didn't I, Firebrand?"

"The only way you could get me," agreed Eunice, saucily.

"Oh, I don't know!" and Embury smiled. "You weren't so desperately opposed."

"No; but she was undecided," said Aunt Abby; "why, for weeks before your engagement was announced, Eunice couldn't make up her mind for certain. There was Mason Elliott and Al Hendricks, both as determined as you were."

"I know it, Aunt. Good Lord, I guess I knew those boys all my life, and I knew all their love affairs as well as they knew all mine."

"You had others, then?" and Eunice opened her brown eyes in mock amazement.

"Rather! How could I know you were the dearest girl in the world if I had no one to compare you with?"

"Well, then I had a right to have other beaux."

"Of course you did! I never objected. But now, you're my wife, and though all the men in Christendom may admire you, you are not to give one of them a glance that belongs to me."

"No, sir; I won't," and Eunice's long lashes dropped on her cheeks as she assumed an absurdly overdone meekness.

"I was surprised, though," pursued Aunt Abby, still reminiscent, "when Eunice married you, Sanford. Mr. Mason is so much more intellectual and Mr. Hendricks so much better looking."

"Thank you, lady!" and Embury bowed gravely. "But you see, I have that—er—indescribable charm—that nobody can resist."

"You have, you rascal!" and Miss Ames beamed on him. "And I think this a favorable moment to ask a favor of your Royal Highness."

"Out with it. I'll grant it, to the half of my kingdom, but don't dip into the other half."

"Well, it's a simple little favor, after all. I want to go out to Newark to-morrow in the big car—"

"Newark, New Jersey?"

"Is there any other?"

"Yep; Ohio."

"Well, the New Jersey one will do me, this time. Oh, Sanford, do let me go! A man is going to will another man—blindfolded, you know—to find a thingumbob that he hid—nobody knows where—and he can't see a thing, and he doesn't know anybody and the guide man is Mr. Mortimer—don't you remember, his mother used to live in Cambridge? she was an Emmins—well, anyway, it's the most marvelous exhibition of thought transference, or mind-reading, that has ever been shown—and I must go. Do let me?—please, Sanford!"

"My Lord, Aunt Abby, you've got me all mixed up! I remember the Mortimer boy, but what's he doing blindfolded?"

"No; it's the Hanlon man who's blindfolded, and I can go with Ferdinand—and—"

"Go with Ferdinand! Is it a servants' ball—or what?"

"No, no; oh, if you'd only listen, Sanford!"

"Well, I will, in a minute, Aunt Abby. But wait till I tell Eunice something. You see, dear, if Hendricks does show up, I can pump him judiciously and find out where the Meredith brothers stand. Then—"

"All right, San, I'll see that he stays. Now do settle Aunt Abby on this crazy scheme of hers. She doesn't want to go to Newark at all—"

"I do, I do!" cried the old lady.

"Between you and me, Eunice, I believe she does want to go," and Embury chuckled. "Where's the paper, Aunt? Let me see what it's all about."

"'A Fair Test,'" he read aloud. "'Positive evidence for or against the theory of thought transference. The mysterious Hanlon to perform a seeming miracle. Sponsored by the Editor of the Newark Free Press, assisted by the prominent citizen, James L. Mortimer, done in broad daylight in the sight of crowds of people, tomorrow's performance will be a revelation to doubters or a triumph indeed for those who believe in telepathy.' H'm —h'm—but what's he going to do?"

"Read on, read on, Sanford," cried Aunt Abby, excitedly.

"'Starting from the Oberon Theatre at two o'clock, Hanlon will undertake to find a penknife, previously hidden in a distant part of the city, its whereabouts known only to the Editor of the Free Press and to Mr. Mortimer. Hanlon is to be blindfolded by a committee of citizens and is to be followed, not preceded by Mr. Mortimer, who is to will Hanlon in the right direction, and to "guide" him merely by mental will-power. There is to be no word spoken between these two men, no personal contact, and no possibility of a confederate or trickery of any sort.

"' Mr. Mortimer is not a psychic; indeed, he is not a student of the occult or even a believer in telepathy, but he has promised to obey the conditions laid down for him. These are merely and only that he is to follow Hanlon, keeping a few steps behind him, and mentally will the blindfolded man to go in the right direction to find the hidden knife.'"

"Isn't it wonderful, Sanford," breathed Miss Abby, her eyes shining with the delight of the mystery.

"Poppycock!" and Embury smiled at her as a gullible child. "You don't mean to say, aunt, that you believe there is no trickery about this!"

"But how can there be? You know, Sanford, it's easy enough to say 'poppycock' and 'fiddle-dee-dee!' and 'gammon' and 'spinach!' But just tell me how it's done— how it can be done by trickery? Suggest a means however complicated or difficult—"

"Oh, of course, I can't. I'm no charlatan or prestidigitateur! But you know as well as I do, that the thing is a trick—"

"I don't! And anyway, that isn't the point. I want to go to see it. I'm not asking your opinion of the performance, I'm asking you to let me go. May I?"

"No, indeed! Why, Aunt Abby, it will be a terrible crowd—a horde of ragamuffins and ruffians. You'd be torn to pieces—"

"But I want to, Sanford," and the old lady was on the verge of tears. "I want to see Hanlon—"

"Hanlon! Who wants to see Hanlon?"

The expected Hendricks came into the room, and shaking hands as he talked, he repeated his question: "Who wants to see Hanlon? Because I do, and I'll take any one here who is interested."

"Oh, you angel man!" exclaimed Aunt Abby, her face beaming. "I want to go! Will you really take me, Alvord?"

"Sure I will! Anybody else? You want to see it, Eunice?"

"Why, I didn't, but as Sanford just read it, it sounded interesting. How would we go?"

"I'll run you out in my touring car. It won't take more'n the afternoon, and it'll be a jolly picnic. Go along, San?"

"No, not on your life! When did you go foolish, Alvord?"

"Oh, I always had a notion toward that sort of thing. I want to see how he does it. Don't think I fall for the telepathy gag, but I want to see where the little joker is,—and then, too, I'm glad to please the ladies."

"I'll go," said Eunice; "that is, if you'll stay and dine now —and we can talk it over and plan the trip."

"With all the pleasure in life," returned Hendricks.

Chapter 2: A Trip To Newark

Perhaps no factor is more indicative of the type of a home life than its breakfast atmosphere. For, in America, it is only a small proportion, even among the wealthy who 'breakfast in their rooms.' And a knowledge of the appointments and customs of the breakfast are often data enough to stamp the status of the household.

In the Embury home, breakfast was a pleasant send-off for the day. Both Sanford and Eunice were of the sort who wake up wide-awake, and their appearance in the dining-room was always an occasion of merry banter and a leisurely enjoyment of the meal. Aunt Abby, too, was at her best in the morning, and breakfast was served sufficiently early to do away with any need for hurry on Sanford's part.

The morning paper, save for its headlines, was not a component part of the routine, and it was an exceptionally interesting topic that caused it to be unfolded.

This morning, however, Miss Ames reached the dining-room before the others and eagerly scanned the pages for some further notes of the affair in Newark.

But with the total depravity of inanimate things and with the invariable disappointingness of a newspaper, the columns offered no other information than a mere announcement of the coming event.

"Hunting for details of your wild-goose chase?" asked Embury, as he paused on the way to his own chair to lean over Aunt Abby's shoulder.

"Yes, and there's almost nothing! Why do you take this paper?"

"You'll see it all to-day, so why do you want to read about it?" laughed a gay voice, and Eunice came in, all fluttering chiffon and ribbon ends.

She took the chair Ferdinand placed for her, and picked up a spoon as the attentive man set grapefruit at her plate. The waitress was allowed to serve the others, but Ferdinand reserved to himself the privilege of waiting on his beloved mistress.

"Still of a mind to go?" she said, smiling at her aunt.

"More than ever! It's a perfectly heavenly day, and we'll have a good ride, if nothing more."

"Good ride!" chaffed Embury. "Don't you fool yourself, Aunt Abby! The ride from this burg to Newark, N.J., is just about the most Godforsaken bit of scenery you ever passed through!"

"I don't mind that. Al Hendricks is good company, and, any way, I'd go through fire and water to see that Hanlon show. Eunice, can't you and Mr. Hendricks pick me up? I want to go to my Psychic Class this morning, and there's no use coming way back here again."

"Yes, certainly; we're going about noon, you know, and have lunch in Newark."

"In Newark!" and Embury looked his amazement.

"Yes; Alvord said so last night. He says that new hotel there is quite all right. We'll only have time for a bite, anyway."

"Well, bite where you like. By the way, my Tiger girl, you didn't get that information from our friend last evening."

"No, San, I couldn't, without making it too pointed. I thought I could bring it in more casually to-day—say, at luncheon."

"Yes; that's good. But find out, Eunice, just where the Merediths stand. They may swing the whole vote."

"What vote?" asked Aunt Abby, who was interested in everything.

"Our club, Auntie," and Embury explained. "You know Hendricks is president—has been for years—and we're trying to oust him in favor of yours truly."

"You, Sanford! Do you mean you want to put him out and put yourself in his place?"

"Exactly that, my lady."

"But-how queer! Does he know it?"

"Rather! Yes—even on calm second thought, I should say Hendricks knows it!"

"But I shouldn't think you two would be friends in such circumstances."

"That's the beauty of it, ma'am; we're bosom friends, as you know; and yet, we're fighting for that presidency like two cats of Kilkenny."

"The New York Athletic Club, is it?"

"Oh, no, ma'am! Not so, but far otherwise. The Metropolitan Athletic Club if you please."

"Yes, I know—I'd forgotten the name."

"Don't mix up the two—they're deadly rivals."

"Why do you want to be president, Sanford?"

"That's a long tale, but in a nutshell, purely and solely for the good of the club."

"And that's the truth," declared Eunice. "Sanford is getting himself disliked in some quarters, influential ones, too, and he's making life-long enemies—not Alvord, but others—and it is all because he has the real interests of the club at heart. Al Hendricks is running it into—into a mud-puddle! Isn't he, San?"

"Well, yes, though I shouldn't have thought of using that word. But, he is bringing its gray hairs in sorrow to the grave—or will, if he remains in office, instead of turning it over to a well-balanced man of good judgment and unerring taste—say, like one Sanford Embury."

"You certainly are not afflicted with false pride, Sanford," and Aunt Abby bit into her crisp toast with a decided snap.

"Why, thank you," and Embury smiled as he purposely misinterpreted her words. "I quite agree, Aunt, that my pride is by no means false. It is a just and righteous pride in my own merits, both natural and acquired."

He winked at Eunice across the table, and she smiled back appreciatively. Aunt Abby gave him what was meant to be a scathing glance, but which turned to a nod of admiration.

"That's so, Sanford," she admitted. "Al Hendricks is a nice man, but he falls down on some things. Hasn't he been a good president?"

"Until lately, Aunt Abby. Now, he's all mixed up with a crowd of intractables—sporty chaps, who want a lot of innovations that the more conservative element won't stand for."

"Why, they want prize-fights and a movie theatre-right in the club!" informed Eunice. "And it means too much expense, besides being a horrid, low-down—"

"There, there, Tiger," and Sanford shook his head at her. "Let us say those things are unpalatable to a lot of us old fogies—"

"Stop! I won't have you call yourself old—or fogyish, either! You're the farthest possible removed from that! Why, you're no older than Al Hendricks."

"You were all children together," said Aunt Abby, as if imparting a bit of new information; "you three, and Mason Elliott. Why, when you were ten or eleven, Eunice, those three boys were eternally camping out in the front yard, waiting for you to get your hair curled and go out to play. And later, they all hung around to take you to parties, and then, later still —not so much later, either—they all wanted to marry you."

"Why, Auntie, you're telling the 'whole story of my life and what's my real name!'—Sanford knows all this, and knows that he cut out the other two—though I'm not saying they wanted to marry me."

"It goes without saying," and her husband gave her a gallant bow. "But, great heavens, Eunice, if you'd married those other two—I mean one of 'em—either one—you'd have been decidedly out of your element. Hendricks, though a bully chap, is a man of impossible tastes, and Elliott is a prig—pure and simple! I, you see, strike a happy medium. And, speaking of such things, are your mediums always happy, Aunt Abby?"

"How you do rattle on, Sanford! A true medium is so absorbed in her endeavors, so wrapped up in her work, she is, of course, happy—I suppose. I never thought about it."

"Well, don't go out of your way to find out. It isn't of vital importance that I should know. May I be excused, Madam Wife? I'm called to the busy marts—and all that sort of thing." Embury rose from the table, a big, tall man, graceful in his every motion, as only a trained athlete can be. Devoted to athletics, he kept himself in the pink of condition physically, and this was no small aid to his vigorous mentality and splendid business acumen.

"Wait a minute, San," and for the first time that morning there was a note of timidity in Eunice's soft voice. "Please give me a little money, won't you?"

"Money, you grasping young person! What do you want it for?"

"Why—I'm going to Newark, you know—"

"Going to Newark! Yes, but you're going in Hendricks' car—that doesn't require a ticket, does it?"

"No—but I—I might want to give the chauffeur something when I get out—"

"Nonsense! Not Hendricks' chauffeur. That's all right when you're with formal friends or Comparative strangers—but it would be ridiculous to tip Hendricks' Gus!"

Embury swung into the light topcoat held by the faithful Ferdinand.

"But, dear," and Eunice rose, and stood by her husband, "I do want a little money," she fingered nervously the breakfast napkin she was still holding.

"What for?" was the repeated inquiry.

"Oh, you see—I might want to do a little shopping in Newark."

"Shop in Newark! That's a good one! Why, girlie, you never want to shop outside of little old New York, and you know it. Shop in Newark!"

Embury laughed at the very idea.

"But—I might see something in a window that's just what I want."

"Then make a note of it, and buy it in New York. You have an account at all the desirable shops here, and I never kick at the bills, do I, now?"

"No; but a woman does want a little cash with her—"

"Oh, that, of course! I quite subscribe to that. But I gave you a couple of dollars yesterday."

"Yes, but I gave one to a Red Cross collector, and the other I had to pay out for a C.O.D. charge."

"Why buy things C.O.D. when you have accounts everywhere?"

"Oh, this was something I saw advertised in the evening paper—"

"And you bought it because it was cheap! Oh, you women! Now, Eunice, that's just a case in point. I want my wife to have everything she wants—everything in reason, but there's no sense in throwing money away. Now, kiss me, sweetheart, for I'm due at a directors' meeting in two shakes—or thereabouts."

Embury snapped the fastening of his second glove, and, hat in hand, held out his arms to his wife.

She made one more appeal.

"You're quite right, San, maybe I didn't need that C.O.D. thing. But I do want a little chickenfeed in my purse when I go out to-day. Maybe they'll take up a collection."

"A silver offering for the Old Ladies' Home,—eh? Well, tell 'em to come to me and I'll sign their subscription paper! Now, good-by, Dolly Gray! I'm off!"

With a hearty kiss on Eunice's red lips, and a gay wave of his hand to Aunt Abby, Embury went away and Ferdinand closed the door behind him.

"I can't stand it, Aunt Abby," Eunice exclaimed, as the butler disappeared into the pantry; "if Sanford were a poor man it would be different. But he's made more money this year than ever before, and yet, he won't give me an allowance or even a little bit of ready money."

"But you have accounts," Aunt Abby said, absently, for she-was scanning the paper now.

"Accounts! Of course, I have! But there are a thousand things one wants cash for! You know that perfectly well. Why, when our car was out of commission last week and I had to use a taxicab, Sanford would give me just enough for the fare and not a cent over to fee the driver. And lots of times I need a few dollars for charities, or some odds and ends, and I can't have a cent to call my own! Al Hendricks may be of coarser clay than Sanford Embury, but he wouldn' treat a wife like that!"

"It is annoying, Eunice, but Sanford is so good to you—"

"Good to me! Why shouldn't he be? It isn't a question of goodness or of generosity—it's just a fool whim of his, that I mustn't ask for actual cash! I can have all the parties I want, buy all the clothes I want, get expensive hats or knick-knacks of any sort, and have them all charged. He's never even questioned my bills—but has his secretary pay them. And I must have some money in my purse! And I will! I know ways to get it, without begging it from Sanford Embury!"

Eunice's dark eyes flashed fire, and her cheeks burned scarlet, for she was furiously angry.

"Now, now, my dear, don't take it so to heart," soothed Aunt Abby; "I'll give you some money. I was going to make you a present, but if you'd rather have the money that it would cost, say so."

"I daren't, Aunt Abby. Sanford would find it out and he'd be terribly annoyed. It's one of his idiosyncrasies, and I have to bear it as long as I live with him!"

The gleam in the beautiful eyes gave a hint of desperate remedies that might be applied to the case, but Ferdinand returned to the room, and the two women quickly spoke of other things.

Hendricks' perfectly appointed and smooth-running car made the trip to Newark in minimum time. Though the road was not a picturesque one, the party was in gay spirits and the host was indefatigable in his efforts to be entertaining.

"I've looked up this Hanlon person," he said. "and his record is astonishing. I mean, he does astonishing feats. He's a juggler, a sword swallower and a card sharp—that is, a card wizard. Of course, he's a faker, but he's a clever one, and I'm anxious to see what his game is this time. Of course, it's, first of all, advertisement for the paper that's backing him, but it's a new game. At least, it's new over here; they tell me it's done to death in England."

"Oh, no, Alvord, it isn't a game," insisted Miss Ames; "if the man is blindfolded, he can't play any tricks on us. And he couldn't play tricks on newspaper men anyway— they're too bright for that!"

"I think they are, too; that's why I'm interested. Warm enough, Eunice?"

"Yes, thank you," and the beautiful face looked happily content as Eunice Embury nestled her chin deeper into her fur collar.

For, though late April, the day was crisply cool and there was a tang in the bright sunshiny air. Aunt Abby was almost as warmly wrapped up as in midwinter, and when, on reaching Newark, they encountered a raw East wind, she shrugged into her coat like a shivering Esquimau.

"Where do we go to see it?" asked Eunice, as later, after luncheon, she eagerly looked about at the crowds massed everywhere.

"We'll have to reconnoiter," Hendricks replied, smiling at her animated face. "Drive on to the Oberon, Gus."

As they neared the theatre the surging waves of humanity barred their progress, and the big car was forced to come to a standstill.

"I'll get out," said Hendricks, "and make a few inquiries. The Free Press office is near here, and I know some of the people there."

He strode off and was soon swallowed up in the crowd.

"I think I see a good opening," said Gus, after a moment. "I'll get out for a minute, Mrs. Embury. I must inquire where cars can be parked."

"Go ahead, Gus," said Eunice; "we'll be all right here, but don't go far. I'll be nervous if you do."

"No, ma'am; I won't go a dozen steps."

"Extry! Extry! All about the Great Magic! Hanlon the Wonderful and his Big Stunt! Extry!"

"Oh, get a paper, Eunice, do," urged Aunt Abby from the depths of her fur coat. "Ask that boy for one! I must have it to read after I get home—I can't look at it now, but get it! Here, you —Boy—say, Boy!"

The newsboy came running to them and flung a paper into Eunice's lap.

"There y'are, lady," he said, grinning; "there's yer paper! Gimme a nickel, can't yer? I ain't got time hangin' on me hands!"

His big black eyes stared at Eunice, as she made no move toward a purse, and he growled: "Hurry up lady; I gotta sell some papers yet. Think nobuddy wants one but you?"

Eunice flushed with annoyance.

"Please pay him, Aunt Abby," she said, in a low voice; "I —haven't any money."

"Goodness gracious me! Haven't five cents! Why, Eunice, you must have!"

"But I haven't, I tell you! I can't see Alvord, and Gus is too far to call to. Go over there, boy, to that chauffeur with the leather coat—he'll pay you."

"No, thanky mum! I've had that dodge tried afore! Pity a grand dame like you can't scare up a nickel! Want to work a poor newsie! Shame for ya, lady!"

"Hush your impudence, you little wretch!" cried Aunt Abby. "Here, Eunice, help me get my purse. It's in my inside coat pocket—under the rug—there, see if you can reach it now."

Aunt Abby tried to extricate herself from the motor rug that had been tucked all too securely about her, and failing in that, endeavored to reach into her pocket with her gloved hand, and became hopelessly entangled in a mass of fur, chiffon scarf and. eyeglass chain.

"I can't get at my purse, Eunice; there's no use trying," she wailed, despairingly. "Let us have the paper, my boy, and come back here when the owner of this car comes and he'll give you a quarter."

"Yes—he will!" shouted the lad, and he'll give me a di'mon' pin an' a gold watch! I'd come back, willin' enough, but me root lays the other way, an' I must be scootin' or I'll miss the hull show. Sorry!" The boy, who had no trouble in finding customers for his papers, picked up the one he had laid on Eunice's lap and made off.

"Never mind, Auntie," she said, "we'll get another. It's too provoking—but I haven't a cent, and I don't blame the boy. Now, find your purse—or, never mind; here comes Alvord."

"Just fell over Mortimer!" called out Hendricks as the two men came to the side of the car. "I made him come and speak to you ladies, though I believe its holding up the whole performance. Let me present the god in the machine!"

"Not that," said Mr. Mortimer, smiling; "only a small mechanical part of to-day's doings. I've a few minutes to spare, though but a few. How do you do, Miss Ames? Glad to see you again. And Mrs. Embury; this brings back childhood days!"

"Tell me about Hanlon," begged Miss Ames. "Is he on the square?"

"So far as I know, and I know all there is to know, I think. I was present at a preliminary test this morning, and I'll tell you what he did." Mortimer looked at his watch and proceeded quickly. "In at the Free Press office one of the men took a piece of chalk and drew a line from where we were to a distant room of the building. The line went up and down stairs, in and out of various rooms, over chairs and under desks, and finally wound up in a small closet in the city editor's office. Well —and I must jump away now—that wizard, Hanlon, being securely blindfolded—I did it myself—followed that line, almost without deviation, from start to finish. Through a building he had never seers before, and groping along in complete darkness."

"How in the world could he do it?" Aunt Abby asked, breathlessly.

"The chap who drew the line was behind him— behind, mind you—and he willed him where to go. Of course, he did his best, kept his mind on the job, and earnestly used his mentality to will Hanlon along. And did! There, that's all I know, until this afternoon's stunt is pulled off. But what I've told you, I do know—I saw it, and I, for one, am a complete convert to telepathy!"

The busy man, hastily shaking hands, bustled away, and Hendricks told in glee how, through his acquaintance with Mortimer, he had secured a permit to drive his car among the front ones that were following the performance, which was to begin very soon now.

Gus returned, and they were about to start when Aunt Abby set up a plea for a copy of the paper that she wanted.

Good-natured Gus tried his best, Hendricks himself made endeavors, but all in vain. The papers were gone, the edition exhausted. Nor could any one whom they asked be induced to part with his copy even at a substantial premium.

"Sorry, Miss Ames," said Hendricks, "but we can't seem to nail one. Perhaps later we can get one. Now we must be starting or we'll soon lose our advantage."

The crowd was like a rolling sea by this time, and only the efficiency of the fine police work kept anything like order.

Cautiously the motor car edged along while the daring pedestrians seemed to scramble from beneath the very wheels.

And then a cheer arose which proclaimed the presence of Hanlon, the mysterious possessor of second sight, or the marvelous reader of another's mind—nobody knew exactly which he was.

CHAPTER 3: THE STUNT

Doctor Remson's police call had been imperative, and Inspector Mason came in with two men.

"What's this? What's wrong here?" the big burly inspector said, as he faced the few of us who had remained.

"Come in here, inspector," said the doctor, from the dining-room door.

And from that moment the whole aspect of the house seemed to change. No longer a gay little bijou residence, it became a court of justice.

One of the men was stationed at the street door and one at the area door below. Headquarters was notified of details. The coroner was summoned, and we were all for the moment under detention.

"Where is Miss Van Allen? Where is the lady of the house?" asked Mason. "Where are the servants? Who is in charge here?"

Was ever a string of questions so impossible of answers!

Doctor Remson told the main facts, but he was reticent. I, too, hesitated to say much, for the case was strange indeed.

Mrs. Reeves looked gravely concerned, but said nothing.

Ariadne Gale began to babble. That girl didn't know how to be quiet.

"I guess Miss Van Allen is upstairs," she volunteered. "She was in the dining-room, but she isn't here now, so she must be upstairs. Shall I go and see?"

"No!" thundered the inspector. "Stay where you are. Search the house, Breen. I'll cover the street door."

The man he called Breen went upstairs on the jump, and Mason continued. "Tell the story, one of you. Who is this man? Who killed him?"

As he talked, the inspector was examining Somers' body, making rapid notes in a little book, keeping his eye on the door, and darting quick glances at each of us, as he tried to grasp the situation.

I looked at Bert Garrison, who was perhaps the most favored of Miss Van Allen's friends, but he shook his head, so I threw myself into the breach.

"Inspector," I said, "that man's name is Somers. Further than that I know nothing. He is a stranger to all of us, and he came to this house to-night for the first time in his life."

"How'd he happen to come? Friend of Miss Van Allen?"

"He met her to-night for the first time. He came here with—" I paused. It was so hard to know what to do. Steele had gone home, ought I to implicate him?

"Go on—came here with whom? The truth, now."

"I usually speak the truth" I returned, shortly. "He came with Mr. Norman Steele."

"Where is Mr. Steele?"

"He has gone. There were a great many people here, and, naturally, some of them went away when this tragedy was discovered."

"Humph! Then, of course, the guilty party escaped. But we are getting nowhere. Does nobody know anything of this man, but his name?"

Nobody did; but Ariadne piped up, "He was a delightful man. He told me he was a great patron of art, and often bought pictures."

Paying little heed to her, the inspector was endeavoring to learn from the dead man's property something more about him.

"No letters or papers," he said, disappointedly, as he turned out the pockets. "Not unusual—in evening togs—but not even a card or anything personal—looks queer—"

"Look in his watch," said Ariadne, bridling with importance.

Giving her a keen glance, the inspector followed her suggestion. In the back of the case was a picture of a coquettish face, undoubtedly that of an actress. It was not carefully fastened in, but roughly cut out and pressed in with ragged edges.

"Temporary," grunted the inspector, "and recently stuck in. Some chicken he took out to supper. He's a club man, you say?"

"Yes, Mr. Steele said so, and also vouched for his worth and character." I resented the inspector's attitude. Though I knew nothing of Somers, and didn't altogether like him, yet, I saw no reason to think ill of the dead, until circumstances warranted it.

Further search brought a thick roll of money, some loose silver, a key-ring with seven or eight keys, eyeglasses in a silver case, handkerchiefs, a gold pencil, a knife, and such trifles as any man might have in his pockets, but no directly identifying piece of property.

R. S. was embroidered in tiny white letters on the handkerchiefs, and a monogram R. S. was on his seal ring.

His jewelry, which was costly, the inspector did not touch. There were magnificent pearl studs, a watch fob, set with a black opal and pearl cufflinks. Examination of his hat showed the pierced letters R. S., but nothing gave clue to his Christian name.

"Somers," said the inspector, musingly. "What club does he belong to?"

"I don't know," I replied. "Mr. Steele belongs to several, but Mr. Somers does not belong to any that I do. At least, I've never seen him at any."

"Call in the servants. Let's find out something about this household."

As no one else moved to do it, I stepped to the door of the butler's pantry, and summoned the head waiter of the caterer.

"Where are the house servants?" I asked him.

"There aren't any, sir," he replied, looking shudderingly at the grisly form on the floor.

"No servants? In a house of this type! What do you mean?"

"That's true," said Mrs. Reeves, breaking her silence, at last. "Miss Van Allen has a very capable woman, who is housekeeper and ladies' maid in one. But when guests are here, the suppers are served from the caterer's."

"Then call the housekeeper. And where is Miss Van Allen herself?"

"She's not in the house," said the policeman Breen, returning from his search.

"Not in the house!" cried Mrs. Reeves. "Where is she?"

"I've been all over—every room—every floor. She isn't in the house. There's nobody upstairs at all."

"No housekeeper or maid?" demanded Mason. "Then they've got away! Here, waiter, tell me all you know of this thing."

The Italian Luigi came forward, shaking with terror, and wringing his fingers nervously.

"I d—don't know anything about it," he began, but Mason interrupted, "You do! You know all about it! Did you kill this man?"

"No! Dio mio! No! a thousand no's!"

"Then, unless you wish to be suspected of it, tell all you know."

A commotion at the door heralded the coroner's arrival, also a detective and a couple of plain clothes men. Clearly, here was a mysterious case.

The coroner at once took matters in his own hands. Inspector Mason told him all that had been learned so far, and though Coroner Fenn seemed to think matters had been pretty well bungled, he made no comment and proceeded with the inquiries.

"Sure there's nobody upstairs?" he asked Breen.

"Positive. I looked in every nook and cranny. I've raked the whole house, but the basement and kitchen part."

"Go down there, then, and then go back and search upstairs again. Somebody may be hiding. Who here knows Miss Van Allen the most intimately?"

"Perhaps I do," said Mrs. Reeves. "Or Miss Gale. We are both her warm friends."

"I'm also her friend," volunteered Bert Garrison. "And I can guarantee that if Miss Van Allen has fled from this house it was out of sheer fright. She never saw this man until to-night. He was a stranger to us all."

"Where's the housekeeper?" went on Fenn.

"I think she must be somewhere about," said Mrs. Reeves. "Perhaps in the kitchen. Julie is an all round capable woman. When there are no guests she prepares Miss Van Allen's meals herself. When company is present the caterer always is employed."

"And there are no other servants?"

"Not permanent ones," replied Mrs. Reeves. "I believe the laundress and chore boy come by the day, also cleaning women and such. But I know that Miss Van Allen has no resident servant besides the maid Julie."

"This woman must be found," snapped the coroner. "But we must first of all identify the body. Mason, call up the principal clubs on the telephone, and locate R. Somers. Also find Mr. Norman Steele. Now, Luigi, let's have your story."

The trembling waiter stammered incoherently, and said little of moment.

"Look here," said Fenn, bluntly, "is that your knife sticking in him? I mean, is it one belonging to Fraschini's service? Don't touch it, but look at it, you can tell."

Luigi leaned over the dead man. "Yes, it is one of our boning knives," he said. "We always bring our own hardware."

"Well, then, if you want to clear yourself and your men of doubt, tell all you know."

"I know this," and Luigi braced himself to the ordeal. "I was waiting in the pantry for Miss Van Allen to send me word to serve supper, and I peeped in the dining-room now and then to see if it was time. I heard, presently, Miss Van Allen's voice, also a man's voice. I didn't want to intrude, so waited for a summons. After a moment or two I heard a little scream, and heard somebody or something fall. I had no thought of anything wrong, but thought the guests were unusually—er—riotous."

"Are Miss Van Allen's guests inclined to be riotous?"

"No, sir, oh, no," asseverated the man, while Mrs. Reeves and Ariadne looked indignant. "And for that reason, I felt a little curious, so I pushed the door ajar and peeped in."

"What did you see?"

"I saw," Luigi paused so long that I feared he was going to collapse. But the coroner eyed him sternly, and he went on. "I saw Miss Van Allen standing, looking down at this—this gentleman on the floor, and making as if to pull out the knife. I could scarcely believe my eyes, and I watched her. She didn't pull the knife, but she straightened up, looked around, glanced down at her gown, which—which was stained with blood—and then— she ran out into the hall."

"Where did she go?"

"I don't know. I couldn't see, as the door was but on a crack. Then I thought I ought to go into the dining-room, and I did. I looked at the gentleman, and I didn't know what to do. So I went into the hall, to the parlor door, and called for help, for a doctor or somebody. And then they all came out here. That's all I know."

Luigi's nerve gave way, and he sank into a chair with a sob. Fenn looked at him, and considerately left him alone for the time.

"Can this be true?" he said, turning to us. "Can you suspect Miss Van Allen of this crime?"

"No!" cried Bert Garrison and the women, at once. And, "No!" said I. "I am positive Miss Van Allen did not know Mr. Somers and could not have killed an utter stranger—on no provocation whatever."

"You do not know what provocation she may have had," suggested Fenn.

"Now, look here, Mr. Coroner," said Mrs. Reeves very decidedly, "I won't have Miss Van Allen spoken of in any such way. I assume you mean that this man, though a stranger, might have said or done something to annoy or offend Miss Van Allen. Well, if he had done so, Victoria Van Allen never would have killed him! She is the gentlest, most gay and light-hearted girl, and though she never tolerates any rudeness or familiarity, the idea of her killing a man is too absurd. You might as well suspect a dove or a butterfly of crime!"

"That's right, Mr. Coroner," said Garrison. "That waiter's story is an hallucination of some sort—if it isn't a deliberate falsification. Miss Van Allen is a dainty, happy creature, and to connect her with anything like this is absurd!"

"That's to be found out, Mr. Garrison. "Why did Miss Van Allen run away?"

"I don't admit that she did run away—in the sense of flight. If she were frightened at this thing—if she saw it— she may have run out of the door in hysterics or in a panic of terror. But she the perpetrator! Never!"

"Never!" echoed Mrs. Reeves. "The poor child! If she did come out here—and saw this awful sight—why, I think it would unhinge her mind!"

"Who is Miss Van Allen?" asked Fenn. "What is her occupation?"

"She hasn't an occupation," said Mrs. Reeves. "She is a young lady of independent fortune. As to her people or immediate relatives, I know nothing at all. I've known her a year or so, and as she never referred to such matters I never inquired. But she's a thorough little gentlewoman, and I'll defend her against any slander to my utmost powers."

"And so will I," said Miss Gale. "I'm sure of her fineness of character, and lovely nature—"

"But these opinions, ladies, don't help our inquiries," interrupted Fenn. "What can you men tell us? What I want first, is to identify this body, or, rather to learn more of R. Somers, and to find Miss Van Allen. I can't hold an inquest until these points are cleared up. Mason, have you found out anything?"

"No," said the inspector, returning from his long telephone quest. "I called up four clubs. Norman Steele belongs to three of them, but this man doesn't seem to belong to any. That is, there are Somerses and even R. Somerses, but they all have middle names, and, too, their description doesn't fit this Somers."

"Then Mr. Steele misrepresented him. Did you get Steele, Mason?"

"No, he wasn't at any of the clubs. I found his residence, a bachelor apartment house, but he isn't there, either."

"Find Steele; find Miss Van Allen; find the maid, what's her name—Julia?"

"Julie, she was always called," said Mrs. Reeves. "If Miss Van Allen went away, I've no doubt Julie went with her. She is a most devoted caretaker of her mistress."

"An oldish woman?"

"No. Perhaps between thirty-five and forty."

"What's she look like?"

"Describe her, Ariadne, you're an artist."

"Julie," said Miss Gale, "is a good sort. She's medium-sized, she has brown hair and rather hazel eyes. She wears glasses, and she stoops a little in her walk. She has perfect training and correct manners, and she is a model servant, but she gives the impression of watching over Miss Van Allen, whatever else she may be engaged in at the same time."

"Wears black?"

"No; usually gray gowns, or sometimes white. Inconspicuous aprons and no cap. She's not quite a menial, but yet, not entirely a housekeeper."

"English?"

"English speaking, if that's what you mean. But I think she's an American. Don't you, Mrs Reeves?"

"American? Yes, of course."

Bowing in response to the mighty cheer that greeted his appearance, Hanlon stood, smiling at the crowd.

A young fellow he seemed to be, slender, well-knit and with a frank, winning face. But he evidently meant business, for he turned at once to Mr. Mortimer, and asked that the test be begun.

A few words from one of the staff of the newspaper that was backing the enterprise informed the audience that the day before there had been hidden in a distant part of the city a penknife, and that only the hider thereof and the Hon. Mr. Mortimer knew where the hiding place was.

Hanlon would now undertake to go, blindfolded, to the spot and find the knife, although the distance, as the speaker was willing to disclose, was more than a mile. The blindfolding was to be done by a committee of prominent citizens and was to be looked after so carefully that there could be no possibility of Hanlon's seeing anything.

After that, Hanlon engaged to go to the hiding place and find the knife, on condition that Mr. Mortimer would follow him, and concentrate all his willpower on mentally guiding or rather directing Hanlon's footsteps.

The blindfolding, which was done in full view of the front ranks of spectators, was an elaborate proceeding. A heavy silk handkerchief had been prepared by folding it in eight thicknesses, which were then stitched to prevent Clipping. This bandage was four inches wide and completely covered the man's eyes, but as an additional

precaution pads of cotton wool were first placed over his
closed eyelids and the bandage then tied over them.

Thus, completely blindfolded, Hanlon spoke earnestly
to Mr. Mortimer.

"I must ask of you, sir, that you do your very best to
guide me aright. The success of this enterprise depends
quite as much on you as on myself. I am merely
receptive, you are the acting agent. I strive to keep my
mind a blank, that your will may sway it in the right
direction. I trust you, and I beg that you will keep your
whole mind on the quest. Think of the hidden article,
keep it in your mind, look toward it. Follow me—not too
closely—and mentally push me in the way I should go. If
I go wrong, will me back to the right path, but in no case
get near enough to touch me, and, of course, do not speak
to me. This test is entirely that of the influence of your
will upon mine. Call it telepathy, thought-transference,
will-power—anything you choose, but grant my request
that you devote all your attention to the work in hand. If
your mind wanders, mine will; if your mind goes straight
to the goal, mine will also be impelled there."

With a slight bow, Hanlon stood motionless, ready to
start.

The preliminaries had taken place on a platform,
hastily built for the occasion, and now, with Mortimer
behind him, Hanlon started down the steps to the street.

Reaching the pavement, he stood motionless for a few
seconds and then, turning, walked toward Broad Street.
Reaching it, he turned South, and walked along, at a
fairly rapid gait. At the crossings he paused
momentarily, sometimes as if uncertain which way to go,
and again evidently assured of his direction.

The crowd surged about him, now impeding his
progress and now almost pushing him along. He gave
them no heed, but made his way here or there as he chose
and Mortimer followed, always a few steps behind, but
near enough to see that Hanlon was in no way interfered
with by the throng.

Indeed, so anxious were the onlookers that fair play should obtain, the ones nearest to the performer served as a cordon of guards to keep his immediate surroundings cleared.

Hanlon's actions, in all respects, were those that might be expected from a blindfolded man. He groped, sometimes with outstretched hands, again with arms folded or hands clasped and extended, but always with an expression, so far as his face could be seen, of earnest, concentrated endeavor to go the right way. Now and then he would half turn, as if impelled in one direction, and then hesitate, turn and march off the other way. One time, indeed, he went nearly half a block in a wrong street. Then he paused, groped, stumbled a little, and gradually returned to the vicinity of Mortimer, who had stood still at the corner. Apparently, Hanlon had no idea of his detour, for he went on in the right direction, and Mortimer, who was oblivious to all but his mission, followed interestedly.

One time Hanlon spoke to him. "You are a fine 'guide,' sir," he said. "I seem impelled steadily, not in sudden thought waves, and I find my mind responds well to your will. If you will be so good as to keep the crowd away from us a little more carefully. I don't want you any nearer me, but if too many people are between us, it interferes somewhat with the transference of your guiding thought."

"Do you want to hear my footsteps?" asked Mortimer, thoughtfully.

"That doesn't matter," Hanlon smiled. "You are to follow me, sir, even if I go wrong. If I waited to hear you, that would be no test at all. Simply will me, and then follow, whether I am on the right track or not. But keep your mind on the goal, and look toward it—if convenient. Of course, the looking toward it is no help to me, save as it serves to fix your mind more firmly on the matter."

And then Hanlon seemed to go more carefully. He stepped slowly, feeling with his foot for any curbstone, grating or irregularity in the pavement. And yet he failed in one instance to feel the edge of an open coalhole, and his right leg slipped down into it.

Some of the nearby watchers grabbed him, and pulled him back without his sustaining injury, for which he thanked them briefly and continued.

Several times some sceptical bystanders put themselves deliberately in front of the blindfolded man, to see if he would turn out for them.

On the contrary, Hanlon bumped into them, so innocently, that they were nearly thrown down.

He smiled good-naturedly, and said, "All right, fellows; I don't mind, if you don't. And I don't blame you for wanting to make sure that I'm not playing 'possum!"

Of course, Hanlon carried no light cane, such as blind men use, to tap on the stones, so he helped himself by feeling the way along shop windows and area gates, judging thus, when he was nearing a cross street, and sometimes hesitating whether to cross or turn the corner.

After a half-hour of this sort of progress he found himself in a vacant lot near the edge of the city. There had been a building in the middle of the plot of ground, but it had been burned down and only a pile of blackened debris marked the place.

Reaching the corner of the streets that bounded the lot, Hanlon made no pause, but started on a straight diagonal toward the center of the lot. He stepped into a tangle of charred logs and ashes, but forged ahead unhesitatingly, though slowly, and picked his way by thrusting the toe of his shoe tentatively forward.

Mortimer, about three paces behind him, followed, unheeding the rubbish he stalked through, and very evidently absorbed in doing his part to its conclusion.

For the knife was hidden in the very center of the burned-down house. A bit of flooring was left, on which Hanlon climbed, Mortimer getting up on it also.

Hanlon walked slowly round in a circle, the floor being several yards square. Mortimer stepped behind him, gravely looking toward the hiding-place, and exerting all his mentality toward "guiding" Hanlon to it. At no time was he nearer than two feet, though once, making a quick turn, Hanlon nearly bumped into him. Finally, Hanlon, poking about in the ashes with his right foot, kicked against something. He picked it up and it proved to be only a bit of wire. But the next moment he struck something else, and, stooping, brought up triumphantly the hidden penknife, which he waved exultantly at the crowd.

Loud and long they cheered him. Cordially Mr. Mortimer grasped the hands of the hero, and it was with some difficulty that Alvord Hendricks restrained Miss Abby Ames from getting out of his car and rushing to congratulate the successful treasure- seeker.

"Now," she exclaimed; "no one can ever doubt the fact of telepathy after this! How else could that young man have done what he has done. Answer me that!"

"It's all a fake," asserted Hendricks, "but I'm ready to acknowledge I don't know how it's done. It's the best game I ever saw put up, and I'd like to know how he does it."

"Seems to me," put in Eunice, a little dryly, "one oughtn't to insist that it is a fake unless one has some notion, at least, of how it could be done. If the man could see—could even peep —there might be a chance for trickery. But with those thick cotton pads on his eyes and then covered with that big, thick, folded silk handkerchief—it's really a muffle-there's no chance for his faking."

"And if he could see—if his eyes were wide open—how would he know where to go?" demanded Aunt Abby. "That blindfolding is only so he can't see Mr. Mortimer's face, if he turns round, and judge from its expression.

And also, I daresay, to help him concentrate his mind, and not be diverted or distracted by the crowd and all."

"All the same, I don't believe in it," and Hendricks shook his head obstinately. "There is no such thing as telepathy, and this 'willing' business has all been exposed years ago."

"I remember," and Aunt Abby nodded; "you mean that Bishop man and all that. But this affair it quite different. You don't believe Mr. Mortimer was a party to deceit, do you?"

"No, I don't. Mortimer is a judge and a most honest man, besides. He wouldn't stoop to trickery in a thing of this sort. But he has been himself deceived."

"Then how was it done?" cried Eunice, triumphantly; "for no one else knew where the knife was hidden, except that newspaper man who hid it, and he was sincere, of course, or there'd be no sense in the whole thing."

"I know that. Yes, the newspaper people were hoodwinked, too."

"Then what happened?" Eunice persisted. "There's no possible explanation but telepathy. Is there, now?"

"I don't know of any," Hendricks was forced to admit. "After the excitement blows over a little, I'll try to speak with Mortimer again. I'd like to know his opinion."

They sat in the car, looking at the hilarious crowds of people, most of whom seemed imbued with a wild desire to get to the hero of the hour and demand his secret.

"There's a man who looks like Tom Meredith," said Eunice, suddenly. "By the way, Alvord, where do the Merediths stand in the matter of the club election?"

"Which of them?"

"Either—or both. I suppose they're on your side— they never seemed to like Sanford much."

"My dear Eunice, don't be so narrow-minded. Club men don't vote one way or another because of a personal like or dislike—they consider the good of the club—the welfare of the organization."

"Well, then, which side do they favor as being for the good of the club?"

"Ask Sanford."

"Oh—if you don't want to tell me."

Eunice looked provokingly pretty and her piquant face showed a petulant expression as she turned it to Hendricks.

"Smile on me again and I'll tell you anything you want to know: if I know it myself."

A dazzling smile answered this speech, and Hendricks' gaze softened as he watched her.

"But you'll have to ask me something else, for, alas, the brothers Meredith haven't made a confidant of me."

"Story-teller" and Eunice's dark eyes assumed the look of a roguish little girl. "You can't fool me, Alvord; now tell me, and I'll invite you in to tea when we get home."

"I'm going in, anyway."

"Not unless you tell me what I ask. Why won't you? Is it a secret? Pooh! I'd just as lief ask Mr. Tom Meredith myself, if I could see him. Never mind, don't tell me, if you don't want to. You're not my only confidential friend; there are others."

"Who are they, Euny? I flattered myself I was your only really, truly intimate friend—not even excepting your husband!"

"Oh, what a naughty speech! If you weren't Sanford's very good friend, I'd never speak to you again!"

"I don't see how you two men can be friends," put in Aunt Abby, "when you're both after that same presidency."

"That's the answer!" Eunice laughed. "Alvord is San's greatest friend, because it's going to be an easy thing for Sanford to win the election from him! If there were a more popular candidate in Alvord's place, or a less popular one in Sanford's place, it wouldn't be such a walkover!"

"You—you—" Hendricks looked at Eunice in speechless admiration. The dancing eyes were impudent, the red lips curved scornfully, and she made a daring little moue at him as she readjusted her black lace veil so that a heavy bit of its pattern covered her mouth.

"What do you do that for? Move that darned flower, so I can see you talk!"

She laughed then, and wrinkled her straight little nose until the veil billowed mischievously.

"I wish you'd take that thing off," Hendricks said, irritatedly; "it annoys me."

"And pray, sir, who are you, that I should shield you from annoyance? My veil is a necessary part of my costume."

"Necessary nothing! Take it off, I tell you!"

"Merry Christmas!" and Eunice gave him such a scornful shrug of her furred shoulders that Hendricks laughed out, in sheer enjoyment of her audacity.

"Tell me about the Merediths, and I'll take off the offending veil," she urged, looking at him very coaxingly.

"All right; off with it."

Slowly, and with careful deliberation, Eunice unpinned her veil, took it off and folded it in a small, compact parcel. This she put in her handbag, and then, with an adorable smile, said: "Now!"

"You beautiful idiot," and Hendricks devoured her with his eyes. "All I can tell you about the Merediths is, that I don't know anything about their stand on the election."

"What do you guess, assume, surmise, imagine or predict?" she teased, still fascinating him with her magnetic charm.

"Well, I think this: they're a little too old-timey to take up all my projects. But, on the other hand, they're far from willing to subscribe to your husband's views. They do not approve of the Sunday-school atmosphere he wants to bring about, nor do they shut their eyes to the fact that the younger element must be considered."

"Younger element! Do you call Sanford old?"

"No; he's only twenty-eight this minute. But there are a lot of new members even younger than that strange as it may seem! These boys want gayety—yea, even unto the scorned movies and the hilarious prize-fights—and as they are scions of the wealthy and aristocratic families of our little old town, I think we should consider them. And, since you insist on knowing, it is my firm belief, conviction and—I'm willing to add—my hope that the great and influential Meredith brothers agree with me! So there now, Madam Sanford Embury!"

"Thank you, Alvord; you're clear, at least. Do you think I could persuade them to come over to Sanford's side?"

"I think you could persuade the statue of Jupiter Ammon to climb down from his pedestal and take you to Coney Island, if you looked at him like that! But I also think that friend husband will not consent to your electioneering for him. It isn't done, my dear Eunice."

"As if I cared what is 'done' and what isn't, if I want to help Sanford."

"Go ahead, then, fair lady; but remember that Sanford Embury stands for the conservative element in our club, and anything you might try to do by virtue of your blandishments or fascinations would be frowned upon and would react against your cause instead of for it. If I might suggest, my supporters, the younger set, the—well—the gayer set, would more readily respond to such a plan. Why don't you electioneer for me?"

Eunice disdained to reply, and Aunt Abby broke into the discussion by exclaiming: "Oh, Alvord, here comes Mr. Mortimer, and he has Mr. Hanlon with him!"

Sure enough the two heroes of the day were walking toward the Hendricks car, which, still standing near the scene of Hanlon's triumph, awaited a good chance for a getaway.

"I wonder if you ladies wouldn't like to meet this marvel," began Mr. Mortimer, genially, and Aunt Abby's delight was convincing, indeed.

Eunice, too, greeted Mr. Hanlon cordially, and Hendricks held out a welcoming hand.

"Tell us how you did it," he said, smiling into the intelligent face of the mysterious "mind-reader."

"You saw," he returned, simply, with a slight gesture of out-turned palms, as if to disavow any secrets.

"Yes, I saw," said Hendricks, "but with me, seeing is not believing."

"Don't listen, Hanlon," Mr. Mortimer said, smiling a little resentfully. "That sort of talk would go before the test, but not now. What do you mean, Hendricks, by not believing? Do you suspect me of complicity?"

"I do not, Mortimer. I believe you have been taken in with the rest, by a very clever trick." He looked sharply at Hanlon, who returned his gaze serenely. "I believe this young man is unusually apt as a trickster, and I believe he hoodwinked the whole community. The fact that I cannot comprehend, or even guess how he did it, in no way disturbs my conviction that he did do it by trickery. I will change this opinion, however, if Mr. Hanlon will look me in the eye and assure me, on his honor, that he found the penknife by no other means or with no other influence to guide him than Mr. Mortimer's will-power."

"I am not on trial," he said. "I am not called upon to prove or disprove anything. I promised to perform a feat and I have done so. It was not nominated in the bond that I should defend my honor by asseverations."

"Begging the question," laughed Hendricks, but Mr. Mortimer said: "Not at all. Hanlon is right. If he has any secret means of guidance, it is up to us to discover it. But I hold that he cannot have, or it would have been discovered by some of the eager observers. We had thousands looking on to-day. There must have been some one clever enough to suspect the deceit, if deceit there were."

"Thank you, Mr. Mortimer," Hanlon spoke quietly. "I made no mystery of my performance; I had no confederate, no paraphernalia. All there was to see could be seen by all. You willed me; I followed your will. That is all."

The simple manner and pleasant demeanor of the young man greatly attracted Eunice, who smiled at him kindly.

"I came here very sceptical," she admitted; "and even now I can't feel entirely convinced—"

"Well, I can!" declared Aunt Abby. "I am willing to own it, too. These people who really believe in your sincerity, Mr. Hanlon, and refuse to confess it, make me mad! I wish you'd give an exhibition in New York."

"I'm sorry to disappoint you, madam, but this is my last performance."

"Good gracious why?" Aunt Abby looked curiously at him.

"I have good reasons," Hanlon smiled. "You may learn them later, if you care to."

"I do. How can I learn them?"

"Read the Newark Free Press next Monday."

"Oh!" and Eunice had an inspiration—a premonition of the truth. "May I speak to you alone a minute, Mr. Hanlon?"

She got out of the car and walked a few steps with the young man, who politely accompanied her.

They paused a short distance away, and held a brief but animated conversation. Eunice laughed gleefully, and it was plain to be seen her charming smiles played havoc with Hanlon's reserved demeanor. Soon he was willingly agreeing to something she was proposing and finally they shook hands on it.

They returned to the car; he assisted Eunice in, and then he told Mr. Mortimer they had stayed as long as was permissible and were being eagerly called back to the committee in charge of the day's programme.

"That's so," said Mortimer. "I begged off for a few minutes. Good-by, all." He raised his hat and hurried away after Hanlon.

"Well," said Hendricks as they started homeward, "what did you persuade him to do, Eunice? Give a parlor exhibition for you?"

"The boy guessed nearly right the very first time!" cried Eunice, gleefully; "it was all a fake, and he's coming to our house Sunday afternoon to tell how he did it. It's all coming out in the paper on Monday."

"My good land!" and Aunt Abby sank back in her seat, utterly   disgusted.

CHAPTER 4: THE EMBURYS

"And that's my last word on the subject."

Embury lighted one cigarette from the stub of another, and deposited the stub in the ash-tray at his elbow. It was Sunday afternoon, and the peculiar relaxedness of that day of rest and gladness had somewhat worn on the nerves of both Sanford and Eunice.

Aunt Abby was napping, and it was too early yet to look for their expected visitor, Hanlon.

Eunice had been once again endeavoring to persuade her husband to give her an allowance—a stated sum, however small, that she might depend upon regularly. The Emburys fulfilled every requirement of the condition known as "happily married" save for this one item. They were congenial, affectionate, good-natured, and quite ready to make allowances for each other's idiosyncrasies or whims.

With this one exception. Eunice found it intolerable to be cramped and pinched for small amounts of ready cash, when her husband was a rich man. Nor was Embury mean, or even economical of nature. He was more than willing that his wife should have all the extravagant luxuries she desired. He was entirely ready to pay any and all bills that she might contract. Never had he chided her for buying expensive or unnecessary finery—even more, he had always admired her taste and shown pleasure at her purchases. He was proud of her beauty and willing it should be adorned. He was proud of her grace and charm and willing that the household appointments should provide an appropriate setting for her hospitality. They were both fond of entertaining and never was there a word of protest from him as to the amounts charged by florists and caterers.

And yet, by reason of some crank, crotchet or perverse notion, Embury was unwilling to give his wife what is known as "pin money."

"Buy your pins at the best jewelers'," he would laugh, "and send the bills to me; buy your hats and gowns from the Frenchiest shops—you can get credit anywhere on my name—Good Lord! Tiger, what more can a woman want?"

Nor would he agree to her oft-repeated explanations that there were a thousand and one occasions when some money was an absolute necessity. Or, if persuaded, he gave her a small amount and expected it to last indefinitely.

It is difficult to know just what was the reason for this attitude. Sanford Embury was not a miser. He was not penurious or stingy. He subscribed liberally to charities, many of them unknown to the public, or even to his wife, but some trick of nature, some twist in his brain, made this peculiarity of his persistent and ineradicable.

Now, Eunice Embury was possessed of a quick, sometimes ungovernable temper. It was because of this that her husband called her Tiger. And also, as he declared, because her beautiful, lithe grace was suggestive of "the fearful symmetry" of the forest tribe.

She had tried honestly to control her quick anger, but it would now and then assert itself in spite of her, and Embury delighted to liken her to Katherine, and declared that he must tame her as Petruchio tamed his shrew.

This annoyed Eunice far more than she let him know, for she was well aware that if he thought it teased her, he would more frequently try Petruchio's methods.

So, when she flew into a rage, and he countered with a fiercer anger, she knew he was assuming it purposely, and she usually quieted down, as the better part of valor.

On this particular occasion Eunice had taken advantage of a quiet, pleasant tete-a-tete to bring up the subject.

Embury had heard her pleading, not unkindly, but with a bored air, and had finally remarked, as she paused in her arguments, "I refuse, Eunice, to give you a stated allowance. If you haven't sufficient confidence in your husband's generosity to trust him to give you all you want or need, and even more than that, then you are ungrateful for what I have given you. And that's my last word on the subject."

The rank injustice of this was like iron entering her soul. She knew his speech was illogical, unfair and even absurd, but she knew no words of hers could make him see it so.

And in utter exasperation at her own impotence, she flung her self-control to the winds, and let go of her temper.

"Well, it isn't my last word on the subject!" she cried. "I have something further to say!"

"That is your woman's privilege," and Embury smiled irritatingly at her.

"Not only my privilege, but my duty! I owe it to my self-respect, to my social position, to my standing as your wife—the wife of a prominent man of affairs—to have at my command a sum of ready money when I need it. You know perfectly well, I do not want it for anything wrong— or for anything that I want to keep secret from you. You know I have never had a secret from you nor do I wish to have! I simply want to do as other women do—even the poorest, the meanest man, will give his wife an allowance, a little something that is absolutely her own. Why, most of the women of my set have a checking account at the bank—they all have a personal allowance!"

"So?" Embury took up another cigarette. "You may remember, Eunice, I have spoken my last word on the subject."

"And you may remember that I have not! But I will—and right now. And it is simply that since you refuse me the pleasure and convenience of some money for everyday use, I shall get some from another source."

Embury's eyes narrowed, and he surveyed his wife with a calm scrutiny. Then he smiled.

"Stenography and typewriting?" he said; "or shall you take in plain sewing? Cut out the threats, Eunice; they won't get you anywhere!"

"They'll get me where I want to arrive! Don't say I didn't warn you—I repeat, I shall get money for my personal use, and you will have no right to criticize my methods, since you refuse me a paltry sum by way of allowance."

Eunice was standing, her two hands tightly grasping a chair-back as she looked angrily at Embury, who still seated lazily, blew smoke rings toward her. She was magnificent in her anger, her cheeks burned crimson, her dark eyes had an ominous gleam in them and her curved lips straightened into a determined line of scarlet. Her muscles were strained and tense, her breath came quickly, yet she had full control of herself and her pose was that of a crouching, waiting tiger rather than a furious ode.

Embury was full of admiration at the beautiful picture she made, but pursuant of his inexorable plan, he rose to "tame" her.

"'Tiger, tiger, burning bright,'" he quoted, "you must take back that speech—it is neither pretty nor tactful—"

"I have no wish to be tactful! Why should I? I am not trying to coax or cajole you! You refuse my request—you have repeatedly refused me—now, I am at the end of my patience, and I shall take matters into my own hands!"

"Lovely hands!" he murmured, taking them in his own. "You have unusually pretty hands, Eunice; it would be a pity to use them to earn money."

"Yet that is my intention. I shall get money by the work of these hands. It will be in a way that you will not approve, but you have forfeited your right to approve or disapprove."

"That I have not! I am your husband—you have promised to obey me—"

"A mere form of words—it meant nothing!"

"Our marriage ceremony meant nothing?"

"If it did, remember that you endowed me with all your worldly goods—"

"And I give them to you, too! Do you know that nine-tenths of my yearly expenditures are for your pleasure and benefit! I enjoy our home, too, but it would not be the elaborate, luxurious establishment that it is, but that it suits your taste to have it so! And then, you whine and fret for what you yourself call a paltry matter! Ingrate!"

"Don't you dare call me ingrate! I owe you no gratitude! Do you give me this home as a charity? As a gift, even! It is my right! And it is also my right to have a bank account of my own! It is my right to uphold my head among other women who laugh at me, who ridicule me, because, with all your wealth, I have no purse of my own! I will not stand it! I rebel! And you may rest assured things are going to be different hereafter. I will get money—"

"You shall not!" Embury grasped the wrists of the hands he still held, and his face was fiercely frowning. "You are my wife, and whatever you may or may not owe to me, you owe it to our position, to our standing in the community to do nothing beneath your dignity or mine!"

"You care nothing for my dignity, for my appearance before other women, so why should I consider your dignity? You force me to it, and it is therefore your fault if I—"

"What is it you propose to do? How are you going to get this absurd paltry sum you are making such a fuss about?"

"That I decline to tell you—"

"Don't you dare to do needlework or anything that would make me look foolish. I forbid it!"

"And I scorn your forbidding! Make you look foolish, indeed! When you make me look foolish every day of my life, because I can't do as other women do—can't have what other wives have—"

"Now, now, Tiger, don't make such a row over nothing—let's talk it over seriously—"

"There's nothing to talk over. I've asked you time and again for an allowance of money—real money, not charge accounts—and you always refuse—"

"And always shall, if you are so ugly about it! Why must you fly into a rage over it? Your temper is—"

"My temper is roused by your cruelty—"

"Cruelty!"

"Yes; it's as much cruelty as if you struck me! You deny me my heart's dearest wish for no reason whatever—"

"It's enough that I don't approve of an allowance—"

"It ought to be enough that I do!"

"No, no, my lady! I love you, I adore you, but I am not the sort of man to lie down and let you walk over me! I give you everything you want and if I reserve the privilege of paying for it myself, it does not seem to me a crime!"

"Oh, do hush up, Sanford! You drive me frantic! You prate the same foolishness. over and over! I don't want to hear any more about it. You said you had spoken the last word on the subject, now stop it! I, too, have said my final say. I shall do as I please, and I shall not consider myself accountable to you for my actions."

"Confound it! Do what you please, then! I wash my hands of your nonsense! But be careful how you carry the name I have given you!"

"If you keep on, I may decide not to carry it at all—"

Eunice was interrupted by the entrance of Ferdinand, announcing the arrival of Mason Elliott.

Trained in the school of convention, both the Emburys became at once the courteous, cordial host and hostess.

"Hello, Elliott," sang out Sanford, "glad to see your bright and happy face. Come right along and chum in."

Eunice offered her hand with a welcoming smile.

"Just the boy I was looking for," she said, we've the jolliest game on for the afternoon. Haven't we, San?"

"Fool trick, if you ask me! Howsumever, everything goes. Interested in thought-transference bunk, Elliott?"

"I know what you're getting at." Mason Elliott nodded his head understandingly. "Hendricks put me wise. So, I says to myself, s'posin' I hop along and listen in. Yes, I am interested, sufficiently so not to mind your jeers about bunk and that."

"Oh, do you believe in it, Mason?" said Eunice, animatedly; "for this is a faked affair—or, rather, the explanation of one. It's the Hanlon boy, you know—"

"Yes; I know. But what's the racket with you two turtle-doves? I come in, and find Eunice wearing the pet expression of a tragedy queen and Sanford, here, doing the irate husband. Going into the movies?"

"Yes, that's it," and Eunice smiled bravely, although her lips still quivered from her recent turbulent quarrel, and a light, jaunty air was forced to conceal her lingering nervousness.

"Irate husband is good!" laughed Embury, "considering we are yet honeymooners."

"Good dissemblers, both of you," and Elliott settled himself in an easy chair, "but you don't fool your old friend. Talk about thought-transference—it doesn't take much of that commodity to read that you two were interrupted by my entrance in the middle of a real, honest-to-goodness, cats'-and-dogs' quarrel."

"All right, have it your own way," and Embury laughed shortly; "but it wasn't the middle of it, it was about over."

"All but the making up! Shall I fade away for fifteen minutes?"

"No," protested Eunice. "It was only one of the little tiffs that happen in the best families! Now, listen, Mason—"

"My dear lady, I live but on the chance of being permitted to listen to you—only in the hope that I may listen early and often—"

"Oh, hush! What a silly you are!"

"Silly, is it? Remember I was your childhood playmate. Would you have kept me on your string all these years if I were silly? And here's another of my childhood friends! How do you do, most gracious lady?"

With courtly deference Elliott rose to greet Aunt Abby, who came into the living-room from Eunice's bedroom.

Her black silk rustled and her old point lace fell yellowly round her slender old hands, for on Sunday afternoon Miss Ames dressed the part.

"How are you, Mason," she said, but with a preoccupied air. "What time is Mr. Hanlon coming, Eunice?"

"Soon now, I think," and Eunice spoke with entire composure, her angry excitement all subdued. It was characteristic of her that after a fit of temper, she was more than usually soft and gentle. More considerate of others and even, more roguishly merry.

"You know, Mason, that what we are to be told to-day is a most inviolable secret—that is, it is a secret until tomorrow."

"Never put off till to-morrow what you can tell tonight," returned Elliott, but he listened attentively while Eunice and Aunt Abby described the performance of the young man Hanlon.

"Of course," Elliott observed, a little disappointedly, "if he says he hoaxed the crowd, of course he did; but in that case I've no interest in the thing. I'd like it better if he were honest."

"Oh, he's honest enough," corrected Embury; "he owns right up that it was a trick. Why, good heavens, man! if it hadn't been, he couldn't have done it at all. I'm rather keen to know just how he managed, though, for the yarn of Eunice and Aunt Abby is a bit mystifying."

"Don't depend too much on the tale of interested spectators. They're the worst possible witnesses! They see only what they wish to see."

"Only what Hanlon wished us to see," corrected Eunice, gaily. And then Hanlon, himself, and Alvord Hendricks arrived together.

"Met on the doorstep," said Hendricks as he came in. "Mr. Hanlon is a little stage-struck, so it's lucky I happened along."

Willy Hanlon, as he was called in the papers, came shyly forward and Eunice, with her ready tact, proceeded to put him at once at his ease.

"You came just at the right minute to help me out," she said, smiling at him. "They are saying women are no good at describing a scene! They say that we can't be relied on for accuracy. So, now you're here and you can tell what really happened."

"Yes, ma'am," and Hanlon swallowed, a little embarrassedly; "that's what I came for, ma'am. But first, are you all straight goods? Will you all promise not to tell what I tell you before tomorrow morning?"

They all promised on their honor, and, satisfied, Hanlon began his tale.

"You see, it's a game that can't be played too often or too close together," he said; "I mean, if I put it over around here, I can't risk it again nearer than some several states away. And even then it's likely to get caught on to."

"Have you put it over often?" asked Hendricks, interestedly.

"Yes, sir—well, say, about a dozen times altogether. Now I'm going to chuck it, for it's too risky. And so, I've sold the story of how I do it to the newspaper syndicate for more than I'd make out of it in a dozen performances. You can read it all in to-morrow's papers, but Mrs. Embury, she asked me to tell it here and I said yes— 'cause-'cause—well, 'cause I wanted to!"

The boyish outburst was so unmistakably one of admiration, of immediate capitulation to Eunice's charm, that she blushed adorably, and the others 'laughed outright.

"One more scalp, Euny," said Elliott; "oh, you can't help it, I know."

"Go on, Mr. Hanlon," said Eunice, and he went on.

"You see, to make you understand it rightly, I must go back a ways. I've done all sorts of magic stunts and I'm kinda fond of athletics. I've given exhibitions along both those lines in athletic clubs and in ladies' parlors, too. Well, I had a natural talent for making my ears move— lots of fellows do that, I know; but I got pretty spry at it."

"What for?" asked Embury.

"Nothing particular, sir, only one thing led to another. One day I read in an English magazine about somebody pulling off this trick—this blindfold chase, and I said to myself I b'lieved I could do it first rate and maybe make easy money. I don't deny I'm out after the coin. I've got to get my living, and if I'd rather do it by gulling the public, why, it's no more than many a better man does."

"Right you are," said Elliott.

"So, 's I say, I read this piece that told just how to do it, and I set to work. You may think it's funny, but the first step was working my forehead muscles."

"Whatever for?" cried Aunt Abby, who was listening, perhaps most intently of all.

"I'll tell you, in a jiffy, ma'am," and Hanlon smiled respectfully at the eager old face.

"You see, if you'll take notice, the muscles of your forehead, just above your eyebrows, work whenever you shut or open your eyes. Yes, try it, ma'am," as Aunt Abby wrinkled her forehead spasmodically. "Shut your eyes, ma'am. Now, cover them closely with the palm of your left hand. Press it close—so. Now, with your hand there, open your eyes slowly, and feel your forehead muscles go up. They have to, you can't help it. Now, that's the kcynote of the whole thing."

"Clear as Erebus!" remarked Hendricks. "I don't get you, Steve."

"Nor I," and Eunice sat with her hand against her eyes, drawing her lovely brows into contortions.

"Well, never mind trying; I'll just tell you about it." Hanlon laughed good-naturedly at the frantic attempts of all of them to open their eyes in accordance with his directions.

"Anyhow, you gentleman know, for I know you all belong to a big athletic club, that if you exercise any set of muscles regularly and for a long time, they will develop and expand and become greatly increased in size and strength."

"Sure," said Hendricks. "I once developed my biceps—"

"Yes, that's what I mean. Well, sir, I worked at my forehead muscles some hours a day for months and I kept at it until I had those muscles not only developed and in fine working condition but absolutely under my control. Look!"

They gazed, fascinated, while the strange visitor moved the skin of his forehead up and down and sideways, and in strange circular movements. He seemed distinctly proud of his accomplishment and paused for approbation.

"Marvelous, Holmes, marvelous!" exclaimed Hendricks, who had discovered that Hanlon did not resent jocularity, "but—what for?"

"Can't you guess?" and the young man smiled mysteriously. "Try."

"Give it up," and Hendricks shook his head. "I think it's more wonderful to get thought-transference by wiggling your forehead than any other way I ever heard of, but I can't guess how it helps."

"Can't any of you?" and Hanlon looked around the circle.

"Wait a minute," said Aunt Abby, who was thinking hard. "Let me try. Is it because when the thought waves jump from the `guide' to you they strike your forehead first—"

"And it acts as a wireless receiving station? No, ma'am, that isn't it. And, too, ma'am, I owned up, you know, that the whole thing was a fake, a trick. You see, there was no 'thought-transference,'—not any—none at all."

"Then what do you accomplish with your forehead muscles?" asked Eunice, unable to restrain her impatience.

CHAPTER 5: THE EXPLANATION

"Just this, Mrs. Embury, the impossibility of my being blindfolded. As a matter of fact, it is practically impossible to blindfold anybody, anyway."

"Why, what do you mean?" interrupted Hendricks. "Why is it?"

"Because the natural formation of most people's noses allows them to see straight down beneath an ordinary bandage. I doubt if one child out of a hundred who plays 'Blind Man's Buff' is really unable to see at all."

"That's so," said Embury, "when I played it, as a kid, I could always see straight down—though not, of course, laterally."

"And noses are different," went on Hanlon. "Some prominent beaks could never be blindfolded, but some small, flat noses might be. However, this refers to ordinary blindfolding with an ordinary handkerchief. When it comes to putting fat cotton pads in one's eye sockets, before the thick bandage is added, it necessitates previous preparation. So, my powers of contracting and expanding my forehead muscles allow me to push the pads out of the way, and enable me to see straight down the sides of my nose from under the bandage. Of course, I can see only the ground, and that but in a circumscribed area around my feet, but it's enough."

"How?" asked Eunice, her piquant face eagerly turned to the speaker. "How did you know which way to turn?"

"I don't like it," declared Aunt Abby. "I hate it—I'm absolutely disgusted with the whole performance! I detest practical jokes!"

"Oh, come now, Miss Ames," and Hendricks chuckled; "this isn't exactly a joke—it's a hoax, and a new one, but it's a legitimate game. From the Davenport Brothers and

Herrmann, on down through the line of lesser lights in the conjuring business—even our own Houdini—we know there is a trick somewhere; the fun is in finding it. Hanlon's is a new one and a gem—I don't even begin to see through it yet."

"Neither do I," agreed Mason Eliott. "I think to do what he did by a trick is really more of a feat than to be led by real thought-transference."

"Except that the real thing isn't available—and trick-work is." Hanlon smiled genially as he said this, and Embury, a little impatiently, urged him to go on, and begged the others to cease their interruptions.

"Well," Hanlon resumed, "understand, then, that I cannot be really blindfolded. No committee of citizens, however determined, can bandage my eyes in such a manner that I can't wiggle my forehead about sufficiently to get the pads up or down or one side or the other until I can see—all I want to." Hanlon knotted up his frontal muscles to prove that a bandage tied tightly would become loose when he relaxed the strain." Understand that I can see the ground only for a few inches directly at the front of me or very close to my sides. That is all."

"O.K.," said Hendricks. "Now, with your sight assured for that very limited space, what is next?"

"That, sir, is enough to explain the little game I put over in the newspaper office, before trying the out-of-door test. You remember, ladies, Mr. Mortimer told you how I followed a chalk line, drawn on the floor, and which led me up and down stairs, over chairs, under desks, and all that. Well, it was dead easy, because I could see the line on the floor all the time. Their confidence in their 'secure' blindfolding made them entirely unsuspicious of my ability to see. So, that was easy."

"Clever, though," and Embury looked at young Hanlon with admiration. "Simple, but most perfectly convincing."

"Yes, sir, it was the very simplicity of it that gulled 'em. And, of course, I'm some actor. I groped around, and felt my way by chairs and railings and door-frames, though I needn't have touched one of 'em. My way was plainly marked, and I could see the chalk line and all I had to do was to follow it. But it was that preliminary test that fixed it in their minds about the 'willing' business. I kept asking the 'guide' to keep his mind firmly on his efforts to 'will' me. I begged him to use all his mental powers to keep me in the right direction—oh, I have that poppycock all down fine—just as the mediums at the seances have."

Aunt Abby sniffed disdainfully, and Embury chuckled at her expression. Though not a 'spiritualist,' Miss Ames was greatly interested in telepathy and kindred subjects and like all the apostles of such cults she disliked to hear of frauds committed in their names.

"Go on," said Eunice, her eyes dancing with anticipation. "I love a hoax of this sort, but I can't imagine yet how you did it! I understand about the blindfolding, though, and of course that was half the battle."

"It was, ma'am, and the other half was—boots!"

"Boots!"

"Yes, ma'am. Do you know that you seldom see two pairs of boots or shoes alike on men?"

"I thought they were all alike," exclaimed Eunice. "I mean all street shoes alike, and all pumps alike, and so forth."

"No, not that," and Embury laughed; "but, I say, Hanlon, there are thousands of duplicates!"

"Not so you'd notice it I But let me explain. First, however, here are four men present. Let's compare our shoes."

Eight feet were extended, and it was surprising to note the difference in the footgear. Naturally, Hanlon's were of a cheaper grade than the others, but whereas it might have been expected that the three society men would wear almost identical boots, they were decidedly varied. Each pair was correct in style, and the work of the best bootmakers, but the difference in the design of tip, side cut, sole and fastening was quite sufficient to prevent mistaking one for another.

"You see," said Hanlon. "Well, take a whole lot of your men friends, even if they all go to the same bootmaker, and you'll find as much difference. I don't mean that there are not thousands of shoes turned out in the same factory, as alike as peas, but there is small chance of striking two pairs alike in any group of men. Then, too, there is the wear to be counted on. Suppose two of you men had bought shoes exactly alike, you wear them differently; one may run over his heel slightly, another may stub out the toe. But, these things are observable only to a trained eye. So—I trained my eye. I made a study of it, and now, if I see a shoe once, I never forget it, and never connect it with the wrong man. On the street, in the cars, everywhere I go, I look at shoes— or, rather, I did when I was training for this stunt. It was fascinating, really. Why, sometimes the only identifying mark would be the places worn or rubbed by the bones of the man's foot—but it was there, allee samee! I nailed 'm, every one! Oh, I didn't remember them all—that was only practice. But here's the application; when I started on that trip in Newark, I was introduced to Mr. Mortimer. Mind you, it was the first time I had ever laid eyes on the man. Well, unnoticed by anybody, of course, I caught onto his shoes. They were, probably, to other people, merely ordinary shoes, but to me they were as a flaming beacon light! I stamped them on my memory, every detail of them. They were not brand new, for, of course, anybody would choose an easy old pair for that walk. So there were scratches, bumps, and worn, rubbed places, that, with their general make-up, rendered them unmistakable to yours truly! Then I was ready. The earnest but easily-gulled committee carefully adjusted their useless pads of cotton and their thick bandage over my eyes, and I was led forth to the fray.

"Remember, I asked Mr. Mortimer not only to think of the hidden penknife, and will me toward it, but also to look toward it himself. Now, to look toward any object, a man usually turns his whole body in that direction. So, groping about, clumsily, I managed to get sight of the toes of those well-remembered boots. Seeing which way they were pointed was all the information I needed just then. So, with all sorts of hesitating movements and false starts, I finally trotted off in the direction he had faced. The rest is easy. Of course, coming to a corner, I was absolutely in the dark as to whether I was to turn or to keep straight ahead. This necessitated my turning back to Mr. Mortimer to catch a glimpse of which way his feet were pointing. I covered this by speaking to him, begging him to will me aright —to will me more earnestly—or some such bunk. I could invent many reasons for turning round; pretend I had lost my feeling of 'guidance,' or pretend I heard a sudden noise, as of danger, or even pretend I felt I was going wrong. Well, I got a peek at those feet as often as was necessary, and the rest was just play-acting to mislead the people's minds. Of course, when I stumbled over a stone or nearly fell into a coal hole or grating, it was all pretense. I saw the pavements as well as anybody, and my effort was to seem unaware of what was coming. Had I carefully avoided obstacles, they would know I could see."

"And when you reached that vacant lot?" prompted Eunice.

"I saw friend Mortimer's feet were pointing toward the center of the lot, and not in the direction of either street. So I turned in, and when I got where I could see the burned-down house, I guessed that was the hiding-place. So I circled around it, urging my 'guide' to look toward the place, and then noting his feet. I had to do a bit of scratching about; but remember, I could see perfectly, and I felt sure the knife was in the charred and blackened rubbish, so I just hunted till I found it. That's all."

"Well, it does sound simple and easy as you tell it, but, believe me, Hanlon, I appreciate the cleverness of the thing and the real work you went through in preparation for it all," Hendricks said, heartily, and the other men added words of admiration and approval.

But Miss Ames was distinctly displeased.

"I wouldn't mind, if you'd advertised it as a trick," she said, in an injured tone, "as, say, the conjurors do such tricks, but everybody knows they're fooling their audience. It is expected."

"Yes, lady," Hanlon smiled, "but the fake mediums and spirit-raisers, they don't say they're frauds—but they are."

"Sir, you don't know what you're talking about! Just because there are some tricksters in that, as in all professions, you must not denounce them all."

"They're all fakes, lady," and Hanlon's air of sincerity carried conviction to all but Aunt Abby.

"How do you know?" she demanded angrily.

"I've looked into it—I've looked into all sorts of stunts like these. It's in my nature, I guess. And all professional mediums are frauds. You bank on that, ma'am! If you want to tip tables or run a Ouija Board with some honest friends of yours, go ahead; but any man or woman who takes your money for showing you spiritual revelations of any sort, is a fraud and a charlatan."

"There's no exception?" asked Embury, quite surprised.

"Not among the professionals. They wouldn't keep on in their profession if they didn't put up the goods. And to do that, they've got to use the means."

"Why—why, young man—" cried Aunt Abby, explosively, "you just read 'The Voice of Isis'! You read—"

"That's all right, they are plenty of fake books, more, prob'ly, than fake mediums, but you read some books that

I'll recommend. You read 'Behind the Scenes With the Mediums,' or 'The Spirit World Unveiled,' and see where you're at then! No, ma'am, the only good spook is a dead spook, and they don't come joy-riding back to earth."

"But," and Eunice gazed earnestly at her guest, "is there nothing—nothing at all in telepathy?"

"Now you've asked a question, ma'am. I don't say there isn't, but I do say there isn't two per cent of what the fakers claim there is. I'll grant just about two per cent of real stuff in this talk of telepathy and thought-transference, and even that is mostly getting a letter the very day you were thinking about the writer!"

Embury laughed. "That's as close as I've ever come to it," he said.

"Yep, that's the commonest stunt. That and the ghostly good-by appearance of a friend that's dyin' at the time in a distant land."

"Aren't those cases ever true?" Eunice asked.

"'Bout two per cent of 'em. Most of those that have been traced down to actual evidence have fizzled out. Well, I must be going. You see, now, I've sold this whole spiel that I've just given you folks to a big newspaper syndicate, and I got well paid. That puts me on Easy Street, for the time bein', and I'm going to practice up for a new stunt. When you hear again of Willy Hanlon, it'll be in a very different line of goods!"

"What?" asked Eunice, interestedly.

"'Scuse me, ma'am. I'd tell you, if I'd tell anybody. But, you see, it ain't good business. I just thought up a new line of work and I'm going to take time to perfect myself in it, and then spring it on a long-sufferin' public."

"No, I won't ask you to tell, of course," Eunice agreed, "but when you give an exhibition, if it's near New York, let me know, won't you?"

"Yes, ma'am, I sure will. And now I'll move on."

"Oh, no, you must wait for a cup of tea; we'll have it brought at once."

Eunice left the room for a moment. Aunt Abby in
dudgeon, refused to talk to the disappointing visitor. But
the three men quickly engaged him in conversation and
Hanlon told some anecdotes of his past experiences that
kept them interested.

Ferdinand brought in the tea things, and Eunice, with
her graceful hospitality, saw to it that her guest was in no
way embarrassed or bothered by unaccustomed service.

"I've had a right good time," he said in his boyish way,
as he rose to go. "Thank you, ma'am, for the tea and
things. I liked it all."

His comprehensive glance that swept the room and its
occupants was a sincere compliment and after he had
gone there was only kindly comment on his personality.

Except from Aunt Abby.

"He's an ignorant boor," she announced.

"Now, now," objected Eunice, "you only say that
because he upset your favorite delusions. He punctured
your bubbles and pulled down your air-castles. Give it
up, Aunt Abby, there's nothing in your' Voice of Isis'
racket!"

"Permit me to be the judge of my own five senses,
Eunice, if you please."

"That's just it, Miss Ames," spoke up Hendricks. "Is
your psychic information, or whatever it is, discernible to
your five senses, or any of them?"

"Of course, or how could I realize the presence of the
psychic forces?"

"I don't know just what those things are, but I
supposed they were available only to a sort of sixth
sense—or seventh! Why, I have five senses, but I don't
lay claim to any more than that."

"You're a trifler, and I decline to discuss the subject
seriously with you. You've always been a trifler, Alvord—
remember, I've known you from boyhood, and though
you've a brilliant brain, you have not utilized it to the
best advantage."

"Sorry, ma'am," and the handsome face put on a mock penitence, "but I'm too far advanced in years to pull up now."

"Nonsense! you're barely thirty! That's a young man."

"Not nowadays. They say, after thirty, a man begins to fall to pieces, mentally."

"Oh, Al, what nonsense!" cried Eunice. "Why, thirty isn't even far enough along to be called the prime of life!"

"Oh, yes, it is, Eunice, in this day and generation. Nobody thinks a man can do any great creative work after thirty. Inventing, you know, or art or literature—honestly, that's the attitude now. Isn't it, Mason?"

Elliott looked serious. "It is an opinion recently expressed by some big man," he admitted. "But I don't subscribe to it. Why, I'd be sorry to think I'm a down-and-outer! And I'm in the class with you and Embury."

"You're none of you in the sere and yellow," declared Eunice, laughing at the idea. "Why, even Aunt Abby, in spite of the family record, is about as young as any of us."

"I know I am," said the old lady, serenely. "And I know more about my hobby of psychic lore in a minute than you young things ever heard of in all your life! So, don't attempt to tell me what's what!"

"That's right, Miss Ames, you do!" and Mason Elliott looked earnestly at her. "I'm half inclined to go over to your side myself. Will you take me some time to one of your seances—but wait, I only, want to go to one where, as you said, the psychic manifestations are perceptible to one or more of the five well-known senses. I don't want any of this talk of a mysterious sixth sense."

"Oh, Mason, I wish you would go with me! Madame Medora gives wonderful readings!"

"Mason! I'm ashamed of you!" cried Eunice, laughing. "Don't let him tease you, Aunt Abby; he doesn't mean a word he says!"

"Oh, but I do! I want to learn to read other people's thoughts —not like our friend Hanlon, but really, by means of my senses and brain."

"You prove you haven't any brain, when you talk like that!" put in Hendricks, contemptuously.

"And you prove you haven't any sense," retorted Elliott "I say, who's for a walk? I've got to sweep the cobwebs out of the place where my brain ought to be— even if it is empty, as my learned colleague avers."

"I'll go," and Eunice jumped up. "I want a breath of fresh air. Come along, San?"

"Nixy I've got to look over some papers in connection with my coming election as president of a big club."

"Your coming election may come when you're really in the prime of life," Hendricks laughed, "or, perhaps, not till you strike the sere and yellow, but if you refer to this year's campaign of the Athletic Club, please speak of my coming election."

"Oh, you two deadly rivals!" exclaimed Eunice. "I'm glad to be out of it, if you're going to talk about those eternal prize-fights and club theatres! Come on, Mason, let's go for a brisk walk in the park."

Eunice went to her room, and came back, looking unusually beautiful in a new spring habit. The soft fawn color suited her dark type and a sable scarf round her throat left exposed an adorable triangle of creamy white flesh.

"Get through with your squabbling, little boys," she said, gaily, with a saucy smile at Hendricks and a swift, perfunctory kiss on Embury's cheek, and then she went away with Mason Elliott.

They walked a few blocks in silence, and then Elliott said, abruptly: "What were you and Sanford quarreling about?"

"Aren't you a little intrusive?" but a smile accompanied the words.

"No, Eunice; it isn't intrusion. I have the right of an old friend—more than a friend, from my point of view—and I ask only from the best and kindest motives."

"Could you explain some those motives?" She tried to make her voice cold and distant, but only succeeded in making it pathetic.

"I could—but I think it better, wiser and more honorable not to. You know, dear, why I want to know. Because I want you to be the happiest woman in the whole world—and if Sanford Embury can't make you so—"

"Nobody can!" she interrupted him, quickly. "Don't, Mason," she turned a pleading look toward him; "don't say anything we may both regret. You know how good Sanford is to me; you know how happy we are together"

"Were," he corrected, very gravely.

"Were—and are," she insisted. "And you know, too—no one better—what a fiendish temper I have! Though I try my best to control it, it breaks out now and then, and I am helpless. Sanford thinks he can tame it by giving me as good as I send —by playing, as he calls it, Petruchio to my Katherine—but, somehow, I don't believe that's the treatment I need."

Her dark eyes were wistful, but she did not look at him.

"Of course it isn't!" Elliott returned, in a low voice. "I know your nature, Eunice; I've known it all our lives. You need kindness when you are in a tantrum. The outbursts of temper you cannot help—that I know positively—they're an integral part of your nature. But they're soon over—often the fiercer they are, the quicker they pass,—and if you were gently managed, not brutally, at the time they occur, it would go far to help you to overcome them entirely. But—and I ask you again—what were you discussing to-day when I came?"

"Why do you want to know?"

"I think I do know—and forgive me, if I offend you—I think I can help you."

"What do you mean?   "Eunice looked up with a frightened stare.

"Don't look like that—oh, Eunice, don't!   I only meant—I know you want money—ready money—let me give it to you—or lend it to you—do, Eunice—darling!"

"Thank you, Mason," Eunice forced herself to say, "but I must refuse your offer.   I think—I think we—we'll go home now."

Chapter 6: A Slammed Door

"Don't you call her 'that Desternay woman'!"

"I'll call her what I please! And without asking your permission, either. And I won't have my wife playing bridge at what is practically a gambling house!"

"Nothing of the sort! A party of invited guests, in a private house is a social affair, and you shall not call it ridiculous names! You play for far higher stakes at your club than we ever do at Fifi Desternay's."

"That name is enough! Fancy your associating with a woman who calls herself Fifi!"

"She can't help her name! It was probably wished on her by her parents in baptism—"

"It probably was not! She was probably christened Mary Jane!"

"You seem to know a lot about her."

"I know all I want to; and you have reached the end of your acquaintance with her and her set. You are not to go there, Eunice, and that's all there is about it."

The Emburys were in Eunice's bedroom. Sanford was in evening dress and was about to leave for his club. Eunice, who had dined in a negligee, was donning an elaborate evening costume. She had dismissed her maid when Embury came into the room, and was herself adjusting the finishing touches. Her gown of henna-colored chiffon, with touches of gold embroidery, was most becoming to her dark beauty, and some fine ornaments of ancient carved gold gave an Oriental touch to her appearance. She stood before a long mirror, noting the details of her gown, and showed an irritating lack of attention to Embury's last dictum.

"You heard me, Eunice?" he said, caustically, his hand on the doorknob.

"Not being deaf, I did," she returned, without looking toward him.

"And you will obey me?" He turned back, and reaching her side, he grasped her arm with no uncertain touch. "I demand your obedience!"

"Demands are not always granted!"

She gave him a dazzling smile, but it was defiant rather than friendly.

"I make it a request, then. Will you grant me that?"

"Why should I grant your requests, when you won't grant mine?"

"Good Lord, Eunice, are you going to harp on that allowance string again?"

"I am. Why shouldn't I, when it warps my whole life—"

"Oh, come, cut out the hifalutin' talk!" "Well, then, to come down to plain facts, there isn't a day that I'm not humiliated and embarrassed by the lack of a little cash."

"Bad as that?"

"Yes, quite as bad as that! Why, the day we went out to Newark I didn't have five cents to buy Aunt Abby a newspaper, and she had to get along without one!"

"She seemed to live through it."

"Sanford, you're unbearable! And to-day, at Mrs. Garland's, a woman talked, and then they took up a collection for the 'Belgian Home Fires,' and I didn't have a cent to contribute."

"Who is she? I'll send a check."

"A check! You answer everything by a check! Can't you understand? Oh, there's no use explaining; you're determined you won't understand! So, let us drop the subject. Is to-night the club election?"

"No, to-morrow night. But to-night will probably decide it in my mind. It practically hinges on the Meredith set—if they can be talked over—"

"Oh, Sanford, I do hope they can!" Eunice's eyes sparkled and she smiled as she put her hands on her husband's shoulders. "And, listen, dear, if they are—if you do win the election, won't you —oh, San, won't you give me an allowance?"

"Eunice, you're enough to drive a man crazy! Will you let up on that everlasting whine? No, I won't! Is that plain?"

"Then I shall go and get it for myself!"

"Go to the devil for all I care!"

Sanford flung out of the room, banging the door behind him. Eunice heard him speaking to Ferdinand, rather shortly, and as he left the apartment, she knew that he had gone to the club in their motor car, and if she went out, she would have to call a cab.

She began to take off her gown, half deciding to stay at home. She had never run counter to Embury's expressed orders and she hesitated to do so now.

And yet—the question of money, so summarily dismissed by her husband, was a very real trouble to her. In her social position, she actually needed ready cash frequently, and she had determined to get it. Her last hope of Sanford failed her, when he refused to grant her wish as a sort of celebration of his election, and she persuaded herself that it was her right to get some money somehow.

Her proposed method was by no means a certain one, for it was the hazardous plan of winning at bridge.

Although a first-rate player, Eunice often had streaks of bad luck, and, too, inexpert partners were a dangerous factor. But, though she sometimes said that winnings and losings came out about even in the long run, she had found by keeping careful account, her skill made it probable for her to win more than she lost, and this reasoning prompted her to risk high stakes in hope of winning something worth-while.

Fifi Desternay was a recent acquaintance of hers, and not a member of the set Eunice looked upon as her own. But the gatherings at the Desternay house were gay and pleasant, a bit Bohemian, yet exclusive too, and Eunice had already spent several enjoyable afternoons there.

She had never been in the evening, for Embury wouldn't go, and had refused to let her go without him. Nor did she want to, for it was not Eunice's way to go out alone at night.

But she was desperate and, moreover, she was exceedingly angry. Sanford was unjust and unkind. Also, he had been cross and ugly, and had left her in anger, a thing that had never happened before.

And she wanted some money at once. A sale of laces was to be held next day at a friend's home, and she wanted to go there, properly prepared to purchase some bits if she chose to.

Her cheeks flushed as she remembered Mason Elliott's offer to give or lend her money, but she smiled gently, as she remembered the true friendliness of the man, and his high-mindedness, which took all sting from his offer.

As she brooded, her anger became more fierce, and finally, with a toss of her head, she rose from the chair, rang for the maid, and proceeded to finish her toilette.

"Lend me some money, will you, Aunt Abby?" she asked, as, all ready to go, she stepped into the livingroom.

She had no hesitancy in making this appeal. If she won, she would repay on her return. If she lost, Aunt Abby was a good-natured waiter, and she knew Eunice would pay later.

"Bridge?" said the old lady, smiling at the lovely picture Eunice made, in her low gown and her billowy satin wrap. "I thought Sanford took the car."

"He did. I'm going in a taxi. What a duck you are to let me have this," as she spoke she stuffed the bills in her soft gold mesh-bag. "Don't sir up, dear, I'll be out till all hours."

"Where are you going?"

"To the end of the rainbow—where there's a pot of gold! You read your spook books, and then go to bed and dream of ghosts and specters!"

Eunice kissed her lightly, and gathering up her floating draperies, went out of the room with the faithful and efficient Ferdinand.

On his way to the club, Embury pursued that pleasing occupation known as nursing his wrath. He was sorry he had left Eunice in anger—he realized it was the first time that had ever happened— and he was tempted to go back, or, at least to telephone back, that he was sorry. But that would do little good, he knew, unless he also said he was willing to accede to her request for an allowance, and that he was as sternly set against as ever.

He couldn't quite have told himself why he was so positive in this matter, but it was largely owing to an instinctive sense of the fitness of having a wife dependent on her husband for all things. Moreover, it seemed to him that unlimited charge accounts betokened a greater generosity than an allowance, and he felt an aggrieved irritation at Eunice's seeming ingratitude.

The matter of her wanting "chicken-feed" now and then seemed to him too petty to be worthy of serious consideration. He really believed that he gave her money whenever she asked for it, and was all unaware how hard he made it for her to ask.

The more he thought about it, the more he saw Eunice in the wrong, and himself an injured, unappreciated benefactor.

He adored his wife, but this peculiarity of hers must be put an end to somehow. Her temper, too, was becoming worse instead of better; her outbreaks were more frequent, more furious, and he had less power to quell them than formerly.

Clearly, he concluded, Eunice must be taught a lesson, and this occasion must be made a test case. He had left her angrily, and it might turn out that it was the best thing he could have done. Poor girl, she doubtless was sorry enough by now; crying, probably. His heart softened as he conjured up the picture of his wife alone, and in tears, but he reasoned that it would do her good, and he would give her a new jewel to make up for it, after the trouble was all over.

So he went on to the club, and dove into the great business of the last possible chance of electioneering.

Though friendly through all this campaign, the strain was beginning to tell on the two candidates, and both Embury and Hendricks found it a little difficult to keep up their good feeling.

"But," they both reasoned, "as soon as the election is over, we'll be all right again. We're both too good sports to hold rancor, or to feel any jealousy."

And this was true. Men of the world, men of well-balanced minds, clever, logical and just, they were fighting hard, each for his own side, but once the matter was decided, they would be again the same old friends.

However, Embury was just as well pleased to learn that Hendricks was out of town. He had gone to Boston on an important business matter, and though it was not so stated, Embury was pretty sure that the important business was closely connected with the coming election.

In his own endeavor to secure votes, Embury was not above playing the, to him, unusual game of being all things to all men.

And this brought him into cordial conversation with one of the younger club members, who was of the type he generally went out of his way to avoid.

"Try to put yourself in our place, Mr. Embury," the cub was saying. "We want this club to be up-to-date and beyond. Conservatism is all very well, and we all practiced it 'for the duration,' but now the war's over, let's have some fun, say we!"

"I know, Billy, but there is a certain standard to be maintained—"

"We, the people of the United States—and tiddle tya—tya—tya! Why, everybody's doing it! The women—bless 'em!—too. I just left your wife at a table with my wife, and the pile of chips between 'em would make some men's card-rooms hide their diminished walls!"

"That so? You saw my wife this evening? Where?"

"As if you didn't know! But, good heavens! perhaps you didn't! Have I been indiscreet?"

"Not at all. At Mrs. Desternay's, wasn't it?"

"Yes, but you gave me a jolt. I was afraid I'd peached."

"Not at all. They're friends."

"Well, between you and me, they oughtn't to be. I let Gladys go, under protest—I left her there myself—but it's never again for her! I shall tell her so to-night."

Embury changed the subject and by using all his self-control gave no hint of his wrath. So Eunice had gone after all! After his expressly forbidding it! It was almost unbelievable!

And within an hour of his receiving information, Sanford Embury, in his own car, stopped at the Desternay house.

Smiling and debonair as he entered the drawingroom, he greeted the hostess and asked for his wife.

"Oh, don't disturb her, dear Mr. Embury," begged the vivacious Fifi; "she's out for blood! She's in the den, with three of our wizards and the sky's their limit!"

"Tut, tut! What naughtiness!" Embury's manner was just the right degree of playful reproach, and his fine poise and distinguished air attracted attention from many of the players.

The rooms were filled, without being crowded, and a swift mental stock-taking of the appointments and atmosphere convinced the newcomer that his preconception of the place was about right.

"I must take her away before she cleans out the bunch," he laughed, and made progress toward the 'den.'

"Here you are," he said lightly, as he came upon Eunice, with another woman and two men, all of whom were silently concentrating on what was quite evidently a stiff game.

"Yes, here I am," she returned; "don't speak please, until I finish this hand."

Eunice was playing the hand, and though her face paled, and a spot of bright color appeared on either cheek she did not lose her head, and carried the hand through to a successful conclusion.

"Game and rubber!" she cried, triumphantly, and the vanquished pair nodded regretfully.

"And the last game, please, for my wife," Embury said, in calm, courteous tones. "You can get a substitute, of course. Come, Eunice!"

There was something icy in his tones that made Eunice shiver, though it was not noticeable to strangers, and she rose, smiling, with a few gay words of apology.

"Perfectly awful of me to leave, when I'm winning," she said, "but there are times, you know, when one remembers the 'obey' plank in the matrimonial platform! Dear Fifi, forgive me—"

She moved about gracefully, saying a word or two of farewell, and then disappeared to get her wrap, with as little disturbance as possible of the other players.

"You naughty man!" and Mrs. Desternay shook her finger at Embury; "if you weren't so good-looking I should put you in my black books!"

"That would at least keep me in your memory," he returned, but his smile was now quite evidently a forced one.

And his words of farewell were few, as he led Eunice from the house and down to the car.

He handed her in, and then sat beside her, as the chauffeur turned homeward.

Not a word was spoken by either of them during the whole ride.

Several times Eunice decided to break the silence, but concluded not to. She was both angry and frightened, but the anger predominated.

Embury sat motionless, his face pale and stern, and when they arrived at their own house, he assisted her from the car, quite as usual, dismissed the chauffeur, with a word of orders for the next day, and then the pair went into the house.

Ferdinand met them at their door, and performed his efficient and accustomed services.

And then, after a glance at her husband, Eunice went into her own room and closed the door.

Embury smoked a cigarette or two, and at last went to his room.

Ferdinand attended him, and the concerned expression on the old servant's face showed, though he tried to repress it, an anxiety as to the very evident trouble that was brewing.

But he made no intrusive remark or implication, though a furtive glance at his master betokened a resentment of his treatment of Eunice, the idol of Ferdinand's heart.

Dismissed, he left Embury's room, and closed the door softly behind him.

The door between the rooms of Embury and his wife stood a little ajar, and as his hand fell on it to shut it, he heard a stifled gasp of "Sanford!"

He looked in, and saw Eunice, in a very white heat of rage. In all their married life he had never seen her so terribly angry as she looked then. Speechless from very fury, she stood, with clenched hands, trying to command her voice.

She looked wonderfully beautiful like some statue of an avenging angel—he almost fancied he could see a flaming sword!

As he looked, she took a step toward him, her eyes burning with a glance of hate. Judith might have looked so, or Jael. Not exactly frightened, but alarmed, lest she might fly into a passion of rage that would really injure her, Embury closed the door, practically in her very face. Indeed, practically, he slammed it, with all the audible implication of which a slammed door is capable.

The next morning Ferdinand waited for the usual summons from Embury's bedroom. The tea tray was ready, the toast crisp and hot, but the summons of the bell was unusually delayed.

When the clock pointed to fifteen minutes past the hour Ferdinand tapped on Embury's door. A few moments later he tapped again, rapping louder.

Several such attempts brought no response, and the valet tried the door. It would not open, so Ferdinand went to Eunice's door and knocked there.

Jumping from her bed, and throwing a kimono round her, Eunice opened her own door.

Ferdinand started at sight of her white face, but recovered himself, and said, "Mr. Embury, ma'am. He doesn't answer my knock. Can he be ill?"

"Oh, I guess not," Eunice tried to speak casually, but miserably failed. "Go through that way." She pointed to the door between her room and her husband's.

Ferdinand hesitated. "You open it, Mrs. Embury, please," he said, and his voice shook.

"Why, Ferdinand, what do you mean? Open that door!"

"Yes, ma'am," and turning the knob, Ferdinand entered.

"Why, he's still asleep!" he exclaimed. "Shall I wake him?"

"Yes—that is—yes, of course! Wake him up, Ferdinand."

The door on the other side of Eunice's room opened, and Aunt Abby put her head in.

"What's the matter? What's Ferdinand doing in your room, Eunice? Are you ill?"

"No, Aunt Abby—" but Eunice got no further. She sank back on her bed, and buried her face in the pillows.

"Get up, Mr. Embury—it's late," Ferdinand was saying, and then he lightly touched the arm of his master. "He—he—oh, Miss Eunice! Oh, my God! Why, ma'am—he—he looks to be dead!"

With a shriek, Eunice raised her head a moment and then flung it down on the pillows again, crying, "I don't believe it! You don't know what you're saying! It can't be so!"

"Yes, I do, ma'am—he's—why, he's cold!"

"Let me come in!" ordered Aunt Abby, as Ferdinand tried to bar her entrance; "let me see, I tell you! Yes, he is dead! Oh, Eunice—now, Ferdinand, don't lose your head! Go quickly and telephone for Doctor—what's his name? I mean the one in this building—on the ground floor—Harper—that's it—Doctor Harper. Go, man, go!"

Ferdinand went, and Aunt Abby leaned over the silent figure.

"What do you suppose ailed him, Eunice? He was perfectly well, when he went to bed, wasn't he?"

"Yes," came a muffled reply.

"Get up, Eunice; get up, dear. That doctor will be here in a minute. Brush up your hair, and fasten your kimono. You won't have time to dress. I must put on a cap."

Aunt Abby flew to her bedroom, and returned quickly, wearing a lace cap Eunice had given her, and talking as she adjusted it.

"It must be a stroke—and yet, people don't have strokes at his age. It can't be apoplexy—he isn't that build—and, too, he's such an athlete; there's nothing the matter with him. It can't be—oh, mercy gracious! it can't be—Eunice! Sanford wouldn't kill himself, would he?"

"No! no! of course not!"

"Not just now before the election—no, of course he wouldn't! But it can't be-oh, Lord, what can it be?"

CHAPTER 7: A VISION

"I have never been so mystified in all my life!" Dr. Harper spoke in a perplexed, worried way, and a puzzled frown drew his shaggy eyebrows together. Though the family physician of most of the tenants of the large, up-to-date apartment house, he was of the old school type and had the kindly, sociable ways of a smalltown practitioner.

"I know Sanford Embury, bone, blood and muscle," he said; "I've not only been his physician for two years, but I've examined him, watched him and kept him in pink of condition for his athletic work. If I hadn't looked after him, he might have overdone his athletics—but he didn't—he used judgment, and was more than willing to follow my advice. Result—he was in the most perfect possible physical shape in every particular! He could no more have had a stroke of apoplexy or paralysis than a young oak tree could! And there's no indication of such a thing, either. A man can't die of a stroke of any sort without showing certain symptoms. None of these are present—there's nothing present to hint the cause of his death. There's no cut, scratch or mark of any description; there's no suggestion of strangulation or heart failure— well, it's the strangest thing I ever ran up against in all my years of practice!"

The doctor sat at the Embury breakfast table, heartily partaking of the dishes Ferdinand offered. He had prescribed aromatic ammonia for Eunice, and a cup of coffee for Miss Ames, and then he had made a careful examination of Sanford Embury's mortal body.

Upon its conclusion he had insisted that the ladies join him at breakfast and he saw to it that they made more than a pretense of eating.

"You've a hard day ahead of you," he said, in his gentle, paternal way, "and you must be fortified as far as possible. I may seem harsh, Mrs. Embury, but I'm going to ask you to be as brave as you can, right now—at first— as I may say—and then, indulge in the luxury of tears later on. This sounds brutal, I daresay, but I've a reason, dear madam. There's a mystery here. I don't go so far as to say there's anything wrong—but there's a very mysterious death to be looked into, and as your physician and your friend, I want to advise—to urge you to keep up your strength for what may be a trying ordeal. In the first place, I apprehend an autopsy will be advisable, and I trust you will give your consent to that."

"Oh, no!" cried Eunice, her face drawn with dismay, "not that!"

"Now, now, be reasonable, Mrs. Embury. I know you dislike the idea—most people do—but I think I shall have to insist upon it."

"But you can't do it, unless I agree, can you?" and Eunice looked at him sharply.

"No—but I'm sure you will agree."

"I won't! I never will! You shan't touch Sanford! I won't allow it."

"She's right!" declared Aunt Abby. "I can't see, doctor, why it is necessary to have a postmortem. I don't approve of such things. Surely you can, somehow discover what Mr. Embury died of—and if not, what matter? He's dead, and nothing can change that! It doesn't seem to me that we have to know—"

"Pardon me, Miss Ames, it is necessary that I should know the cause of the death. I cannot make a report until—"

"Well you can find out, I should think."

"I never heard of a doctor who couldn't determine the cause of a simple, natural death of one of his own patients!" Eunice's glance was scathing and her tones full of scorn.

But the doctor realized the nervous tension she was under, and forbore to take offense, or to answer her sharply.

"Well, well, we'll see about it," he temporized. "I shall first call in Marsden, a colleague of mine, in consultation. I admit I'm at the end of my own knowledge. Tell me the details of last evening. Was Mr. Embury just as usual, so far as you noticed?"

"Of course he was," said Eunice, biting the words off crisply. "He went to the Athletic Club he's a candidate for the presidency—"

"I know—I know—"

"And I—I was at a party. On his way from the club he called for me and brought me home in our car. Then he went to bed almost at once-and so did I. That's all."

"You heard no sound from him whatever during the night?"

"None."

"As nearly as I can judge, he died about daybreak. But it is impossible to say positively as to that. Especially as I cannot find the immediate cause of death. You heard nothing during the night, Miss Ames?"

"I did and I didn't," was the strange reply.

"Just what does that mean? "and Doctor Harper looked at her curiously.

"Well," and Aunt Abby spoke very solemnly, "Sanford appeared to me in a vision, just as he died—"

"Oh, Aunt Abby," Eunice groaned, "don't begin that sort of talk! Miss Ames is a sort of a spiritualist, doctor, and she has hallucinations."

"Not hallucinations—visions," corrected the old, lady. "And it is not an unheard of phenomenon to have a dying person appear to a friend at the moment of death. It was the passing of Sanford, and I did see him!"

Eunice rose and left the table. Her shattered nerves couldn't stand this, to her mind, foolishness at the moment.

She went from the dining-room into the livingroom, and stood, gazing out of the window, but seeing nothing.

Dr. Harper pushed back his chair from the table.

"Just a word more about that, Miss Ames," he said. "I'm rather interested in those matters myself. You thought you saw Mr. Embury?"

"I did see him. It was a vague, shadowy form, but I recognized him. He came into my room from Eunice's room. He paused at my bedside and leaned over me, as if for a farewell. He said nothing—and in a moment he disappeared. But I know it was Sanford's spirit taking flight."

"This is interesting, but I can't discuss it further now. I have heard of such cases, but never so directly. But my duty now is to Mrs. Embury. I fear she will have a nervous breakdown. May I ask you, Miss Ames, not to talk about you—your vision to her? I think it disturbs her."

"Don't you tell me, doctor, what to talk to Eunice about, and what not to! I brought up that girl from a baby, and I know her clear through! If it upsets her nerves to hear about my experience last night, of course, I shall not talk about it to her, but trust me, please, to know what is best to do about that!"

"Peppery women—both of them!" was Dr. Harper's mental comment; but he only nodded his head pleasantly and went to Eunice.

"If you've no objections, I'll call Marsden here at once," he said, already taking up the telephone.

Eunice listlessly acquiesced, and then the doctor returned to Embury's bedroom.

He looked carefully about. All the details of the room, the position of clothing, the opened book, face down, on the night table, the half-emptied water-glass, the penciled memorandum on the chiffonier—all seemed to bear witness to the well, strong man, who expected to rise and go about his day as usual.

"Not a chance of suicide," mused the doctor, hunting about the room and scrutinizing its handsome appointments. He stepped into Embury's bathroom, and could find nothing that gave him the least hint of anything unusual in the man's life. A chart near the white, enameled scale showed that Embury had recorded his weight the night before in his regular, methodical way. The written figures were clear and firm, as always. Positively the man had no premonition of his swiftly approaching end.

What could have caused it? What could have snapped short the life thread of this strong, sound specimen of human vitality? Dr. Harper could find no possible answer, and he was glad to hear Ferdinand's voice as he announced the arrival of Dr. Marsden. The two men held earnest consultation.

The newcomer was quite as much mystified as his colleague, and they marveled together.

"Autopsy, of course," said Marsden, finally; "the widow must be brought to consent. Why does she object so strongly?"

"I don't know of any reason except the usual dislike the members of the family feel toward it. I've no doubt she will agree, when you advise it."

Eunice Embury did agree, but it was only after the strenuous insistence of Dr. Marsden.

She flew into a rage at first, and the doctor, who was unacquainted with her, wondered at her fiery exhibition of temper.

And, but for the arrival of Mason Elliott on the scene, she might have resisted longer.

Elliott had telephoned, wishing to consult Embury on some matter, and Ferdinand's incoherent and emotional words had brought out the facts, so of course Elliott had come right over to the house.

"What is it, Eunice?" he asked, as he entered, seeing her fiercely quarreling with the doctors. "Let me help you—advise you. Poor child, you ought to be in bed."

His kindly, assertive voice calmed her, and turning her sad eyes to him, she moaned, plaintively, "Don't let them do it—they mustn't do it."

"Do what? "Elliott turned to the doctors, and soon was listening to the whole strange story.

"Certainly an autopsy!" he declared; "why, it's the only thing to do. Hush, Eunice, make no further objection. It's absolutely necessary. Give your consent at once."

Almost as if hypnotized, Eunice Embury gave her consent, and the two doctors went away together.

"Tell me all about it," said Elliott; "all you know—" And then he saw how weak and unnerved Eunice was, and he quickly added, "No, not now. Go and lie down for a time—where's Miss Ames?"

"Here," and Aunt Abby reappeared from her room. "Yes, go and lie down, Eunice; Maggie has made up our rooms, and your bed is in order. Go, dear child."

"I don't want to," and Eunice's eyes looked unusually large and bright. "I'm not the sort of woman who can cure everything by 'lying down'! I'd rather talk. Mason, what happened to Sanford?"

"I don't know, Eunice. It's the strangest thing I ever heard of. If you want to talk, really, tell me what occurred last night. Did you two have a quarrel?"

"Yes, we did—" Eunice looked defiant rather than penitent. "But that couldn't have done it! I mean, we didn't quarrel so violently that San burst a blood-vessel— or that sort of thing!"

"Of course not; in that case the doctors would know. That's the queerest thing to me. A man dies, and two first-class physicians can't say what killed him!"

"But what difference does it make, Mason? I'm sure I don't care what he died of—I mean I don't want him all cut up to satisfy the curiosity of those inquisitive doctors!"

"It isn't that, Eunice; they have to know the cause, to make out a death certificate."

"Why do they have to make it out? We all know he's dead."

"The law requires it. The Bureau of Vital Statistics must be notified and must be told the cause of death. Try to realize that these matters are important—you cannot put your own personal preferences above them. Leave it to me, Eunice; I'll take charge and look after all the details. Poor old San—I can't realize it! He was so big and strong and healthy. And so full of life and vitality. And, by Jove, Eunice, think of the election!"

Though a warm friend of Embury, it was characteristic of Elliott that his thoughts should fly to the consequences of the tragic death outside the family circle. He was silent as he realized that the removal of the other candidate left Alvord Hendricks the winner in the race for president of the club.

That is, if the election should be held. It was highly probable that it would be postponed—the club people ought to be notified at once—Hendricks ought to be told.

"I say, Eunice, there's lots of things to do. I think I ought to telephone the club, and several people. Do you mind?"

"No; of course not. Do whatever is right, Mason. I'm so glad to have you here, it takes a load of responsibility off of me. You're a tower of strength."

"Then do what you can to help me, Eunice. Try, won't you, to be quiet and calm. Don't get so wrought up over these things that are unpleasant but unavoidable. I don't underrate your grief or your peculiarly hard position. The nervous shock is enough to make you ill—but try to control yourself—that's a goody girl."

"I will, Mason. Honest I will."

Soon after noon Hendricks arrived. He had returned from Boston on an early morning train, and hearing of the tragedy, came at once to the Embury home.

At sight of his grave, sympathetic face, Eunice burst into tears, the first she had been able to shed, and they were a real relief to her overburdened heart.

"Oh, Alvord," she cried, hysterically, "now you can be president!"

"Hush, hush, Eunice, dear," he soothed her; "don't let's speak of that now. I'm just in from Boston—I hurried over as soon as I heard. Tell me, somebody—not you, Eunice—you tell me, Aunt Abby, how it happened."

"That's the strange part," said Elliott, who was sitting at the telephone, and was, at the moment, waiting for a response to a call, "the doctors can't tell what ailed Sanford!"

"What! Can't tell what made him die!"

"No;" Aunt Abby took up the tale, as Elliott turned hack to the telephone; "and I think it's very queer. Did you ever know a man to die, Alvord, and nobody be able to tell what killed him?"

"I certainly never did! What had he eaten?"

"Oh, it's nothing like that," Eunice spoke up; "it must be that something gave way—his heart, or lungs—"

"Never! Sanford was a sound as a dollar!"

"That's what Dr. Harper says. They're—they're going to have an autopsy."

"Of course. We'd never be satisfied without that. They'll find the cause that way, of course. Dear Eunice, I'm so sorry for you."

"It's awful for Eunice," said Aunt Abby "the excitement and the mystery—oh, Alvord, do let me tell you what I saw!"

"What?" he asked, with interest.

"Why, it was almost dawn—just beginning to be daylight, and, you know—Dr. Harper says Sanford died about daybreak—he thinks—and I was sort of between asleep and awake—don't you know how you are like that sometimes—"

"Yes."

"And I saw—"

"Aunt Abby, if you're going to tell that yarn over again, I'll go away! I can't stand it!"

"Go on, Eunice," and Aunt Abby spoke gently. "I wish you would go to your room and lie down for awhile. Even if you don't want to, it will rest your nerves."

To her surprise, Eunice rose and without a word went to her own room.

Aunt Abby sent Maggie to look after her, and resumed her story.

"I'm going to tell you, Alvord, for I must tell somebody, and Eunice won't listen, and Mason is busy telephoning—he's been at it all day—off and on—"

"Fire away, Aunt Abby, dear," Hendricks said. He had small desire to hear her meandering tales, but he felt sorry for the pathetic face she showed and listened out of sheer charity.

"Yes, it was near dawn, and I was sort of dozing but yet, awake, too—and I heard a step—no, not a step, just a sort of gliding footfall, like a person shufing in slippers.

"And then, I saw a vague shadowy shape—like Sanford's—and it passed slowly through the room—not stepping, more like floating —and it stopped right at my bedside, and leaned over me—"

"You saw this!"

"Well, it was so dark, I can't say I saw it—but I was— I don't know how to describe it—I was conscious of its presence, that's all!"

"And you think it was Sanford's ghost?"

"Don't put it that way, Al. It was Sanford's spirit, leaving the earth, and bidding me good-by as it wafted past."

"Why didn't he bid his wife good-by?" Hendricks was blunt, but he deemed it best to speak thus, rather than to encourage the ghost talk.

"He probably tried to, but Eunice must have been asleep. I don't know as to that—but, you know, Alvord, it is not an uncommon thing for such experiences to happen—why, there are thousands of authenticated cases—"

"Authenticated fiddlesticks!"

"Your scorn doesn't alter the truth. I saw him, I tell you, and it was not a dream, or my imagination. I really saw him, though dimly."

"What did he have on?"

"That's the queer part. Not his usual clothes, but that sort of a jersey he wears when he's doing his exercise."

"Oh, his gym suit? You saw it plainly?"

"Not so very plainly—but—I felt it!"

"Felt it! What are you talking about?"

"I did, I tell you. He leaned over me, and I put out my hand and touched his arm, and I—I think I felt a tight woolen jersey sleeve."

"Oh, you think you did! Well, that's all right, then, but you mustn't say you felt a ghost. They're not material, you know."

"You're making fun of me, Alvord, but you mustn't. I know more about these things than you do. Why shouldn't I? I've made a study of them—I've read lots of books, and been to lots of seances, and lectures—oh, I know it was a manifestation of San himself!"

"Well, Aunt Abby, if it gives you any comfort to think it was, why, just keep right on thinking. I don't say there aren't such happenings. I only say I don't believe there are. I don't doubt your word, you understand, but I can't make my hard common sense take it in. My mind isn't built that way. Did you hear anything?"

"I heard—" Aunt Abby paused, and blushed a little— "you'll laugh, I know, but I heard—his watch ticking!"

"Oh, come now, Aunt Abby, that's a little too much! I can't help smiling at that! For I'm sure ghosts don't carry watches, and anyway not in a gymnasium suit!"

"I knew you'd jeer at it, but I did hear the ticking, all the same."

"Wasn't your own watch under your pillow?"

"Yes."

"Oh, all right. I haven't a word to say."

"But it wasn't any watch I heard—it was a different sort of tick."

"Yes, of course it was. Ghosts' watches have a peculiar tick of their own—"

"Alvord, stop! It's mean of you to poke fun at me!"

"Forgive me, do; I apologize. It was mean, and I'll stop. What else happened?"

"Nothing," Aunt Abby was clearly piqued.

"Yes, tell me. What became of the—the figure?"

"Why, it disappeared. Gradually you know—just seemed to float away into nothingness."

"He gave you no message?"

"Not in words, no. They rarely do. But the appearance, the visibility is the usual way of manifestation. I'm glad it occurred. Oh, I'm awfully sorry Sanford is dead—I didn't mean that but, since he had to go, I'm glad he bade me good-by, as he passed on."

"Well, I'm glad, too, if it is any comfort to you. Are you sure Eunice had no such experience?"

"Oh, no—if she had she'd have told me. She hates all such ideas. I suppose if she had seen Sanford—as I did—she would have become a believer—but I'm sure she didn't."

"Poor Eunice. She is terribly broken up."

"Yes, of course. They were so devoted. They had a tiff now and then, but that was because of Eunice's quick temper. She flares up so easily," Aunt Abby sighed. "San couldn't manage her at times."

"I know. Poor girl, I don't blame her for those spasms of rage. She can't help it, you know. And she's improving every day."

"That's what Sanford said. He thought he helped her, and I dare say he did. But sometimes he had to speak pretty sharply to her. Just as one would to a naughty child."

"That's what she is, bless her heart! Just a naughty child. We must be very considerate of her now, Aunt Abby, mustn't we?"

"Yes, indeed. She is sorely to be pitied. She adored Sanford. I don't know what she will do."

Chapter 8: The Examiner

When after the autopsy, Dr. Harper announced that it was necessary to send for the Medical Chief Examiner, Eunice cried out, "Why, what do you mean? He's the same as a Coroner!"

"He takes the place of the Coroner, nowadays," rejoined Harper, "and in Dr. Marsden's opinion his attendance is necessary."

"Do you mean Sanford was murdered?"

Eunice whispered, her face white and drawn.

"We can't tell, Mrs. Embury. It is a most unusual case. There is absolutely no indication of foul play, but, on the other hand, there is no symptom or condition that tells the reason of his death. That is your finding, Dr. Marsden?"

"Yes," agreed the other. "Mr. Embury died because of a sudden and complete paralysis of respiration and circulation. There is nothing we can find to account for that and by elimination of all other possible causes we are brought to the consideration of poison. Not any known or evident poison, but a subtle, mysteriously administered toxic agent of some sort—"

"You must be crazy!" and Eunice faced him with scornful glance and angry eyes. "Who would poison my husband? How could any one get at him to do it? Why would they, anyway?"

Dr. Marsden looked at her curiously. "Those questions are not for me, madame," he said, a little curtly. "I shall call Examiner Crowell, and he will take charge of the case."

"He's the same as a coroner! I won't have him!" Eunice declared.

"It isn't for you to say," Dr. Marsden was already at the telephone. "The course of events makes it imperative that I should call Dr. Crowell. He is not a coroner. He is, of course, a Civil Service appointee, and as such, in authority. You will do whatever he directs."

Eunice Embury was silent from sheer astonishment. Never before had she been talked to like this. Accustomed to dictate, to give orders, to have her lightest word obeyed, she was dumfounded at being overruled in this fashion.

The men took in the situation more clearly.

"Medical Examiner!" exclaimed Hendricks. "Is it a case for him?"

"Yes," returned Marsden, gravely. "At least, it is a very mysterious death. Mystery implies wrong—of some sort. Had Mr. Embury been a man with a weak heart, or any affected organ, I should have been able to make a satisfactory diagnosis. But his sound, perfect condition precludes any reason for this sudden death. It must be looked into. It may be the Examiner will find a simple, logical cause, but I admit I can find none—and I am not inexperienced."

"But if he were poisoned," began Hendricks, "as you have implied, surely, you could find some trace."

"That's just the point," agreed Marsden. "I certainly think I could. And, since I can't, I feel it my duty to report it as a mysterious and, to me, inexplicable death."

"You're right," said Elliott. "If you can't find the cause, for heaven's sake get somebody who can! I don't for a minute believe it's a murder, but the barest suspicion of such a thing must be set at rest once and for all! Murder! Ridiculous! But get the Examiner, by all means!"

So Eunice's continued objections were set aside and Dr. Crowell was called in.

A strange little man the Examiner proved to be. He had sharp, bird-like eyes, that darted from one person to another, and seemed to read their very thoughts. On his entrance, he went straight to Eunice, and took her hand.

"Mrs. Embury? "he said, positively, rather than interrogatively. "Do not fear me, ma'am. I want to help you, not annoy you."

Impressed by his magnetic manner and his encouraging handclasp, Eunice melted a little and her look of angry scorn changed to a half-pleased expression of greeting.

"Miss Ames—my aunt," she volunteered, as Dr. Crowell paused before Aunt Abby.

And then the newcomer spoke to the two doctors already present, was introduced to Elliott and Hendricks, who were still there, and in a very decided manner took affairs into his own hands.

"Yes, yes," he chattered on; "I will help you, Mrs. Embury. Now, Dr. Harper, this is your case, I understand? Dr. Marsden—yours, too? Yes, yes— mysterious, you say? Maybe so—maybe so. Let us proceed at once."

The little man stood, nervously teetering up and down on his toes, almost like a schoolboy preparing to speak a piece. "Now—if you please—now—" he looked eagerly toward the other doctors.

They all went into Embury's room and closed the door.

Then Eunice's temporary calm forsook her.

"It's awful!" she cried. "I don't want them to bother poor Sanford. Why can't they let him alone? I don't care what killed him! He's dead, and no doctors can help that! Oh, Alvord, can't you make them let San alone?"

"No, Eunice; it has to be. Keep quiet, dear. It can do no good for you to get all wrought up, and if you'd go and lie down—"

"For heaven's sake, stop telling me to go and lie down! If one more person says that to me I shall just perfectly fly!"

"Now, Eunice," began Aunt Abby, "it's only 'for your own good, dear. You are all excited and nervous—"

"Of course, I am! Who wouldn't be? Mason," she looked around at the concerned faces, "I believe you understand me best. You know I don't want to go and lie down, don't you?"

"Stay where you are, child," Elliott smiled kindly at her. "Of course, you're nervous and upset—all you can do is to try to hold yourself together—and don't try that too hard, either—for you may defeat your own ends thereby. Just wait, Eunice; sit still and wait."

They all waited, and after what seemed an interminable time the Examiner reappeared and the other two doctors with him.

"Well, well," Crowell began, his restless hands twisting themselves round each other. "Now, be quiet, Mrs. Embury—I declare, I don't know how to say what I have to say, if you sit there like a chained tiger—"

"Go on!" Eunice now seemed to usurp something of Crowell's own dictatorship. "Go on, Dr. Crowell!"

"Well, ma'am, I will. But there's not much to tell. Our principal evidence is lack of evidence—"

"What do you mean? "cried Eunice. "Talk English, please!"

"I am doing so. There is positively no evidence that Mr. Embury was poisoned, yet owing to the absolute lack of any hint of any other means of death, we are forced to the conclusion that he was poisoned."

"By his own hand?" asked Hendricks, his face grave.

"Probably not. You see, sir, with no knowledge of how the poison was administered—with no suspicion of any reason for its being administered—we are working in the dark—"

"I should say so!" exclaimed Elliott; "black darkness, I call it. Are you within your rights in assuming poison?"

"Entirely; it has to be the truth. No agent but a swift, subtle poison could have cut off the victim's life like that."

Crowell was now walking up and down the room. He was a restless, nervous man, and under stress of anxiety he became almost hysterical.

"I don't know!" he cried out, as one in an extremity of uncertainty. "It must be poison—it must have been—murder!"

He pronounced the last word in a gasping way—as if afraid to suggest it but forced to do so.

Hendricks looked at him with a slight touch of contempt in his glance, but seeing this, Dr. Harper interjected:

"The Examiner is regretting the necessity of thrusting his convictions upon you, but he knows it must be done."

"Yes," said Crowell, more decidedly now, "I have had cases before where murder was committed in such an almost undiscoverable way as this. Never a case quite so mysterious, but nearly so."

"What is your theory of the method?" asked Elliott, who was staggered by the rush of thoughts and conclusions made inevitable by the Examiner's report.

"That's the greatest mystery of all," Crowell replied. He was quite calm now—apparently it was concern for the family that had made him so disturbed.

"Poison was not taken by way of the stomach, that is certain. Therefore, it must have been introduced through some other channel. But we find no trace of a hypodermic needle—"

"How utterly ridiculous!" Eunice exclaimed, her eyes blazing with scorn. "How could any one get in to poison my husband? Why, we lock all our doors at night—we always have."

"Yes'm—exactly, ma'am," Crowell began, rubbing his hands again; "and now, please tell me of the locking up last night. As usual, ma'am, as usual?"

"Precisely. Our sleeping rooms are those three," she pointed to the bedrooms. "When they are locked, they form a unit by themselves, quite apart from the rest of the apartment."

Dr. Crowell looked interested.

The apartment faced on Park Avenue, and being on the corner had also windows on the side street.

Front, enumerating from the corner and running south, were the dining-room, the large living-room, and the good-sized reception hall.

Directly back of these, and with windows on a large court, were the three bedrooms, Eunice's in the middle, Sanford's back of the hall, and Aunt Abby's back of the dining-room. Aunt Abby's room was ordinarily Eunice's boudoir and dressing-room, but was used as a guest chamber on occasion.

These three bedrooms, as was shown to Examiner Crowell, when locked from the inside were shut off by themselves, although allowing free communication from one to another of them.

"Lock with keys?" he asked.

"No," Eunice replied. "There are big, strong, snap-locks on the inside of the doors. I mean locks that fasten themselves when you shut the door, unless you have previously put up the catch."

"Yes, I see," and Crowell looked into the matter for himself. "Spring catches, and mighty strong ones, too. And these were always fastened at night?"

"Always," Eunice declared. "Mr. Embury was not afraid of burglars, but it was his life-long habit to sleep with a locked door, and he couldn't get over it."

"Then," and the bird-like little eyes darted from one to another of his listeners and paused at Aunt Abby; "then, Miss Ames, you were also locked in, each night with your niece and her husband, safe from intruders."

"Yes," and Aunt Abby looked a little startled at being addressed. "I don't sleep with my door locked at home, and it bothered me at first. But, you see, my room has no outlet except through Mrs. Embury's bedroom, so as the door between her room and mine was never locked, it really made little difference to me."

"Oh, is that the way of it?" and Dr. Crowell rose in his hasty manner and dashed in at Eunice's door. This, the middle room, opened on the right to the boudoir, and on the left to Embury's room.

The latter door was closed, and Crowell turned toward the boudoir—now Aunt Abby's bedroom. A small bed had been put up for her there, and the room was quite large enough to be comfortable. It was luxuriously furnished and the appointments were quite in keeping with the dainty tastes of the mistress of the house.

Crowell darted here and there about the room. He looked out of the rear windows, which faced on the court; out of a window that faced on the side street, peeped into the bathroom, and then hurried back to Eunice's own room. Here he observed the one large window, which was a triple bay, and which, of course, opened on the court.

He glanced at Embury's closed door, and then returned to the living-room, and again faced his audience.

"Nobody came in from the outside," he announced. "The windows show a sheer drop of ten stories to the ground. No balconies or fire-escapes. So our problem resolves itself into two possibilities— Mr. Embury was given the poison by someone already inside those locked doors—or, the doors were not locked."

The restless hands were still now. The Examiner bore the aspect of a bomb-thrower who had exploded his missile and calmly awaited the result. His darting eyes flew from face to face, as if he were looking for a criminal then and there. He sat motionless —save for his constantly moving eyeballs—and for a moment no word was spoken by anyone.

Then Eunice said, with no trace of anger or excitement, "You mean some intruder was concealed in there when we went to bed?"

Crowell turned on her a look of undisguised admiration. More, he seemed struck with a sudden joy of finding a possible loophole from the implication he had meant to convey.

"I never thought of that," he said, slowly, piercing her with his intent gaze; "it may be. But Mrs. Embury—in that case, where is the intruder now? How did he get out?"

"Rubbish!" cried Miss Ames, caustically. "There never was any intruder—I mean, not in our rooms. Ridiculous! Of course, the doors were not locked—they were unintentionally left open—I don't believe they're locked half the time!—and your intruder came in through these other rooms."

"Yes," agreed Hendricks; "that must have been the way of it. Dr. Crowell, if you're sure this is a—a—oh, it isn't! Who would kill Embury? Your theory presupposes a motive. What was it? Robbery? Is anything missing?"

Nobody could answer this question, and Ferdinand, as one familiar with his master's belongings was sent into the room of death to investigate.

Unwillingly, and only after a repeated order, the man went.

"No, ma'am," he said, on his return, addressing Eunice. "None of Mr. Embury's things are gone. All his pins and cuff-links are in their boxes and his watch is on the chiffonier where he always leaves it.

"Then," resumed Hendricks, "what motive can you suggest, Dr. Crowell?"

"It's not for me, sir, to go so far as that. I see it this way: I'm positive that the man was killed by foul means. I'm sure he was poisoned, though I can't say how. I—you see, I haven't been Medical Examiner very long—and I never had such a hard duty to perform before. But it is my duty and I must do it. I must report to headquarters."

"You shan't!" Eunice flew across the room and stood before him, her whole body quivering with intense rage. "I forbid it! I am Sanford Embury's wife, and as such I have rights that shall not be imposed upon! I will have no police dragged into this matter. Were my husband really murdered—which, of course, he was not—I would rather never have the murderer discovered or punished, than to have the degradation, the horrors of—a police case!"

The infinite scorn with which she brought out the last phrase showed her earnestness and her determination to have the matter pushed no further.

But Examiner Crowell was by no means the inefficient little man he looked. His eyes took on a new glitter, and narrowed as they looked at the angry woman before him.

"I am sorry, Mrs. Embury," he said, gently, but with a strong decision in his tone, "but your wishes cannot be considered. The law is inexorable. The mystery of this case is deepened rather than lessened by your extraordinary behavior and I must—"

But his brave manner quailed before the lightning of Eunice's eyes.

"What!" she cried; "you defy me! You will call the police against my desire—my command! You will not, sir! I forbid it!"

Crowell looked at her with a new interest. It would seem he had discovered a new species of humanity. Doubtless he had never seen a woman like that in his previous experience.

For Eunice was no shrew. She did not, for a moment, lose her poise or her dignity. Indeed, she was rather more imperious and dominating in her intense anger than when more serene. But she carried conviction. Both Elliott and Hendricks hoped and believed she could sway the Examiner to her will.

Aunt Abby merely sat nodding her head, in corroboration of Eunice's speeches. "Yes—yes—that's so!" she murmured, unheeding whether she were heard or not.

The Examiner, however, paid little attention to the decrees of the angry woman. He looked at Eunice, curiously, even admiringly, and then went across the room to the telephone.

Eunice flew after him and snatched the instrument from his hand.

"Stop!" she cried, fairly beside herself with fury. "You shall not!"

Both Elliott and Hendricks sprang from their chairs, and Dr. Harper rose to take care of Eunice as an irresponsible patient, but Crowell waved them all back.

"Sit down, gentlemen," he said; "Mrs. Embury, think a minute. If you act like that you will—you inevitably will—draw suspicion on yourself!"

"I don't care!" she screamed; "better that than the— the publicity—the shame of a police investigation! Oh, Sanford—my husband!"

It was quite clear that uppermost in her disturbed mind was the dread of the disgrace of the police inquiry. This had dulled her poignant grief, her horror, her sadness—all had been lost in the immediate fear of the impending unpleasantness.

"And, too," the Examiner went on, coldly, "It is useless for you to rant around like that! I'll simply go to another telephone."

Eunice stepped back and looked at him, more in surprise than submission. To be told that she was "ranting around" was not the way in which she was usually spoken to! Moreover, she realized it was true, that to jerk the telephone away from Dr. Crowell could not permanently prevent his sending his message.

She tried another tack.

"I beg your pardon, doctor," she said, and her expression was that of a sad and sorry child. "You're right, I mustn't lose my temper so. But, you know, I am under a severe mental strain—and something should be forgiven me—some allowance made for my dreadful position—"

"Yes, ma'am—oh, certainly, ma'am—" Crowell was again nervous and restless. He proved that he could withstand an angry woman far better than a supplicating one. Eunice saw this and followed up her advantage.

"And, so, doctor, try to appreciate how I feel—a newlymade widow—my husband dead, from some unknown cause, but which I know is not—murder," after a second's hesitation she pronounced the awful word clearly—"and you want to add to my terror and distress by calling in the police—of all things, the police!"

"Yes, ma'am, I know it's too bad—but, my duty, ma'am—"

"Your duty is first, to me!" Eunice's smile was dazzling. It had been a callous heart, indeed, that would not be touched by it!

"To you, ma'am?" The Examiner's tone was innocence itself.

"Yes," Eunice faltered, for she began to realize she was not gaining ground. "You owe me the—don't they call it the benefit of the doubt?"

"What doubt, ma'am?"

"Why, doubt as to murder. If my husband died a natural death you know there's no reason to call the police. And as you're not sure, I claim that you must give me the benefit of your doubt and not call them."

"Now, ma'am, you don't put that just right. You see, the police are the people who must settle that doubt. It's that very doubt that makes it necessary to call them. And, truly, Mrs. Ernbury, it won't be any such horrible ordeal as you seem to anticipate. They're decent men, and all they want to get at is the truth."

"That isn't so!" Eunice was angry again. "They're horrible men! rude, unkempt, low-down, common men! I won't have them in my house! You have no right to insist on it. They'll be all over the rooms, prying into everything, looking here, there and all over! They'll ask impertinent questions; they'll assume all sorts of things that aren't true, and they'll wind up by coming to a positively false conclusion! Alvord, Mason, you're my friends—help me out! Don't, let this man do as he threatens!"

"Listen, Eunice," Elliott said, striving to quiet her; "we can't help the necessity Dr. Crowell sees of notifying the police. But we can help you. Only, however, if you'll be sensible, dear, and trust to our word that it can't be helped, and you must let it go on quietly."

"Oh, hush up, Mason; your talk drives me crazy! Alvord, are you a broken reed, too? Is there nobody to stand by me?"

"I'll try," and Hendricks went and spoke to Dr. Crowell in low tones. A whispered colloquy followed, but it soon became clear that Hendricks' pleas, of whatever nature, were unsuccessful, and he returned to Eunice's side.

"Nothing doing," he said, with an attempt at lightness. "He won't listen to reason—nor to bribery and corruption—" this last was said openly and with a smile that robbed the idea of any real seriousness.

And then Dr. Crowell again lifted the telephone and called up Headquarters.

CHAPTER 9: HAMLET

Of the two detectives who arrived in response to the Examiner's call, one almost literally fulfilled Eunice's prophecy of a rude, unkempt, common man. His name was Shane and he strode into the room with a bumptious, self-important air, his burly frame looking especially awkward and unwieldy in the gentle surroundings.

His companion, however, a younger man named Driscoll, was of a finer type, and showed at least an appreciation of the nature of the home which he had entered.

"We're up from the homicide bureau," Shane said to Dr. Crowell, quite ignoring the others present. "Tell us all you know."

In the fewest possible words the Medical Examiner did this, and Shane paid close attention.

Driscoll listened, too, but his glance, instead of being fixed on the speaker, darted from one to another of the people sitting round.

He noted carefully Eunice's beautiful, angry face, as she sat, looking out of a window, disdaining any connection with the proceedings. He watched Miss Ames, nervously rolling her handkerchief into a ball and shaking it out again; Mason Elliott, calm, grave, and earnestly attentive; Alvord Hendricks, alert, eager, sharply critical.

And in the background, Ferdinand, the well-trained butler, hovering in the doorway.

All these things Driscoll studied, for his method was judging from the manners of individuals, whereas, Shane gathered his conclusions from their definite statements.

And, having listened to Dr. Crowell's account, Shane turned to Eunice and said bluntly, "You and your husband good friends?"

Eunice gasped. Then, after one scathing glance, she deliberately turned back to the window, and neglected to answer.

"That won't do, ma'am," said Shane, in his heavy voice, which was coarse and uncultured but not intentionally rude. "I'm here to ask questions and you people have got to answer 'em. Mebbe I can put it different. Was you and Mr. Embury on good terms?"

"Certainly." The word was forced from Eunice's scornful lips, and accompanied by an icy glance meant to freeze the detective, but which utterly failed.

"No rows or disagreements, eh? "Shane's smile was unbearable, and Eunice turned and faced him like an angry thing at bay.

"I forbid you to speak to me," she said, and looked at Shane as if he were some miserable, crawling reptile. "Mason, will you answer this man for me?"

"No, no, lady," Shane seemed to humor her. "I must get your own word for it. Don't you want me to find out who killed your husband? Don't you want the truth known? Are you afraid to have it told? Hey?"

Shane's secret theory was that of a sort of third degree applied at the very beginning often scared people into a quick confession of the truth and saved time in the long run.

Driscoll knew of this and did not approve.

"Let up, Shane," he muttered; "this is no time for such talk. You don't know anything yet."

"Go ahead, you," returned Shane, not unwillingly, and Driscoll did.

"Of course we must ask questions, Mrs. Embury," he said, and his politeness gained him a hearing from Eunice.

She looked at him with, at least, toleration, as he began to question her.

"When did you last see Mr. Embury alive, ma'am?"

"Last night," replied Eunice, "about midnight, when we retired."

"He was in his usual health and spirits?"

"Yes."

"You have two bedrooms?"

"Yes."

"Door between?"

"Yes."

"Open or shut—after you said good-night to Mr. Embury?"

"Closed."

"Locked?"

"No."

"Who shut it."

"Mr. Embury."

"Bang it?"

"Sir?"

"Did he bang it shut? Slam it?"

"Mr. Embury was a gentleman."

"Yes, I know. Did he slam that door?"

"N—, no."

"He did," and Driscoll nodded his head, as if not minding Eunice's stammered denial, but not believing it, either.

"Now, as he closed that door with a bang, ma'am, I gather that you two had a—well, say, a little tiff—a quarrel. Might as well own up, ma'am,—it'll come out, and it's better you should tell me the truth."

"I am not accustomed to telling anything else!" Eunice declared, holding herself together with a very evident effort. "Mr. Embury and I had a slight difference of opinion, but not enough to call a quarrel."

"What about?" broke in Shane, who had been listening intently.

Eunice did not speak until Elliott advised her. "Tell all Eunice—it is the best way."

"We had a slight discussion," Eunice said, "but it was earlier in the evening. We had spent the evening out—Mr. Embury at his club, and I at the house of a friend. We came home together—Mr. Embury called for me in our own car. On reaching home, we had no angry words—and as it was late, we retired at once. That is all. Mr. Embury closed the door between our bedrooms, and that is the last I ever saw of him until—this morning—"

She did not break down, but she seemed to think she had told all and she ceased speaking.

"And then he was dead," Shane mused. "What doctor did you call?"

Dr. Crowell took up the narrative and told of Dr. Harper and Dr. Marsden, who were not now present. He told further of the mysterious and undiscoverable cause of the death.

"Let me see him," said Shane, rising suddenly.

Most of this man's movements were sudden—and as he was in every respect awkward and uncouth, Eunice's dislike of him grew momentarily.

"Isn't he dreadful!" she cried, as the two detectives and the Medical Examiner disappeared into Embury's room.

"Yes," agreed Hendricks, "but, Eunice, you must not antagonize him. It can't do any good—and it may do harm."

"Harm? How?" and Eunice turned her big, wondering eyes on Hendrick.

"Oh, it isn't wise to cross a man like that. He's a common clod, but he represents authority—he represents the law, and we must respect that fact, however his personal manner offends us."

"All right, Alvord, I understand; but there's no use in my seeing him again. Can't you and Mason settle up things and let Aunt Abby and me go to our rooms?"

"No, Eunice," Hendricks' voice was grave. "You must stay here. And, too, they will go through your room, searching."

"My room! My bedroom! They shan't! I won't have it! Mason, must I submit to such horrible things?"

"Now, Eunice, dear," Mason Elliott spoke very gently, "we can't blink matters. We must face this squarely. The police think Sanford was murdered. They're endeavoring to find out who killed him. To do their duty in the matter they have to search everywhere. It's the law, you know, and we can't get away from it. So, try to take it as quietly as you can."

"Oh, my! oh, my!" wailed Aunt Abby; "that I should live to see this day! A murder in my own family! No wonder poor Sanford's troubled spirit paused in its passing to bid me farewell."

Eunice shrieked. "Aunt Abby, if you start up that talk, I shall go stark, staring mad! Hush! I won't have it!"

"Let up on the spook stuff, Miss Ames," begged Hendricks. "Our poor Eunice is just about at the end of her rope."

"So am I!" cried Aunt Abby. "I'm entitled to some consideration! Here's the whole house turned upside down with a murder and police and all that, and nobody considers me! It's all Eunice!" Then, with a softened voice, she added, "And Lord knows, she's got enough to bear!"

"Yes, I have!" Eunice was composed again, now. "But I can bear it. I'm not going to collapse! Don't be afraid for me. And I do consider you, Aunt Abby. It's dreadful for you—for both of us."

Eunice crossed the room and sat by the cider lady, and they comforted one another.

Shane came back to the living-room.

"Here's the way it is," he said, gruffly. "Those three bedrooms all open into each other; but when their doors that open out into these here other rooms are locked they're quite shut off by themselves, and nobody can get into 'em. Now that last room, the one the old lady sleeps

in, that don't have a door except into Mrs. Embury's
room. What I'm gettin' at is, if Mr. and Mrs. Embury's
room doors is locked—not meanin' the door between—
then those three people are locked in there every night,
and can't get out or in, except through those two locked
doors.

"Well, this morning—where's that butler man?"

"Here, sir," and Ferdinand appeared promptly, and
with his usual correct demeanor.

"Yes, you. Now, this morning, those two doors to the
sleeping rooms was locked, I understand?"

"Yes, sir. They were."

"Usually—what happens?"

"What—what happens, sir?"

"Yes; what's your first duty in the morning? Does Mr.
Embury call you—or ring for you?"

"Oh, that, sir. Why, generally Mr. Embury unlocked
his door about eight o'clock—"

"And you went to help him dress?"

"No, sir. Mr. Embury didn't require that. I valeted
his clothes, like, and kept them in order, but he dressed
by himself. I took him some tea and toast—he had that
before the regular breakfast—"

"And this morning—when he didn't ring or make any
sound, what did you do?"

"I waited a little while and then I rapped at Mrs.
Embury's door."

"Yes; and she—now, be careful, man—" Shane's voice
was impressive. "How did she act? Unusual, or
frightened in any way?"

"Not a bit, sir. Mrs. Embury was surprised, and when
I said Mr. Embury didn't answer my knock, she let me go
through her room to his."

"Exactly. And then you found your master dead?"

"Yes, sir."

"Now-what is your name?"

"Ferdinand."

"Yes. Now, Ferdinand, you know Mr. and Mrs. Embury had a quarrel last night."

"Yes, sir."

The trap had worked! Shane had brought about the admission from the servant that Eunice had refused to make. A smile of satisfaction settled on his ugly features, as he nodded his head and went on.

"At what time was this?"

"Ferdinand, be quiet," said Eunice, her own voice low and even, but her face was ablaze with wrath. "You know nothing of such things!"

"That's right, sir, I don't."

Clearly, the butler, restored to his sense of the responsibilities of his position, felt he had made a misstep and regretted it.

"Be quiet, madam!" Shane hurled at Eunice, and turning to the frightened Ferdinand, said: "You tell the truth, or you'll go to jail! At what time was this quarrel that you have admitted took place?"

Eunice stood, superbly indifferent, looking like a tragedy queen. "Tell him, Ferdinand; tell all you know, but tell only the truth."

"Yes, ma'am. Yes, sir; why, it was just before they went out."

"Ah, before. Did they go out together?"

"No, sir. Mrs. Embury went later—by herself."

"I told you that!" Eunice interposed. "I gave you a detailed account of the evening."

"You omitted the quarrel. What was it about?"

"It was scarcely important enough to call a quarrel. My husband and I frequently disagreed on trifling matters. We were both a little short-tempered, and often had altercations that were forgotten as soon as they occurred."

"And that's true," put in Miss Ames. "For two people who loved each other to distraction, I often thought the Emburys were the most quarrelsome I ever saw."

Shane looked sharply at the old lady. "Is that so?" he said. "Did you hear this particular quarrel, ma'am?"

"Not that I remember. If I did, I didn't take' much notice of it."

"What was it about?"

"Oh, the same old subject. Mrs. Embury wanted—"

"Aunt Abby, hush! What are you talking about! Leave me to tell my own secrets, pray!"

"Secrets, ma'am?" Shane's cold blue eyes glistened. "Who's talking of secrets?"

"Nobody," offered Hendricks. "Seems to me, Shane, you're trying to frighten two nervous women into a confession—"

"Who said anything about a confession? What's to be confessed? Who's made any accusations?"

Hendricks was silent. He didn't like the man Shane at all, but he saw plainly that he was a master of his craft, and depended on his sudden and startling suggestions to rouse antagonism or fear and so gather the facts he desired.

"I'm asking nobody's secrets," he went on, "except in so far as I'm obliged to, by reason of my duty. And in that connection, ma'am, I ask you right here and now, what you meant by your reference to secrets?"

Eunice looked at him a moment in silence. Then she said, "You have, I daresay, a right to ask that. And I've not the least objection to answering. Mr. Embury was the kindest of husbands, but it did not suit his ideas to give me what is known as an allowance. This in no way reflects on his generosity, for he insisted that I should have a charge account at any shops I wished. But, because of a whim, I often begged that I be given a stated and periodical allowance. This, I have no reason for not admitting, was the cause of most of our so-called 'quarrels.' This is what I should prefer to keep 'secret' but not if it is for any reason a necessary admission."

Shane looked at her in undisguised admiration.

"Fine!" he ejaculated, somewhat cryptically. "And you quarreled about this last night?"

"Last evening, before we went out."

"Not after you came home?"

"No; the subject was not then mentioned."

"H'm. And you two were as friendly as ever? No coolness—sorta left over, like?"

"No!" Eunice spoke haughtily, but the crimson flood that rose to her cheeks gave the lie to her words.

Driscoll came in.

"I've found out what killed Mr. Embury," he said, in his quiet fashion.

"What?" cried the Examiner and Shane, at the same time.

"Can't tell you—just yet. I'll have to go out on an errand. Stay here—all of you—till I get back."

The dapper little figure disappeared through the hall door, and Shane turned back to the group with a grunt of satisfaction.

"That's Driscoll, all over," he said. "Put him on a case, and he don't say much, and he don't look like he's doing anything, and then all in a minute he'll bring in the goods."

"I'd be glad to hear the cause of that death," said Dr. Crowell, musingly. "I'm an old, experienced practitioner, and I've never seen anything so mysterious. There's absolutely no trace of any poison, and yet it can be nothing else."

"Poison's a mighty sly proposition," observed Shane. "A clever poisoner can put over a big thing."

"Perhaps your assumption of murder is premature," said Hendricks, and he gave Shane a sharp look.

"Maybe," and that worthy nodded his head. "But I'm still standing pat. Now, here's the proposition. Three people, locked into a suite—you may say—of three rooms. No way of getting in from this side—those locks are heavy brass snap-catches that can't be worked from outside. No way, either, of getting in at the windows. Tenth-story apartment, and the windows look straight down to the ground, no balconies or anything like that. Unless an aryoplane let off its passengers, nobody could get in the windows. Well, then, we have those three people shut up alone there all night. In the morning one of 'em is dead —poisoned. What's the answer?"

He stared at Eunice as he talked. It was quite evident he meant to frighten her—almost to accuse her.

But with her strange contradictoriness, she smiled at him.

"You have stated a problem, Mr. Shane, to which there can be no answer. Therefore, that is not the problem that confronts us."

"Fine talk—fine talk, lady, but it won't get you anywhere. To the unbiased, logical mind, the answer must be that it's the work of the other two people."

"Then yours is not a logical or unbiased mind," Hendricks flared out, "and I object to your making implications. If you are making accusations, do so frankly, and let us know where we stand! If not, shut up!"

Shane merely looked at him, without resenting this speech. The detective appeared to be marking time as he awaited the return of his partner.

And Driscoll returned, shortly. His manner betokened success in his quest, whatever it may have been, and yet he looked distressed, too.

"It's a queer thing," he said, half to himself, as he fell into a chair Shane pushed toward him. "Mrs. Embury, do you keep an engagement book?"

"Why, yes," replied Eunice, amazed at the question put to her.

"Let me see it, please."

Eunice went for it, and, returning, handed the detective a finely bound volume.

Hastily he ran over the dates, looking at notes of parties, concerts and theatres she had attended recently.

At last, he gave a start, read over one entry carefully, and closed the book.

Abruptly, then, he went back to Embury's room, asking Dr. Crowell to go with him.

When they reappeared, it was plain to be seen the mystery was solved.

"There is no doubt," said the Medical Examiner, "that Sanford Embury met his death by foul play. The means used was the administering of poison—through the ear!"

"Through the ear!" repeated Elliott, as one who failed to grasp the sense of the words.

"Yes; it is a most unusual, almost a unique case, but it is proved beyond a doubt. The poison was inserted in Mr. Embury's ear, by means—"

He paused, and Driscoll held up to view a small, ordinary glass medicine dropper, with a rubber bulb top. In it still remained a portion of a colorless liquid.

"By means of this," Driscoll declared. "This fluid is henbane —that is the commercial name of it—known to the profession, however, as hyoscyamus or hyoscyamine. This little implement, I found, in the medicine chest in Miss Ames' bathroom "

"No! no!" screamed Aunt Abby. "I never saw it before!"

"I don't think you did," said Driscoll, quietly. "But here is a side light on the subject. This henbane was used, in this very manner, we are told, in Shakespeare's works, by Hamlet's uncle, when he poisoned Hamlet's father. He used, the play says, distilled hebenon, supposed to be another form of the word henbane. And this is what is, perhaps, important: Mrs. Embury's engagement book shows that about a week ago she attended the play of Hamlet. The suggestion there received—the presence of this dropper, still containing the stuff, the finding of traces of henbane in the ear of the dead man—seem to lead to a conclusion—"

"The only possible conclusion! It's an openand—shut case!" cried Shane, rising, and striding toward Eunice. "Mrs. Embury, I arrest you for the wilful murder of your husband!"

Chapter 10: A Confession

"Don't you dare touch me!" Eunice Embury cried, stepping back from the advancing figure of the burly detective. "Go out of my house—Ferdinand, put this person out!"

The butler appeared in the doorway, but Shane waved a dismissing hand at him.

"No use blustering, Mrs. Embury," he said, gruffly, but not rudely. "You'd better come along quietly, than to make such a fuss."

"I shall make whatever fuss I choose—and I shall not 'come along,' quietly or any other way! I am not intimidated by your absurd accusations, and I command you once more to leave my house, or I will have you thrown out!"

Eunice's eyes blazed with anger, her voice was not loud, but was tense with concentrated rage, and she stood, one hand clenching a chair-back while with the other she pointed toward the door.

"Be quiet, Eunice," said Mason Elliott, coming toward her; "you can't dismiss an officer of the law like that. But you can demand an explanation. I think, Shane, you are going too fast. You haven't evidence enough against Mrs. Embury to think of arrest! Explain yourself!"

"No explanation necessary. She killed her husband, and she's my prisoner."

"Hush up, Shane; let me talk," interrupted Driscoll, whose calmer tones carried more authority than those of his rough partner.

"It's this way, Mr. Elliott. I'm a detective, and I saw at once, that if the doctors couldn't find the cause of Mr. Embury's death, it must be a most unusual cause. So I hunted for some clue or some bit of evidence pointing to

the manner of his death. Well, when I spied that little
medicine dropper, half full of something, I didn't know
what, but—" Here he paused impressively. "But there
was no bottle or vial of anything in the cupboard, from
which it could have been taken. There was no fluid in
there that looked a bit like the stuff in the dropper. So I
thought that looked suspicious—as if some one had
hidden it there. I didn't see the whole game then, but I
went around to a druggist's and asked him what was in
that dropper. And he said henbane. He further
explained that henbane is the common name for
hyoscyamin, which is a deadly poison. Now, the doctors
were pretty sure that Mr. Embury had not been killed by
anything taken into the stomach, so I thought a minute,
and, like a flash, I remembered the play of 'Hamlet' that I
saw last week.

"I guess everybody in New York went to see it—the
house was crowded. Anyway, I've proved by Mrs.
Embury's engagement book that she went—one
afternoon, to a matinee—and what closer or more
indicative hint do you want? In that play, the murder is
fully described, and though many people might think
poison could not be introduced through the intact ear in
sufficient quantity to be fatal, yet it can be—and I read
an article lately in a prominent medical journal saying so.
I was interested, because of the Hamlet play. If I hadn't
seen that, I'd never thought of this whole business. But,
if I'm wrong, let Mrs. Embury explain the presence of
that dropper in her medicine chest."

"I don't know anything about the thing! I never saw
or heard of it before! I don't believe you found it where
you say you did!" Eunice faced him with an accusing look.
"You put it there yourself—it's what you call a frame-up!
I know nothing of your old dropper!"

"There, there, lady," Shane put in; "don't get excited—
it only counts against you. Mr. Driscoll, here, wouldn't
have no reason to do such a thing as you speak of! Why
would he do that, now?"

"But he must have done it," broke in Miss Ames. "For I use that bathroom of Eunice's and that thing hasn't been in it, since I've been here."

"Of course not," and Shane looked at her as at a foolish child; "why should it be? The lady used it, and then put it away."

"Hold on, there, Shane," Hendricks interrupted. "Why would any one do such a positively incriminating thing as that?"

"They always slip up somewhere," said Driscoll, "after committing a crime, your criminal is bound to do something careless, that gives it all away. Mrs. Embury, how did that dropper get in that medicine chest in your bathroom?"

"I scorn to answer!" The cold tones showed no fear, no trepidation, but Eunice's white fingers interlaced themselves in a nervous fashion.

"Do you know anything about it, Miss Ames?"

"N—no," stammered Aunt Abby, trembling, as she looked now at the detectives and then at Eunice.

"Well, it couldn't have put itself there," went on Driscoll. "Who else has access to that place?"

Eunice gave no heed to this speech. She gave no heed to the speaker, but stared at him, unseeingly, her gaze seeming to go straight through him.

"Why, the maid," said Aunt Abby, with a helpless glance toward Elliott and Hendricks, as if beseeching assistance.

"The servants must be considered," said Hendricks, catching at a straw. "They may know something that will help."

"Call the maid," said Shane, briefly, and, as neither of the women obeyed, he turned to Ferdinand, who hovered in the background, and thundered: "Bring her in—you!"

Maggie appeared, shaken and frightened, but when questioned, she answered calmly and positively.

"I put that dropper in the medicine closet," she said, and every one looked toward her.

"Where did you get it?" asked Shane.

"I found it—on the floor."

"On the floor? Where?"

"Beside Miss Ames' bed." The girl's eyes were cast down; she looked at nobody, but gave her answers in a dull, sing-song way, almost as if she had rehearsed them before.

"When?"

"This morning—when I made up her room."

"Had you ever seen it before?"

"No, sir."

"Why did you think it belonged to Miss Ames?"

"I didn't think anything about it. I found it there, and I supposed it belonged to Miss Ames, and I put it away."

"Why did you put it in the medicine chest?"

The girl looked up, surprised.

"That seemed to me the proper place for it. Whenever I find a bottle of camphor or a jar of cold cream—or anything like that —I always put it in the medicine chest. That's where such things belong. So I thought it was the right place for the little dropper. Did I do wrong?"

"No, Maggie," Driscoll said, kindly, "that was all right. Now tell us exactly where you found it."

"I did tell you. On the floor, just beside Miss Ames' bed. Near the head of the bed."

"Well, Miss Ames—I guess it's up to you. What were you doing with this thing?"

"I didn't have it at all! I never saw it before!"

"Come, come, that won't do! How could it get there?"

"I don't know, but I didn't put it there." The old lady trembled pitifully, and looked from one to another for help or guidance.

"Of course, she didn't!" cried Eunice. "You sha'n't torment my aunt! Cease questioning her! Talk to me if you choose—and as you choose—but leave Miss Ames alone!"

She faced her inquisitors defiantly, and even Shane quailed a little before her scornful eyes.

"Well, ma'am, as you see, I ain't got much choice in the matter. Here's the case. You and your aunt and Mr. Embury was shut in those three rooms. Nobody else could get in. Come morning, the gentleman is dead—murdered. One of you two done it. It's for us to find out which—unless the guilty party sees fit to confess."

"I do! I confess!" cried Aunt Abby. "I did it, and I'm willing to go to prison!" She was clearly hysterical, and though her words were positive, they by no means carried conviction.

"Now, that's all bosh," declared Shane. "You're sayin' that, ma'am, to shield your niece. You know she's the murderer and—"

Eunice flew at Shane like a wild thing. She grasped his arm and whirled him around toward her as she glared into his face, quivering with indignation.

"Coward!" she flung at him. "To attack two helpless women—to accuse me—me, of crime! Why, I could kill yon: where you stand —for such an insinuation!"

"Say, you're some tiger!" Shane exclaimed, in a sort of grudging admiration. "But better be careful of your words, ma'am! If you could kill me—ah, there!"

The last exclamation was brought forth by the sudden attack of Eunice, as she shook the big man so violently that he nearly lost his balance.

"Say, you wildcat! Be careful what you do! You are a tiger!"

"Yes," Aunt Abby giggled, nervously. "Mr. Embury always called her 'Tiger'."

"I don't wonder!" and Shane stared at Eunice, who had stepped back but who still stood, like a wild animal at bay, her eyes darting angry fire.

"Now, Mrs. Embury, let's get down to business. Who's your lawyer?

"I am," declared Alvord Hendricks. "I am her counsel.
I represent Mrs. Embury. Eunice, say nothing more.
Leave it to me. And, first, Shane, you haven't enough
evidence to arrest this lady. That dropper thing is no
positive information against her. It might be the work of
the servants—or some intruder. The story of that
housemaid is not necessarily law and gospel. Remember,
you'd get in pretty bad if you were to arrest Mrs. Sanford
Embury falsely! And my influence with your superiors is
not entirely negligible. You're doing your duty, all right,
but don't overstep your authority—or, rather, don't let
your desire to make a sensational arrest cloud your
judgment."

"That's what I think, Mr. Hendricks," said Driscoll,
earnestly; "we've found the method, but I'm by no means
sure we've found the criminal. Leastways, it don't look
sure to me. Eh, Shane?"

"Clear enough to me," the big man growled; but he
was quite evidently influenced by Hendricks' words.
"However, I'm willing to wait—but we must put Mrs.
Embury under surveillance—"

"Under what!" demanded Eunice, her beautiful face
again contorted by uncontrollable anger. "I will not be
watched or spied upon!"

"Hush, Eunice," begged Elliott. "Try to keep yourself
calm. It does no good to defy these men—they are not
really acting on their own initiative, but they are merely
carrying out their duty as they see it."

"Their duty is to find out who killed my husband!" and
Eunice gave Shane another stormy glare. "They cannot
do that by accusing two innocent women!"

"If you two women can be proved innocent, nobody
will be more glad than me," Shane announced, in a hearty
way, that was really generous after Eunice's treatment of
him. "But it beats me to see how it can be proved. You
admit, ma'am, nobody could get into Mr. Embury's room,
except you and Miss Ames, don't you?"

"I don't admit that at all, for the murderer DID get in—and DID commit the murder—therefore, there must be some means of access!"

"Oho! And just how can you suggest that an intruder got in, and got out again, and left those doors fastened on the inside?"

"That I don't know—nor is it my business to find out."

"Maybe you think a flyin' machine came at the window, ma'am! For nothin' else could negotiate a ten-story apartment."

"Don't talk nonsense! But I have heard of keys that unlock doors from the outside—skeleton keys, I think they are called."

"Yes, ma'am, there are such, sure! But they're keys—and they unlock doors. These doors of yours have strong brass catches that work only on the inside, snap-bolts, they are. And when they're fastened, nothing from the other side of the door could undo 'em. But, I say—here you, Ferdinand!"

The butler came forward, his face surprised rather than alarmed, and stood at attention.

"What do you know of events here last night? "Shane asked him.

"Nothing, sir," and Ferdinand's face was blankly respectful.

"You'd better tell all you know, or you'll get into trouble."

"Could you—could you make your question a little more definite?"

"I will. When Mr. and Mrs. Embury came home last night, were they in good humor?"

"I don't know, sir."

"You do know! You know your employers well enough to judge by their manner whether they were at odds or not. Answer me, man!"

"Well, sir, they were, I should judge, a little at odds."

"Oh, they were! In what way did they show it? By quarreling?"

"No, sir."

"How, then?"

"By not saying anything. But it's not uncommon for them to be at odds, sir—"

"Speak when you're spoken to! After Mr. Embury went to his room, did you attend him?"

"I was in his room, yes."

"Mrs. Embury was in her own room then?"

"Yes."

"Her outer door was closed?"

"Yes."

"And, therefore, fastened by the snap-bolt?"

"Yes, I suppose so."

"Don't you know so? Don't you know that it must have been?"

"Yes."

"And then—then, when you left Mr. Embury's room—when you left him for the night-did you close his door?"

"I did."

"And that, of itself, locked that door?"

"Yes, I suppose so."

"Stop saying you suppose so. You know it did! You've lived in this house two years; you know how those doors work—you know your closing that door locked it? Didn't it?"

"Yes, it did. I turned the knob afterward to make sure. I always do that."

Ferdinand now seemed to be as discursive as he was reticent before. "And I know Miss Eunice's—Mrs. Embury's door was locked, because she had to unbolt it before I could get in this morning."

"But look here," Driscoll broke in, "are these doors on that snap-bolt all day? Isn't that rather an inconvenience?"

"Not all day," vouchsafed Ferdinand. "They can be turned so the bolt doesn't catch, and are turned that way in the daytime, usually."

"But," and Driscoll looked at him intently, "you can swear that the bolts were on last night?"

"Yes, sir—"

"You can't!" Hendricks shot at him. The lawyer had been listening in silence, but he now refuted Ferdinand. "You don't KNOW that Mrs. Embury put on the catch of her door when she closed it."

"I do, sir; I heard it click."

"You are very observant," said Shane; "peculiarly so, it seems to me."

"No, sir," and Ferdinand looked thoughtful; "but, you see, it's this way. Every night I hear the click of those locks, and it sort of seems natural to me to listen for it. If it should be forgotten, I'd think it my duty to call attention to it."

"A most careful butler, on my word!" Shane's tone was a little sneering.

"He is, indeed!" Eunice defended; "and I can assert that it is because of his faithfulness and efficiency that we have always felt safe at night from intrusion by marauders."

"And you did lock your door securely last night, Mrs. Embury?"

"I most assuredly did! I do every night. But that does not prove that I killed my husband. Nor that Miss Ames did."

"Then your theory—"

"I have no theory. Mr. Embury was killed—it is for you detectives to find out how. But do not dare to say—or imply —that it was by the hand of his wife—or his relative!"

She glanced fondly at Miss Ames, and then again assumed her look of angry defiance toward the two men who were accusing her.

"It is for you to find out how," said Mason Elliott, gravely. "It is incredible that Mrs. Embury is the guilty one, though I admit the incriminating appearance of the henbane. But I've beet thinking it over, and while Mr. Driscoll's surmise that the deed can possibly be traced to one who recently saw the play of 'Hamlet,' yet he must remember that thousands of people saw that play, and that therefore it cannot point exclusively toward Mrs. Embury."

"That's so," agreed Driscoll. "Who went with you to the play, Mrs. Embury?"

"My aunt, Miss Ames; also a friend, Mrs. Desternay. And, I understand you went yourself, Mr. Driscoll. Why single out me for a suspect?"

The haughty face turned to him was quite severely critical.

"True, Mrs. Embury, why should I? The answer is, motive. You must admit that I had neither motive nor opportunity to kill your husband. Mrs. Desternay, let us say, had neither opportunity nor motive. Miss Ames had opportunity but no motive. And so you, we must all admit, are the only human being who had both opportunity—and motive."

"I did not have motive!" Eunice flushed back. "You talk nonsense! I have had slight differences of opinion with my husband hundreds of time, but that is not a motive for murder! I have a high temper, and at times I am unable to control it. But that does not mean I am a murderess!"

"Not necessarily, but it gives a reason for suspecting you, since you are the only person who can reasonably be suspected."

"But hold on, Driscoll, don't go too fast," said Mason Elliott; "there may be other people who had motives. Remember Sanford Embury was a man of wide public interests outside of his family affairs. Suppose you turn your attention to that sort of thing."

"Gladly, Mr. Elliott; but when we've proved no outsider could get into Mr. Embury's room, why look for outside motives?"

"It seems only fair, to my mind, that such motives should be looked into. Now, for instance, Embury was candidate in a hotly contested coming election—"

"That's so," cried Hendricks; "look for your murderer in some such connection as that."

"Election to what? "growled Shane.

"President of the Metropolitan Athletic Club—a big organization—"

"H'm! Who's the opposing candidate?"

"I am," replied Hendricks, quietly.

"You! Well, Mr. Hendricks, where were you last night, when this man was killed?"

"In Boston." Hendricks did not smile, but he looked as if the question annoyed him.

"You can prove that?"

"Yes, of course. I stayed at the Touraine, was with friends till well after midnight, and took the seven o'clock train this morning for New York, in company with the same men. You can look up all that, at your leisure; but there is a point in what Mr. Elliott says. I can't think that any of the club members would be so keen over the election as to do away with one of the candidates, but there's the situation. Go to it."

"It leaves something to be looked into, at any rate," mused Shane.

"Why didn't you think of it for yourself?" said Hendricks, rather scathingly. "It seems to me a detective ought to look a little beyond his nose!"

"I can't think we've got to, in this case," Shane persisted; "but I'm willing to try. Also, Mrs. Embury, I'll ask you for the address of the lady who went with you to see that play."

"Certainly," said Eunice, in a cold voice, and gave the address desired.

"And, now, we'll move on," said Shane, rising.

"You ain't under arrest, Mrs. Embury—not yet—but I advise you not to try to leave this house without permission—"

"Indeed, I shall! Whenever and as often as I choose! The idea of your forbidding me!"

"Hush, Eunice," said Hendricks. "She will not, Mr. Shane; I'm her guaranty for that. Don't apprehend any insubordination on the part of Mrs. Embury."

"Not if she knows what's good for herself!" was Shane's parting shot, and the two detectives went away.

Chapter 11: Fifi

"Oh, yes, indeed, Mr. Shane, Mrs. Embury is a dear friend of mine —a very, very dear friend—and I'd so gladly go to see her—and comfort her—console with her—and try to cheer her up—but —well, I asked her last night, over the telephone, to let me go to see her to-day—and—she—she—"

Mrs. Desternay's pretty blue eyes filled with tears, and her pretty lips quivered, and she dabbed a sheer little handkerchief here and there on her countenance. Then she took up her babbling again.

"Oh, I don't mean she was unfriendly or—or cross, you know—but she was a little—well, curt, almost—I might say, cool. And I'm one of her dearest friends—and I can't quite understand it."

"Perhaps you must make allowances for Mrs. Embury," Shane suggested. "Remember the sudden and mysterious death of her husband must have been a fearful shock—"

"Oh, terrible! Yes, indeed, I do appreciate all that! And of course when I telephoned last evening, she had just had that long interview with you—and your other detective, Mr. What's-his-name—and—oh, yes, Mr. Elliott answered my call and he told me just how things were—but I did think dear Eunice would want to see me—but it's all right—of course, if she doesn't want my sympathy. I'm the last one to intrude on her grief! But she has no one—no one at all—except that old aunt, who's half foolish, I think—"

"What do you mean, half foolish?"

"Oh, she's hipped over those psychic studies of hers, and she's all wrapped up in Spiritualism and occult thingamajigs—I don't know what you call 'em."

"She seems to me a very sane and practical lady."

"In most ways—yes; but crazy on the subject of spooks, and mediums and things like that! Oh, Mr. Shane, who do you suppose killed Mr. Embury? How awful! To have a real murder right in one's owns circle of acquaintances—I had almost said friends —but dear Eunice doesn't seem to look on me as her friend—"

The blue eyes made a bid for sympathy, and Shane, though not always at ease in the presence of society ladies, met her half way.

"Now, that's a pity, Mrs. Desternay! I'm sure you'd be the greatest help to her in her trouble."

Fifi Desternay raised her hands and let them fall with a pretty little gesture of helplessness. She was a slip of a thing, and —it was the morning of the day after the Embury tragedy—she was garbed in a scant but becoming negligee, and had received the detective in her morning room, where she sat, tucked into the corner of a great davenport sofa, smoking cigarettes.

Her little face was delicately made up, and her soft, fair hair was in blobs over her ears. For the rest, the effect was mostly a rather low V'd neck and somewhat evident silk stockings and beribboned mules.

She continually pulled her narrow satin gown about her, and it as continually slipped away from her lace petticoat, as she crossed and recrossed her silken legs.

She was entirely unself-conscious and yet, the detective felt instinctively that she carefully measured every one of the words she so carelessly uttered.

"Well, Mr. Shane," she said, suddenly, "we're not getting anywhere. Just exactly what did you come here for? What do you want of me?"

The detective was grateful for this assistance.

"I came," he stated, without hesitation, "to ask you about the circumstances of the party which Mrs. Embury attended here night before last, the night her husband— died."

"Oh, yes; let me see—there isn't much to tell. Eunice Embury spent the evening here—we had a game of cards—and, before supper was served, Mr. Embury called for her and took her home —in their car. That's all I know about it."

"What was the card game?"

"Bridge."

"For high stakes?"

"Oh, mercy, no! We never really gamble!" The fluttering little hands deprecated the very idea. "We have just a tiny stake—to —why, only to make us play a better game. It does, you know."

"Yes'm. And what do you call a tiny stake? Opinions differ, you know."

"And so do stakes!" The blue eyes flashed a warning. "Of course, we don't always play for the same. Indeed, the sum may differ at the various tables. Are you prying into my private affairs?"

"Only so far as I'm obliged to, ma'am. Never mind the bridge for the moment. Was Mr. Embury annoyed with his wife—for any reason—when he called to take her home?"

"Now, how should I know that?" a pretty look of perplexity came into the blue eyes. "I'm not a mind reader!"

"You're a woman! Was Mr. Embury put out?"

Fifi laughed a ringing peal. "Was he?" she cried, as if suddenly deciding to tell the truth. "I should say he was! Why, he was so mad I was positively afraid of him!"

"What did he say?"

"That's just it! He didn't say anything! Oh, he spoke to me pleasantly—he was polite, and all that, but I could see that he was simply boiling underneath!"

"You are a mind reader, then!"

"I didn't have to be, to see that!" The little figure rocked back and forth on the sofa, as, with arms clasped round one knee, Fifi gave way to a dramatic reconstruction of the scene.

"'Come, Eunice,' he said, just like that! And you bet Eunice went!"

"Was she angry, too?"

"Rather! Oh, you know her temper is something fierce! When she's roused, she's like a roaring lion and a raging bear—as it says in the Bible—or Shakespeare, or somewhere.'"

"Speaking of Shakespeare, you and Mrs. Embury went to see 'Hamlet' recently, I believe."

"Oh, yes; when the Avon Players put it on. Everybody went. Didn't you? You missed it, if you didn't! Most marvelous performance. 'Macbeth,' too. That was perfectly darling! I went to that with—"

"Excuse me. As to 'Hamlet,' now. Did you notice particularly the speech about the poisoning of—"

"Of Hamlet's father! I should say I did! Why, that speech by Mr. Postlewaite—he was 'The Ghost,' you know—was stunning, as much applauded as the 'Soliloquy' itself! He fairly made you see that poisoning scene!"

"Was Mrs. Embury interested?"

"Oh, we both were! We were at school together, and we both loved Shakespeare—we took it 'Special.' And we were terribly interested in the Avon Players' 'Hamlet'—it was unlike any representation we had ever seen."

"Ah—yes; and did you—you and Mrs. Embury— discuss the poison used by the wicked uncle?"

"Not lately. But in class we discussed that—years ago—oh, that's one of the regulation Shakespearean puzzles. You can't trip us up on our Shakespeare—either of us! I doubt if you can find two frivolous society women who know it better than we do!"

"Did you know that Mr. Embury was killed in a manner identical with the Hamlet murder?"

"No! What do you mean? I've really not heard the details. As soon as I heard of his death, I called up

Eunice, but, as I said, she wasn't cordial at all. Then I was busy with my own guests after that—last night and this morning—well, I'm really hardly awake yet!"

Fifi rubbed her eyes with the back of her hand—a childish gesture, and daintily smothered a slight yawn.

"But I'm awfully interested," she went on, "only—only I can't bear to hear about—a—murder! The details, I mean. I should think Eunice would go crazy! I should think she'd be glad to come here—I was going to ask her, when she called me down! But, what do you mean— killed like Hamlet's father?"

"Yes; there was poison introduced into his ear as Mr. Embury slept—"

"Really! How tragic; How terrible! Who did it?"

"That's what we're trying to discover. Could—do you think Mrs. Embury could have had sufficient motive—"

"Eunice!" Fifi screamed. "What an idea! Eunice Embury to kill her own husband! Oh, no!"

"But only she and that aunt of hers had opportunity. You know how their bedrooms are?"

"Oh, yes, I know. Miss Ames is using Eunice's dressing-room—and a nuisance it is, too."

"Then you know that at night those three bedrooms are shut off from the rest of the house by strong bolts on the inside of the doors."

"Yes, I know."

"Then, don't you see, as Mr. Embury was killed—the doctors say about daybreak, or earlier—nobody could have done it except somebody who was behind those locked doors."

"The windows?"

"Tenth story, and no balconies. And, too, they all have flower-boxes, except one, and the flowers were undisturbed. The one that hasn't a flower-box is on the side street, in Miss Ames' room. And that—I looked out myself—has no balcony, nor even abroad ledge. It

couldn't be reached from the next apartment—if that's
what you're thinking of."

"I'm not thinking of anything," returned Fifi. "I'm too
dazed to think! Eunice Embury! Do you mean she is
really suspected?"

"I mean that, very decidedly, ma'am. And I am here
to ask you if you can give any additional evidence, any—"

"Any evidence! Evidence against my dear friend!
Why, man, if I knew anything, I wouldn't tell it, if it
would go against Eunice!"

"Oh, yes, you would; the law would force you to. But
do you know anything definite?"

"No, of course, I don't! I know that Mr. and Mrs.
Embury were not always cooing like turtle-doves! She
had the devil's own temper—and he wasn't much better!
I know he drove her frantic because he wouldn't give her
some privileges she wanted—wouldn't allow her certain
latitudes, and was generally pretty dictatorial. I know
Eunice resented this, and I know that lots of times she
was pretty nearly at the end of her rope, and she said all
sorts of things—that, of course, she didn't mean—but she
wouldn't kill him! Oh, I don't think she would do that!"

"H'm! So they lived like cats and dogs, did they?"

"What an awful way to put it! But, well, Sanford
didn't make Eunice's life a bed of roses—nor did she go
out of her way to please him!"

"Mr. Embury was often a guest here?"

"He was not! Eunice came here, against his will—
against his expressed commands."

"Oho! She did! And her visit here night before last—
that was an act of insubordination?"

"It was! I wouldn't tell this—but it's sure to come out.
Yes, he had especially and positively forbidden her to
come to that party here, and after he went to his club—
Eunice ran away from home and came. Naughty girl!
She told us she had played hookey, when she first came
in! But, good gracious, Mr. Shane, that was no crime! In

this day and generation a wife may disobey her husband—and get away with it!"

The arch little face smiled saucily, and Fifi cuddled into her corner, and again fell a-thinking.

"I can't believe you really mean you think Eunice did it!" she broke out. "Why, what are you going to do? Arrest her?"

"Not quite. Although she is under strict surveillance at present."

"What! Can't she go out, if she likes?"

"No."

"How perfectly absurd! Oh, I've a notion to telephone and ask her to go for a drive. What fun!"

Shane looked at the mischievous face in astonishment. He was experienced in human nature, but this shallow, frivolous attitude toward a tragedy was new to him.

"I thought you and Mrs. Embury were friends," he said, reprovingly.

"Oh, we are—Or rather, we were. I'm not sure I can know her —after this! But, you see, I can't take it seriously. I can't really believe you mean that you think Eunice—guilty! Why, I'd a thousand times rather suspect the old aunt person!"

"You would!" Shane spoke eagerly. "Could that be possible?"

"It could be possible this way," Fifi was serious now. "You see, Miss Ames adores Eunice. She found it hard to forgive Sanford for his tyrannical ways—and they were tyrannical. And Miss Ames might have, by way of ridding Eunice from a cruel husband—might have—oh, I can't say it—it sounds too absurd! But, after all, it's no more absurd than to suspect Eunice. Why don't you look for somebody else?"

"How could anybody get in?"

"I know," impatiently; "but I've read detective stories, and 'most always, the murder is committed in what they call 'a hermetically sealed room,' and yet somebody did get in!"

"There's no such thing as a hermetically sealed room! Don't you know what hermetically sealed means?"

"Yes, of course I do, literally. But that phrase is used—in detective stories, to mean an inaccessible room. Or a seemingly inaccessible one. But always it comes out that it could be entered."

"That's all very well in fiction, ma'am; but it won't work in this case. Why, I looked over those door locks myself. Nobody could get in."

"Well, leaving aside the way they got in, let's see whom we can suspect. There's two men that I know of who are dead in love with Mrs. Embury—and I daresay there are a lot more, who can see a silver lining in this cloud!"

"What—what do you mean?"

Shane was fascinated by the lovely personality of Mrs. Desternay, and he began to think that she might be of some real help to him. Though a skilled detective, he was of the plodding sort, and never had brilliant or even original ideas. He had had a notion it would have been better to send Driscoll on this errand he was himself attempting, but a touch of jealousy of the younger and more quick-witted man made him determine to attend to Mrs. Desternay himself.

"Well, Mr. Stupid, if you were in the presence of Mrs. Embury and Mr. Elliott and Mr. Hendricks,—as you said you were—and didn't size up how matters stand with those two men, you are a queer sort of detective!"

Her light laughter rippled pleasantly, and Shane forgave her reproof by reason of her charm.

"Both of them?" he said, helplessly.

"Yes, sir, both of them!" She mimicked his tone. "You see, Mr. Shane, it's an old romance, all 'round. When Eunice Ames was a girl, three men fought for her hand, the two we've just mentioned, and Mr. Embury, who was the successful suitor. And he succeeded only by sheer force of will. He practically stole her from the other two and married her out of hand."

"I suppose the lady agreed?"

"Of course, but it was a marriage in haste, and—I imagine that it was followed by the proverbial consequences."

"What do you mean?" asked the dull-witted Shane.

"That they repented at leisure. At least, Eunice did— I don't believe Sanford ever regretted."

"But those two men are Embury's friends."

"Sure they are! Oh, friend Shane, were you born yesterday? I thought detectives were a little more up-to-date than that! Of course, they're all friends, always have been, since they made mud-pies together in their Boston backyards."

"Did you belong to that childish group?

"Me? Lord, no! I'm Simon Pure Middle West! And I glory in it! I'd hate to be of New England descent—you have to live up to traditions and things! I'm a law unto myself, when it comes to life and living!"

"And you met Mrs. Embury?"

"At boarding-school. We spent four years together— chums, and all that. Then after we were both married, we drifted together again, here in New York—and somehow Eunice's husband didn't take to poor little Fifi one bit! I wonder why!"

Her look of injured innocence was charming, and Shane had to make an effort to keep to the subject in hand.

"So those two men admire Mrs. Embury?"

"Admire is a silly word! They adore her—they worship the ground she walks on! They are, no doubt, decently decorous at the passing of their old friend, but as soon as the funeral baked meats are cold enough, look out for a marriage table on which to serve them!"

"Did—did Mr. Embury realize that his friends so admired his wife?"

"Probably. Yes, of course, he did. But he didn't care. She was his—she gave them no encouragement—such things aren't done—" Fifi's eyes rolled upward—"and, I only tell you, to show you that there are, at least, other directions in which to look!"

"But—let me see—Mr. Hendricks was in Boston at the time of Mr. Embury's death."

"Then that lets him out. And Mr. Elliott? Where was he?"

"I haven't made definite inquiry. Probably he—"

"Probably he has an alibi! Oh, yes, of course he has! And if he killed Sanford Embury, he's more likely than ever to have a fine alibi! Look here, Mr. Shane, I believe I could give you cards and spades and beat you at your little detective games!"

"You mix me all up, with your ridiculous suggestions!" Shane tried to speak sternly, but was forced to smile at the roguish, laughing face that mocked him.

"All right, play your own game. I tried to help, by suggesting more suspects—in a multitude of suspects there is safety—for our dear Eunice! And she never did it! If you can't contrive a way for either of those two men to get through those bolted doors, then turn your eagle eyes toward Aunt Abby! She's a queer Dick—if you ask me, and Eunice Embury—well, I admit I resent her coolness last night, but I freely own up that I think her incapable of such a crime."

"But you two discussed the poisoning business in the play—" "We did. But we discussed lots of other points about that play and compared it with other presentations we have seen, and, oh, you're too absurd to hang a murder on that woman, just because she saw a murder on the stage—or rather heard the description of one!"

"But that's the coincidence! She did hear that murder described fully. She did talk it over with you. She did show a special interest in it. Then, a week or so later, her husband is killed by identically the same method. She, and she alone—except for a mild old lady—has opportunity to do the deed; the instrument of death is found in her cupboard; and she flies into a rage at the first hint of accusation, of the crime! By the way, if as you hint, one of those men did it, would they leave the medicine dropper that conveyed the poison, in Mrs. Embury's rooms. Would they want to bring suspicion against the woman they love? Answer me that?"

"There might be another solution," Fifi nodded her wise little head thoughtfully. "Perhaps whoever did it, tried to throw suspicion on Miss Ames."

"That makes him a still more despicable villain. To implicate falsely a harmless old lady—no, I can't think that."

"Yet you think Mrs. Embury did!"

"I don't know. Perhaps the two women worked in collusion. Or Miss Ames might have wakened and learned the truth, and agreed to keep the secret. In fact, Miss Ames confessed that she did the murder, but we know she was not telling the truth then. However, she knows who did do it—I've no doubt of that. Well, Mrs. Desternay, I can't subscribe to your original, if rather impossible, suggestions, but I thank you for this interview, and I may say you have helped me."

"I have? How? Not against Eunice?"

"Never mind, ma'am, I must get off by myself, and straighten out my notes, and see where I stand. Are you going to telephone to Mrs. Embury again?"

"No!" and the little head was tossed proudly. "If she wants me, let her call me up. I did my part, now I'll subside. And, too —if she is—is—oh, I can't say it! But I'll wait further developments before I decide just where I stand in regard to Eunice Embury!"

Chapter 12: In Hanlon's Office

In an office building, away downtown, a little old lady stood in the lobby studying the great bulletin board of room numbers.

"Can I help you, ma'am? "asked the elevator starter, seeing her perplexity.

"I want Sykes and Barton, Scenic Sign Painters," she said, positively enough; "but there are so many S's, I can't seem to find them!"

"All right, ma'am; here they are. Sixth floor, Room 614."

"Thank you," the old lady said, and entered the elevator he indicated.

She seemed preoccupied, and made no move to leave the car, until the elevator man spoke to her twice.

"This is the floor you want, lady," he said. "Room 614. That way, just round that first corner."

Miss Ames started off in the way he pointed, and stood for a moment in front of the door numbered 614.

Then, with a determined shake of her thin shoulders, she opened the door and walked in.

"I want to see Mr. Hanlon," she said to the girl at the first desk.

"By appointment?"

"No; but say it is Miss Ames—he'll see me."

"Why, Miss Ames, how do you do?" and the man who had so interested the beholders of his feat in Newark came forward to greet her. "Come right into my office," and he led her to an inner room. "Now, what's it all about?"

The cheery reception set his visitor at ease, and she drew a long breath of relief as she settled herself in the chair he offered.

"Oh, Mr. Hanlon, I'm so frightened—or, at least, I was. It's all so noisy and confusing down here! Why, I haven't been downtown in New York for twenty years!"

"That so? Then I must take you up on our roof and show you a few of the skyscrapers—"

"No, no, I've not time for anything like that. Oh, Mr. Hanlon —you—have you read in the papers of our—our trouble?"

"Yes," and the young man spoke gravely, "I have, Miss Ames. Just a week ago to-day, wasn't it?"

"Yes; and they're no nearer a solution of the mystery than ever. And, oh, Mr. Hanlon, they're still suspecting Eunice—Mrs. Embury—and I must save her! She didn't do it—truly she didn't, and—I think I did."

"What!"

"Yes, I truly think so. But I wasn't myself, you know—I was —hypnotized—"

"Hypnotized! By whom?"

"I don't know—by some awful person who wanted Sanford dead, I suppose."

"But that's ridiculous, Miss Ames—"

"No, it isn't. I'm a very easy subject—"

"Have you ever been hypnotized?"

"Not very successfully. But no real hypnotizer ever tried it. I'm sure, though, I'd be a perfect subject—I'm so—so psychic, you know—"

"Bosh and nonsense! You know, Miss Ames, what I think of that sort of thing! You know how I played on people's gullibility when I used to do that fake 'thought-transference'—"

"I know, Mr. Hanlon," and Miss Ames was very earnest, "but, and this is why I'm here—you told me that in all the foolery and hocus-pocus there was, you believed, two per cent of genuine telepathy—two per cent of genuine communication with spirits of the dead"

"But I said that merely in a general way, Miss Ames. I didn't mean to say it was a proven proposition—"

"That isn't the point—you told me there were a few—a very few real, sincere mediums—now I'm here to get the address of the best one you know of. I want to go to him—or her—and have a seance, and I want to get into communication with Sanford—with Mr. Embury's spirit, and learn from him who killed him. It's the only way we can ever find out."

Miss Ames' gray eyes took on a strange look; she seemed half hypnotized at the moment, as she looked at Hanlon. He moved uncomfortably under her gaze.

"Well," he said, at length, "I can give you the address of the best—the only real medium I know. That I will do with pleasure, but I cannot guarantee his bringing about a materialization of —of Mr. Embury."

"Never mind about materialization, if he can get in touch and get a message for me. You see—I haven't said much about this—but Mr. Embury's spirit appeared to me as—as he died."

"What?"

"Yes; just at the moment his soul passed from earth, his astral body passed by me and paused at my bedside for a farewell."

"You amaze me! You are indeed psychic. Tell me about it."

"No; I won't tell you the story—I'll tell the medium. But I know I saw him—why, he was discernible to all my five senses—"

"To your senses! Then it was no spirit!"

"Oh, yes, it was. Sanford's body still lay on his own bed, but his passing spirit materialized sufficiently for me to see it—to hear it—to feel it"

"Miss Ames, you mustn't go to a medium! You are too imaginative —too easily swayed—don't go, dear lady, it can do no good."

Young Hanlon looked, as he felt, very solicitous for the aged spinster, and he cast an anxious glance at her disturbed face.

"I must," she insisted; "it is the only way. I had great trouble to find you, Mr. Hanlon. I had to communicate with Mr. Mortimer, in Newark—and at last we traced you here. Are you all through with your fake tricks?"

"Yes," Hanlon laughed. "I wore them out. I've gone into a legitimate business."

"Sign painting?"

"Yes, as you see."

"But such big signs!" and the old lady's eyes wandered to photographs and sketches of enormous scenic signs, such as are painted on high buildings or built on housetops.

"That's the specialty of this firm. I'm only learning, but it strongly appeals to me. It's really more of an art than a trade. Now, as to this man you want to see, Miss Ames, I'll give you his address, but I beg of you to think it over before you visit him. Consult with some one—not Mrs. Embury—some man, of good judgment and clear mind. Who is advising you?"

"Mr. Hendricks and Mr. Elliott—you saw them both the day you were at our house—they advise my niece and myself in all matters. Shall I ask them?"

Miss Abby was pathetic in her simple inquiry, and Hanlon spoke gently as he replied.

"Yes, if you are determined to try the experiment. But I do not advise you to see Mr. Marigny, the medium I spoke of. Here is the address, but you talk it over with those two men you mentioned. I know they are both practical, logical business men, and their advice on the subject will be all right. I thank you, Miss Ames, for honoring me with a call. I hope if you do go to see Marigny, it will prove a satisfactory seance, but I also hope you will decide not to go. You are, as I said, too emotional, too easily swayed by the supernatural to go very deeply into those mysteries. Shall I take you to the elevator?"

"If you please, Mr. Hanlon," and still in that half oblivious mood, Miss Ames allowed herself to be led through the halls.

Hanlon went down with her, for he feared to leave her to her own devices. He was relieved to find she had a taxicab in waiting, and as he put her into it, he cautioned the driver to take his fare straight home.

"But I want to go to Marigny's now," objected Miss Ames, as she heard what Hanlon said.

"Oh, you can't. You must make an appointment with him—by mail or by telephone. And, too, you promised me you'd put it up to Mr. Hendricks or Mr. Elliott first."

"So I did," and the old head nodded submissively, as the taxi drove away.

When Ferdinand admitted Aunt Abby to the Embury home, she heard voices in the living-room that were unmistakably raised in anger.

"You know perfectly well, Fifi," Eunice was saying, "that your little bridge games are quite big enough to be called a violation of the law—you know that such stakes as you people play for—"

"It isn't the size of the stake that makes gambling!" Fifi Desternay cried, shrilly; "I've had the advice of a lawyer, and he says that as long as it's my own home and the players are invited guests, there's no possibility of being—"

"Raided!" said Eunice, scathingly. "Might as well call things by their real name!"

"Hush up! Some of the servants might hear you! How unkind you are to me, Eunice. You used to love your little Fifi!"

"Well, she doesn't now!" said Miss Ames, tartly, as she came in. "You see, Mrs. Desternay, you have been instrumental in bringing our dear Eunice under a dreadful, and absolutely unfounded suspicion—"

"Dreadful, but far from unfounded!" declared Mrs. Desternay, her little hands uplifted, and her pretty face

showing a scornful smile. "You and I, Aunt Abby, know
what our dear Eunice's temper is—"

"Don't you 'Aunt Abby' me, you good-for-nothing little
piece! I am surprised Eunice allows you in this house!"

"Now, now—if Eunice doesn't want me, I'll get out—
and jolly well glad to do so! How about it, Eunice? I
came here to help, but if I'm not wanted—out goes little
Fifi!"

She rose, shaking her fur stole into place about her
dainty person, and, whipping out a tiny mirror from her
vanity case, she applied a rouge stick to her already
scarlet lips.

"No—no—" and Eunice wailed despairingly. "Don't
go, Fifi, I —oh, I don't know how I feel toward you! You
see—I will speak plainly—you see, it was my
acquaintance with you that caused the trouble—mostly—
between me and San."

"Thought it was money matters—his stinginess, you
know."

"He wasn't stingy! He wouldn't give me an allowance,
but he was generous in every other way. And that's
why—"

"Why you came to my 'gambling house' to try to pick
up a little ready cash! I know. But now looky here,
Eunice, you've got to decide—either you're with me or
agin me! I won't have any blow hot, blow cold! You're
friends with Fifi Desternay—or—she's your enemy!"

"What do you mean?"

"Just what I say! You like me, you've always liked
me. Now, stand by me, and I'll stand by you."

"How?"

"You think I can't! Well, madame, you're greatly
mistaken! That big blundering fool of a detective person
has been to see me—"

"Shane?"

"The same. And—he grilled me pretty thoroughly as
to our going to see 'Hamlet' and whether we talked the

poison scene over— and so forth and so on. In a word, Eunice Embury, I hold your life in my hands!"

Fifi held out her pretty little hands, dramatically. She still stood, her white fur scarf hanging from one shoulder, her small turban of red breast feathers cocked at a jaunty angle above her straight brows, and one tiny slippered foot tapping decidedly on the floor.

"Yes, ma'am, in my two hands,—me—Fifi! If I tell all we said about that poisoning of the old 'Hamlet' gentleman, through his ear—you know what we said, Eunice Embury—you know how we discussed the impossibility of such a murder ever being discovered— you know if I should give Shane a full account of that talk of ours—the life of Madame Embury wouldn't be worth that!"

A snap of a dainty thumb and finger gave a sharp click that went straight through Eunice's brain, and made her gasp out a frightened "Oh!"

"Yes, ma'am, oh! all you like to—you can't deny it! Shane came to see me three times. I almost told him all the last time, for you steadily refused to see me—until to-day. And now, to-day, I put it to you, Eunice Embury, do you want me for friend—or foe?"

Fifi's blue eyes glittered, her red lips closed in a tight line, and her little pointed face was as the face of a wicked sprite. Eunice stood, surveying her. Tall, stately, beautiful, she towered above her guest, and looked down on her with a fine disdain.

Eunice's eyes were stormy, not glittering—desperate rather than defiant—she seemed almost like a fierce, powerful tiger appraising a small but very wily ferret.

"Is this a bargain?" she cried scathingly. "Are you offering to buy my friendship? I know you, Fifi Desternay! You are—a snake in the grass!"

Fifi clenched her little fists, drew her lips between her teeth, and fairly hissed, "Serpent, yourself! Murderess! I know all —and I shall tell all! You'll regret the day you scorned the friendship—the help of Fifi Desternay!"

"I don't want your help, at the price of friendship with you! I know you for what you are! My husband told me— others have told me! I did go to your house for the sake of winning money—yes, and I am ashamed of it! And I am ready to face any accusation, brave any suspicion, rather than be shielded from it, or helped out of it by you!"

"Fine words! but they mean nothing! You know you're justly accused! You know you're rightly suspected! But you are clever —you also know that no jury, in this enlightened age, will ever convict a woman! Especially a beautiful woman! You know you are safe from even the lightest sentence—and that though you are guilty—yes, guilty of the murder of your husband, you will get off scot free, because"—Fifi paused to give her last shot telling effect—"because your counsel, Alvord Hendricks, is in love with you! He will manage it, and what he can't accomplish, Mason Elliott can! With those two influential men, both in love with you, you can't be convicted—and probably you won't even be arrested!"

"Go!" said Eunice, and she folded her arms as she gazed at her angry antagonist. "Go! I scorn to refute or even answer your words."

"Because they're true! Because there is no answer!" Fifi fairly screamed. "You think you're a power! Because you're tall and statuesque and stunning! You know if those men can't keep you out of the court-room at least you are safe in the hands of any judge or jury, because they are men! You know if you smile at them— pathetically—if you cast those wonderful eyes of yours at them, they'll grovel at your feet! I know you, Eunice Embury! You're banking on your femininity to save you from your just fate."

"You judge me by yourself, Fifi. You are a power among men, most women are, but I do not bank on that—
"

"Not alone! You bank on the fact that either Hendricks or Elliott would go through hell for you, and count it an easy journey. You rest easy in the knowledge that those two men can do just about anything they set their minds to—"

"Will you go?"

"Yes, I will go. And when Mr. Shane comes to see me again, I will tell him the truth—all the truth about the' Hamlet' play —and—it will be enough!"

"Tell him!" Eunice's eyes blazed now. "Tell him the truth—and add to it whatever lies your clever brain can invent! Do your worst Fifi Desternay; I am not afraid of you!"

"I am going, Eunice." Fifi moved slowly toward the door. "I shall tell the truth, but I shall add no lies—that will not be necessary!"

She disappeared, and Eunice stood, panting with excitement and indignation.

Aunt Abby came toward her. The old lady had been a witness of the whole scene—had, indeed, tried several times to utter a word of pacification, but neither of the women had so much as noticed her.

"Go away, Auntie, please," said Eunice. "I can't talk to you. I'm expecting Mason at any time now, and I want to get calmed down a little."

Miss Ames went to her room, and Eunice sat down on the davenport.

She sat upright, tensely quiet, and thought over all Fifi had said—all she had threatened.

"It would have been far better," Eunice told herself, "for my cause if I had held her friendship. And I could have done it, easily—but—Fifi's friendship would be worse than her enmity!"

When Mason Elliott came, Detective Driscoll was with him.

The net of the detectives was closing in around Eunice, and though both Elliott and Hendricks—as Fifi

152

A Resurrected Press Mystery

had truly surmised —were doing all in their power, the denouement was not far off —Eunice was in imminent danger of arrest at any moment.

"We've been talking about the will—Sanford's will," Elliott said, in a dreary tone, after the callers were seated, "and, Eunice, Mr. Driscoll chooses to think that the fact that San left practically everything to you, without any restraint in the way of trustees, or restriction of any sort, is another count against you."

Eunice smiled bravely. "But that isn't news," she said; "we all knew that my husband made me his sole—or rather principal —beneficiary. I know the consensus of opinion is that I murdered my husband that I might have his money—and full control of it. This is no new element."

"No;" said Driscoll, moved by the sight of the now patient, gentle face; "no; but we've added a few more facts—and look here, Mrs. Embury, it's this way. I've doped it out that there are five persons who could possibly have committed this—this crime. I'll speak plainly, for you have continually permitted me—even urged me to do so. Well, let us say Sanford Embury could have been killed by anyone of a certain five. And they size up like this: Mr. Elliott, here, and Mr. Alvord Hendricks may be said to have had motive but no opportunity."

"Motive?" said Eunice, in a tone of deepest possible scorn.

"Yes, ma'am. Mr. Elliott, now, is an admirer of yours—don't look offended, please; I'm speaking very seriously. It is among the possibilities that he wanted your husband out of his way."

Mason Elliott listened to this without any expression of annoyance. Indeed, he had heard this argument of Driscoll's before, and it affected him not at all.

"But, Mrs. Embury, Mr. Elliott had no opportunity. We have learned beyond all doubt that he was at his club or at his home all that night. Next, Mr. Hendricks had a motive. The rival candidates were both eager for election, and we must call that a motive for Mr. Hendricks to be willing to remove his opponent. But again, Mr. Hendricks had no opportunity. He was in Boston from the afternoon of the day before Mr. Embury's death until noon of the next day. That lets him out positively. Therefore, there are two with motives but no opportunity. Next, we must admit there were two who had opportunity, but no motive. I refer to Ferdinand, your butler, and Miss Ames, your aunt. These two could have managed to commit the deed, had they chosen, but we can find no motive to attribute to either of them. It has been suggested that Miss Ames might have had such a desire to rid you, Mrs. Embury, of a tyrannical husband, that she was guilty. But it is so highly improbable as to be almost unbelievable.

"Therefore, as I sum it up, the two who had motive without opportunity, and the two who had opportunity without motive, must all be disregarded, because of the one who had motive and opportunity both. Yourself, Mrs. Embury."

The arraignment was complete. Driscoll's quiet, even tones carried a sort of calm conviction.

"And so, Eunice," Mason Elliott spoke up, "I'm going to try one more chance. I've persuaded Mr. Driscoll to wait a day or two before progressing any further, and let me get Fleming Stone on this case."

"Very well," said Eunice, listlessly. "Who is he?"

"A celebrated detective. Mr. Driscoll makes no objection—which goes to prove what a good detective he is himself. His partner, Mr. Shane, is not so willing, but has grudgingly consented. In fact, they couldn't help themselves, for they are not quite sure that they have enough evidence to arrest you. Shane thinks that Stone will find out more, and so strengthen the case against you but Driscoll, bless him! thinks maybe Stone can find another suspect."

"I didn't exactly say I thought that, Mr. Elliott," said Driscoll. "I said I hoped it."

"We all hope it," returned Elliott.

"Hope while you may," and Driscoll sighed. "Fleming Stone has never failed to find the criminal yet. And if his findings verify mine, I shall be glad to put the responsibility on his shoulders."

CHAPTER 13: FLEMING STONE

One of the handsomest types of American manhood is that rather frequently seen combination of iron-gray hair and dark, deep-set eyes that look out from under heavy brows with a keen, comprehensive glance.

This type of man is always a thinker, usually a professional man, and almost invariably a man of able brain. He is nearly always well-formed, physically, and of good carriage and demeanor.

At any rate, Fleming Stone was all of these things, and when he came into the Embury living-room his appearance was in such contrast to that of the other two detectives that Eunice greeted him with a pleased smile.

Neither Shane nor Driscoll was present, and Mason Elliott introduced Stone to the two ladies, with a deep and fervent hope that the great detective could free Eunice from the cloud of danger and disgrace that hovered above her head.

His magnetic smile was so attractive that Aunt Abby nodded her head in complete approval of the newcomer.

"And now tell me all about everything," Stone said, as they seated themselves in a cozy group. "I know the newspaper facts, but that's all. I must do my work quite apart from the beaten track, and I want any sidelights or bits of information that your local detectives may have overlooked and which may help us."

"You don't think Eunice did it, do you, Mr. Stone?" Aunt Abby broke out, impulsively, quite forgetting the man was a comparative stranger.

"I am going to work on the theory that she did not," he declared. "Then we will see what we can scare up in the way of evidence against some one else. First, give me a good look at those doors that shut off the bedrooms."

With a grave face, Fleming Stone studied the doors, which, as he saw, when bolted on the inside left no means of access to the three rooms in which the family had slept.

"Except the windows," Stone mused, and went to look at them. As they all had window boxes, save one in Aunt Abby's room, and as that was about a hundred feet from the ground, he dismissed the possibility of an intruder.

"Nobody could climb over the plants without breaking them," said Eunice, with a sigh at the inevitable deduction.

Stone looked closely at the plants, kept in perfect order by Aunt Abby, who loved the work, and who tended them every day. Not a leaf was crushed, not a stem broken, and the scarlet geranium blossoms stood straight up like so many mute witnesses against any burglarious entrance.

Stone returned to Aunt Abby's side window, and leaning over the sill looked out and down to the street below.

"Couldn't be reached even by firemen's ladders," he said, "and, anyway, the police would have spotted any ladder work."

"I tried to think some one came in at that window," said Elliott, "but even so, nobody could go through Miss Ames' room, and then Mrs. Embury's room, and so on to Mr. Embury's room—do his deadly work—and return again, without waking the ladies—"

"Not only that, but how could he get in the window?" said Eunice. "There's no possible way of climbing across from the next apartment—oh, I'm honest with myself," she added, as Stone looked at her curiously. "I don't deceive myself by thinking impossibilities could happen. But somebody killed my husband, and—according to the detectives—I am the only one who had both motive and opportunity!"

"Had you a motive, Mrs. Embury?" Stone asked, quietly.

Eunice stared at him. "They say so," she replied. "They say I was unhappy with him."

"And were you?" The very directness of Stone's pertinent questions seemed to compel Eunice's truthful answers, and she said:

"Of course I was! But that—"

"Eunice, hush!" broke in Elliott, with a pained look. "Don't say such things, dear, it can do no good, and may injure your case."

"Not with me," Stone declared. "My work has led me rather intimately into people's lives, and I am willing to go on record as saying that fifty per cent of marriages are unhappy—more or less. Whether that is a motive for murder depends entirely on the temper and temperament of the married ones themselves. But —it is very rarely that a wife kills her husband."

"Why, there are lots of cases in the papers," said Miss Ames. "And never are the women convicted, either!"

"Oh, not lots of cases," objected Stone, "but the few that do occur are usually tragic and dramatic and fill a front page for a few days. Now, let's sift down this remarkably definite statement of 'motives and opportunities' that your eminent detectives have catalogued. I'm told that they've two people with motive and no opportunity; two more with opportunity and no motive; and one—Mrs. Embury—who fulfills both requirements! Quite an elaborate schedule, to be sure!"

Eunice looked at him with a glimmer of hope. Surely a man who talked like that didn't place implicit reliance on the schedule in question.

"And yet," Stone went on, "it is certainly true. A motive is a queer thing—an elusive, uncertain thing. They say—I have this from the detectives themselves-that Mr. Hendricks and Mr. Elliott both had the motive of deep affection for Mrs. Embury. Please don't be offended, I am speaking quite impersonally, now. Mr. Hendricks, I am advised, also had a strong motive in a desire to

remove a rival candidate for an important election. But—
neither of these gentlemen had opportunity, as each has
proven a perfect and indubitable alibi. I admit the
alibis—I've looked into them, and they are
unimpeachable—but I don't admit the motives. Granting
a man's affection for a married woman, it is not at all a
likely thing for him to kill her husband."

"Right, Mr. Stone!" and Mason Elliott's voice rang out
in honest appreciation.

"Again, it is absurd to suspect one election candidate
of killing another. It isn't done—and one very good
reason is, that if the criminal should be discovered, he
has small chance for the election he coveted. And there is
always a chance—and a strong one—that 'murder will
out! So, personally, I admit I don't subscribe entirely to
the cut-and-dried program of my esteemed colleagues.
Now, as to these two people with opportunity but no
motive. They are, I'm told, Miss Ames and the butler.
Very well, I grant their opportunity—but since they are
alleged to have no motive, why consider them at all? This
brings us to Mrs. Embury."

Eunice was watching the speaker, fascinated. She
had never met a man like this before. Though Stone's
manner was by no means flippant, he seemed to take a
light view of some aspects of the case. But now, he looked
at Eunice very earnestly.

"I am informed," he went on, slowly, "that you have an
ungovernable temper, Mrs. Embury."

"Nothing of the sort!" Eunice cried, tossing her head
defiantly and turning angry eyes on the bland detective.
"I am supposed to be unable to control myself, but it is
not true! As a child I gave way to fits of temper, I
acknowledge, but I have overcome that tendency, and I
am no more hot-tempered now than other people!"

As always, when roused, Eunice looked strikingly
beautiful, her eyes shone and her cheeks showed a
crimson flush. She drew herself up haughtily, and
clenching her hands on the back of a chair, as she stood

facing Stone, she said, "If you have come here to browbeat
me—to discuss my personal characteristics, you may go!
I've no intention of being brought to book by a detective!"

"Why, Eunice, don't talk that way," begged Aunt
Abby. "I'm sure Mr. Stone is trying to get you freed from
the awful thing that is hanging over you!"

"There's no awful thing hanging over me! I don't
know what you mean, Aunt Abby! There can't be
anything worse than to have a stranger come in here and
remark on my unfortunate weakness in sometimes giving
way to my sense of righteous indignation! I resent it! I
won't have it! Mason, you brought Mr. Stone here —now
take him away!"

"There, there, Eunice, you are not quite yourself, and
I don't wonder. This scene is too much for you. I'm sure
you will make allowance, Mr. Stone, for Mrs. Embury's
overwrought nerves—"

"Of course," and Fleming Stone spoke coldly, without
sympathy or even apparent interest. "Let Mrs. Embury
retire to her room, if she wishes."

They had all returned to the big living-room, and
Stone stood near a front window, now and then glancing
out to the trees in Park Avenue below.

"I don't want to retire to my room!" Eunice cried. "I
don't want to be set aside as if I were a child! I did want
Mr. Stone to investigate this whole matter, but I don't
now—I've changed my mind! Mason, tell him to go
away!"

"No, dear," and Elliott looked at her kindly, "you can't
change your mind like that. Mr. Stone has the case, and
he will go on with it and when you come to yourself again,
you will be glad, for he will free you from suspicion by
finding the real criminal."

"I don't want him to! I don't want the criminal found!
I want it to be an unsolved mystery, always and forever!"

"No;" Elliott spoke more firmly. "No, Eunice, that is
not what you want."

"Stop! I know what I want—without your telling me! You overstep your privileges, Mason! I'm not an imbecile, to be ignored, set aside, overruled! I won't stand it! Mr. Stone, you are discharged!"

She stood, pointing to the door with a gesture that would have been melodramatic, had she not been so desperately in earnest. The soft black sleeve fell away from her soft white arm, and her out-stretched hand was steady and unwavering as she stood silent, but quivering with suppressed rage.

"Eunice," and going to her, Elliott took the cold white hand in his own. "Eunice," he said, and no more, but his eyes looked deeply into hers.

She gazed steadily for a moment, and then her face softened, and she turned aside, and sank wearily into a chair.

"Do as you like," she said, in a low murmur. "I'll leave it to you, Mason. Let Mr. Stone go ahead."

"Yes, go ahead, Mr. Stone," said Aunt Abby, eagerly. "I'll show you anywhere you want to go—anything you want to see I'll tell you all about it."

"Why, do you know anything I haven't been told, Miss Ames? I thought we had pretty well sized up the situation."

"Yes, but I can tell you something that nobody else will listen to, and I think you will."

Eunice started up again. "Aunt Abby," she said, "if you begin that pack of fool nonsense about a vision, I'll leave the room—I vow I will!"

"Leave, then!" retorted Aunt Abby, whose patience was also under a strain.

But Stone said, "Wait, please, I want a few more matters mentioned, and then, Miss Ames, I will listen to your 'fool nonsense!' First, what is this talk about money troubles between Mr. and Mrs. Embury?"

"That," Eunice seemed interested, "is utter folly. My husband objected to giving me a definite allowance, but he gave me twice the sum I would have asked for, and more, too, by letting me have charge accounts everywhere I chose."

"Then you didn't kill him for that reason?" and the dark eyes of the detective rested on Eunice kindly.

"No; I did not!" she said, curtly, and Stone returned,

"I believe you, Mrs. Embury; if you were the criminal, that was not the motive. Next," he went on, "what about this quarrel you and Mr. Embury had the night before his death?"

"That was because I had disobeyed his express orders," Eunice said, frankly and bravely, "and I went to a bridge game at a house to which he had forbidden me to go. I am sorry—and I wish I could tell him so."

Fleming Stone looked at her closely. Was she sincere or was she merely a clever actress?

"A game for high stakes, I assume," he said quietly.

"Very high. Mr. Embury objected strongly to my playing there, but I went, hoping to win some money that I wanted."

"That you wanted? For some particular purpose?"

"No; only that I might have a few dollars in my purse, as other women do. It all comes back to the same old quarrel, Mr. Stone. You don't know! can't make you understand—how humiliating, how galling it is for a woman to have no money of her own! Nobody understands—but I have been subjected to shame and embarrassment hundreds of times for the want of a bit of ready money!"

"I think I do understand, Mrs. Embury. I know how hard it must have been for a proud woman to have that annoyance. Did Mr. Embury object to the lady who was your hostess that evening?"

"Yes, he did. Mrs. Desternay is an old school friend of mine, but Mr. Embury never liked her, and he objected more strenuously because she had the bridge games."

"And the lady's attitude toward you?"

"Fifi? Oh, I don't know. We've always been friends, generally speaking, but we've had quarrels now and then—sometimes we'd be really intimate, and then again, we wouldn't speak for six weeks at a time. Just petty tiffs, you know, but they seemed serious at the time."

"I see. Hello, here's McGuire!"

Ferdinand, with a half-apologetic look, ushered in a boy, with red hair, and a very red face. He was a freckled youth, and his bright eyes showed quick perception as they darted round the room, and came to rest on Miss Ames, on whom he smiled broadly. "This is my assistant," Stone said, casually; "his name is Terence McGuire, and he is an invaluable help. Anything doing, son?"

"Not partickler. Kin I sit and listen?"

Clearly the lad was embarrassed, probably at the unaccustomed luxury of his surroundings and the presence of so many high-bred strangers. For Terence, or Fibsy, as he was nicknamed, was a child of the streets, and though a clever assistant to Fleming Stone in his career, the boy seldom accompanied his employer to the homes of the aristocracy. When he did do so, he was seized with a shyness that was by no means evident when he was in his more congenial surroundings.

He glanced bashfully at Eunice, attracted by her beauty, but afraid to look at her attentively. He gazed at Mason Elliott with a more frank curiosity; and then he cast a furtive look at Aunt Abby, who was herself smiling at him.

It was a genial, whole-souled smile, for the old lady had a soft spot in her heart for boys, and was already longing to give him some fruit and nuts from the sideboard.

Fibsy seemed to divine her attitude, and he grinned affably, and was more at his ease.

But he sat quietly while the others went on discussing the details of the case.

Eunice was amazed at such a strange partner for the great man, but she quickly thought that a street urchin like that could go to places and learn of side issues in ways which the older man could not compass so conveniently.

Presently Fibsy slipped from his seat, and quietly went into the bedrooms.

Eunice raise her eyebrows slightly, but Fleming Stone, observing, said, "Don't mind, Mrs. Embury. The lad is all right. I'll vouch for him."

"A queer helper," remarked Elliott.

"Yes; but very worth-while. I rely on him in many ways, and he almost never fails to help me. He's now looking over the bedrooms, just as I did, and he'll disturb nothing."

"Mercy me!" exclaimed Aunt Abby; "maybe he won't— but I don't like boys prowling among my things!" and she scurried after him.

She found him in her room, and rather gruffly said, "What are you up to, boy?"

"Snuff, ma'am," he replied, with a comical wink, which ought to have shocked the old lady, but which, somehow, had a contrary effect.

"Do you like candy?" she asked—unnecessarily, she knew—and offered him a box from a drawer.

Fibsy felt that a verbal answer was not called for, and, helping himself, proceeded to munch the sweets, contentedly and continuously.

"Say," he burst out, after a thoughtful study of the room, "where was that there dropper thing found, anyhow?"

"In this medicine chest—"

"Naw; I mean where'd the girl find it?—the housework girl."

"You seem to know a lot about the matter!"

"Sure I do. Where'd you say?"

"Right here," and Aunt Abby pointed to a place on the rug near the head of her bed. It was a narrow bed, which had been brought there for her during her stay.

"Huh! Now you could'a dropped it there?"

"I know," and Aunt Abby whispered, "Nobody'll believe me, but I know!"

"You do! Say, you're some wiz! Spill it to me, there's a dear!"

Fibsy was, in his way, a psychologist, and he knew by instinct that this old lady would like him better if he retained his ignorant, untutored ways, than if he used the more polished speech, which he had painstakingly acquired for other kinds of occasions.

"I wonder if you'd understand. For a boy, you're a bright one—"

"Oh, yes, ma'am. I am! They don't make 'em no brighter 'n me! Try me, do, Miss Ames! I'm right there with the goods."

"Well, child, it's this: I saw a—a vision—"

"Yes'm, I know—I mean I know what visions are, they're fine, too!" He fairly smacked his lips in gusto, and it encouraged Aunt Abby to proceed.

"Yes, and it was the ghost of—who do you suppose it was?"

"Your grandmother, ma'am?" The boy's attitude was eagerly attentive and his freckled little face was drawn in a desperate interest.

"No!" Aunt Abby drew closer and just breathed the words, "Mr. Embury!"

"Oh!" Fibsy was really startled, and his eyes opened wide, as he urged, "Go on, ma'am!"

"Yes. Well, it was just at the moment that Mr. Embury was—that he died—you know."

"Yes'm, they always comes then, ma'am!"

"I know it, and oh, child, this is a true story!"

"Oh, yes, ma'am—I know it is!"

Indeed one could scarcely doubt it, for Aunt Abby, having found an interested listener at last, poured forth her account of her strange experience, not caring for comment or explanation, since she had found some one who believed!

"Yes, it was just at that time—I know, because it was almost daylight—just before dawn—and I was asleep, but not entirely asleep—"

"Sort'a half dozing—"

"Yes; and Sanford—Mr. Embury, you know, came gliding through my room, and he stopped at my bedside to say good-by—"

"Was he alive?" asked Fibsy, awe-struck at her hushed tones and bright, glittering eyes.

"Oh, no, it was his spirit, you see—his disembodied spirit"

"How could you see it, then?"

"When spirits appear like that, they are visible."

"Oh, ma'am—I didn't know."

"Yes, and I not only saw him but he was evident to all my five senses!"

"What, ma'am? What do you mean?"

Fibsy drew back, a little scared, as Aunt Abby clutched his sleeve in her excitement. He felt uneasy, for it was growing dusk, and the old lady was in such a state of nervous exhilaration that he shrank a little from her proximity.

But Fibsy was game. "Go on, ma'am," he whispered.

"Yes," Aunt Abby declared, with an eerie smile of triumph, "I saw him—I heard him—I felt him—I smelled him—and, I tasted him!"

Fibsy nearly shrieked, for at each enumeration of her marvelous experiences, Miss Ames grasped his arm tighter and emphasized her statements by pounding on his shoulder.

She seemed unaware of his personal presence—she talked more as if recounting the matter to herself, but she used him as a general audience and the boy had to make a desperate effort to preserve his poise.

And then it struck him that the old lady was crazy, or else she really had an important story to tell. In either case, it was his duty to let Fleming Stone hear it, at first hand, if possible. But he felt sure that to call in the rest of the household, or to take the narrator out to them would—as he expressed it to himself "upset her applecart and spill the beans!"

Chapter 14: The Five Senses

However he decided quickly, it must be done, so he said, diplomatically, "This is awful int'restin', Miss Ames, and I'm just dead sure and certain Mr. Stone'd think so, too. Let's go out and get it off where he c'n hear it. What say?"

The boy had risen and was edging toward the door. Rather than lose her audience, Aunt Abby followed, and in a moment the pair appeared in the living-room, where Fleming Stone was still talking to Eunice and Mr. Elliott.

"Miss Ames, now, she's got somethin' worth tellin'," Fibsy announced. "This yarn of hers is pure gold and a yard wide, Mr. Stone, and you oughter hear it, sir."

"Gladly," and Stone gave Aunt Abby a welcoming smile.

Nothing loath to achieve the center of the stage, the old lady seated herself in her favorite arm-chair, and began:

"It was almost morning," she said, "a faint dawn began to make objects about the room visible, when I opened my eyes and saw a dim, gliding figure—"

Eunice gave an angry exclamation, and rising quickly from her chair, walked into her own room, and closed the door with a slam that left no doubt as to her state of mind.

"Let her alone," advised Elliott; "she's better off in there. What is this story, Aunt Abby? I've never heard it in full."

"No; Eunice never would let me tell it. But it will solve all mystery of Sanford's death."

"Then it is indeed important," and Stone looked at the speaker intently.

"Yes, Mr. Stone, it will prove beyond all doubt that Mr. Embury was a suicide."

"Go on, then," said Elliott, briefly.

"I will. In the half light, I saw this figure I just mentioned. It wasn't discernible clearly—it was merely a moving shadow—a vague shape. It came toward me—"

"From which direction? "asked Stone, with decided interest.

"From Eunice's room—that is, it had, of course, come from Mr. Embury's room, through Eunice's room, and so on into my room. For it was Sanford Embury's spirit—get that firmly in your minds!"

The old lady spoke with asperity, for she was afraid of contradiction, and resented their quite apparent scepticism.

"Go on, please," urged Stone.

"Well, the spirit came nearer my bed, and paused and looked down on me where I lay."

"Did you see his face?" asked Elliott.

"Dimly. I can't seem to make you understand how vague the whole thing was—and yet it was there! As he leaned over me, I saw him—saw the indistinct shape— and I heard the sound of a watch ticking. It was not my watch, it was a very faint ticking one, but all else was so still, that I positively heard it."

"Gee!" said Fibsy, in an explosive whisper.

"Then he seemed about to move away. Impulsively, I made a movement to detain him. Almost without volition—acting on instinct—I put out my hand and clutched his arm. I felt his sleeve—it wasn't a coat sleeve—nor a pajama sleeve—it seemed to have on his gymnasium suit—the sleeve was like woolen jersey—"

"And you felt this?"

"Yes, Mr. Stone, I felt it distinctly—and not only with my hand as I grasped at his arm but" Aunt Abby hesitated an instant, then went on, "But I bit at him! Yes, I did! I don't know why, only I was possessed with an impulse to hold him—and he was slipping away. I didn't realize at the time—who—what it was, and I sort of thought it was a burglar. But, anyway, I bit at him, and so I bit at the woolen sleeve—it was unmistakable—and on it I tasted raspberry jam."

"What!" cried her hearers almost in concert.

"Yes—you needn't laugh—I guess I know the taste of raspberry jam, and it was on that sleeve, as sure as I'm sitting here!"

"Gee!" repeated Fibsy, his fists clenched on his knees and his bright eyes fairly boring into the old lady's countenance. "Gee whiz!"

"Go on," said Stone, quietly.

"And—I smelt gasoline," concluded Miss Ames defiantly. "Now, sir, there's the story. Make what you will out of it, it's every word true. I've thought it over and over, since I realized what it all meant, and had I known at the time it was Sanford's spirit, I should have spoken to him. But as it was, I was too stunned to speak, and when I tried to hold him, he slipped away, and disappeared. But it was positively a materialization of Sanford Embury's flitting spirit—and nothing else."

"The vision may argue a passing soul," Stone said kindly, as if humoring her, "but the effect on your other senses, seems to me to indicate a living person."

"No," and Aunt Abby spoke with deep solemnity, "a materialized spirit is evident to our senses—one or another of them. In this case I discerned it by all five senses, which is unusual —possibly unique; but I am very psychic—very sensitive to spiritual manifestations."

"You have seen ghosts before, then?"

"Oh, yes. I have visions often. But never such a strange one."

"And where did this spirit disappear to?"

"It just faded. It seemed to waft on across the room. I closed my eyes involuntarily, and when I opened them again it was gone."

"Leaving no trace behind?"

"The faint odor of gasoline—and the taste of raspberry jam on my tongue."

Fibsy snickered, but suppressed it at once, and said, "And he left the little dropper-thing beside your bed?"

"Yes, boy! You seem clairvoyant yourself! He did. It was Sanford, of course; he had killed himself with the poison, and he tried to tell me so—but he couldn't make any communication—they rarely can—so he left the tiny implement, that we might know and understand."

"H'm, yes;" and Stone sat thinking. "Now, Miss Ames, you must not be offended at what I'm about to say. I don't disbelieve your story at all. You tell it too honestly for that. I fully believe you saw what you call a 'vision.' But you have thought over it and brooded over it, until you think you saw more than you did—or less! But, leaving that aside for the moment, I want you to realize that your theory of suicide, based on the 'vision' is not logical. Supposing your niece were guilty—as the detectives think—might not Mr. Embury's spirit have pursued the same course?"

Aunt Abby pondered. Then, her eyes flashing, she cried, "Do you mean he put the dropper in my room to throw suspicion on me, instead of on his wife?"

"There is a chance for such a theory."

"Sanford wouldn't do such a thing! He was truly fond of me!"

"But to save his wife?"

"I never thought of all that. Maybe he did—or, maybe he dropped the thing accidentally—"

"Maybe." Stone spoke preoccupiedly.

Mason Elliott, too, sat in deep thought. At last he said:

"Aunt Abby, if I were you, I wouldn't tell that yarn to anybody else. Let's all forget it, and call it merely a dream."

"What do you mean, Mason? "The old lady bridled, having no wish to hear her marvelous experience belittled. "It wasn't a dream —not an ordinary dream—it was a true appearance of Sanford, after his death. You know such things do happen—look at that son of Sir Oliver Lodge. You don't doubt that, do you?"

"Never mind those things. But I earnestly beg of you, Aunt Abby, to forget the episode—or, at least, to promise me you'll not repeat it to any one else."

"Why?"

"I think it wiser for all concerned—for all concerned—that the tale shall not become public property."

"But why?"

"Oh, my land!" burst out Fibsy; "don't you see? The ghost was Mrs. Embury!"

The boy had put into words what was in the thoughts of both Stone and Elliott. They realized that, while Aunt Abby's experience might have been entirely a dream, it was so circumstantial as to indicate a real occurrence, and in that case, what solution so plausible as that Eunice, after committing the crime, wandered into her aunt's room, and whether purposely or accidentally, dropped the implement of death?

Stone, bent on investigation, plied Miss Ames with questions.

Elliott, sorely afraid for Eunice, begged the old lady not to answer.

"You are inventing!" he cried. "You are drawing on your imagination! Don't believe all that, Mr. Stone. It isn't fair to—to Mrs. Embury!"

"Then you see it as I do, Mr. Elliott?" and Stone turned to him quickly. "But, even so, we must look into this story. Suppose, as an experiment, we build up a case against Mrs. Embury, for the purpose of knocking it down again. A man of straw—you know."

"Don't," pleaded Elliott. "Just forget the rigmarole of the nocturnal vision—and devote your energies to finding the real murderer. I have a theory—"

"Wait, Mr. Elliott, I fear you are an interested investigator. Don't forget that you have been mentioned as one of those with 'motive but no opportunity.' "

"Since you have raised that issue, Mr. Stone, let me say right here that my regard for Mrs. Embury is very great. It is also honorable and lifelong. I make no secret of it, but I declare to you that its very purity and intensity puts it far above and beyond any suspicion of being 'motive' for the murder of Mrs. Embury's huband."

Mason Elliott looked Fleming Stone straight in the eye and the speaker's tone and expression carried a strong conviction of sincerity.

Fibsy, too, scrutinized Elliott.

"Good egg!" he observed to himself; "trouble is—he'd give us that same song and dance if he'd croaked the guy his own self!"

"Furthermore," Stone went on, "Mrs. Embury shows a peculiarly strong repugnance to hearing this story of Miss Ames' experience. That looks—"

"Oh, fiddlesticks!" cried Miss Ames, who had been listening in amazement; "it wasn't Eunice! Why would she rig up in Sanford's gym jersey?"

"Why wouldn't she?" countered Stone. "As I said, we're building up a supposititious case. Assume that it was Mrs. Embury, not at all enacting a ghost, but merely wandering around after her impulsive deed—for if she is the guilty party it must have been an impulsive deed. You know her uncontrollable temper—her sudden spasms of rage—"

"Mr. Stone, a 'man of straw,' as you call it, is much more easily built up than knocked down." Elliott spoke sternly. "I hold you have no right to assume Mrs. Embury's identity in this story Miss Ames tells."

"Is there anything that points to her in your discernment by your five senses, Miss Ames?" Stone asked, very gravely. "Has Mrs. Embury a faintly ticking watch?"

"Yes, her wrist-watch," Aunt Abby answered, though speaking evidently against her will.

"And it is possible that she slipped on her husband's jersey; and it is possible there was raspberry jam on the sleeve of it. You see, I am not doubting the evidence of your senses. Now, as to the gasoline. Had Mrs. Embury, or her maid, by any chance, been cleaning any laces or finery with gasoline?"

"I won't tell you!" and Aunt Abby shook her head so obstinately that it was quite equivalent to an affirmative answer!

"Now, you see, Aunt Abby," protested Elliott, in an agonized voice, "why I want you to shut up about that confounded 'vision'! You are responsible for this case Mr. Stone is so ingeniously building up against Eunice! You are getting her into a desperate coil, from which it will be difficult to extricate her! If Shane got hold of this absurd yarn—"

"It's not entirely absurd," broke in Stone, "but I agree with you, Mr. Elliott; if Shane learns of it—he won't investigate any further!"

"He shan't know of it," was the angry retort. "I got you here, Mr. Stone—"

"To discover the truth, or to free Mrs. Embury?"

There was a pause, and the two men looked at each other. Then Mason Elliott said, in a low voice, "To free Mrs. Embury."

"I can't take the case that way," Stone replied. "I will abandon the whole affair, or—I will find out the truth."

"Abandon it!" cried a ringing voice, and the door of her bedroom was flung open as Eunice again appeared.

She was in a towering fury, her face was white and her lips compressed to a straight scarlet line.

"Give up the case! I will take my chances with any judge or jury rather than with you!" She faced Stone like the "Tiger" her husband had nicknamed her. "I have heard every word—Aunt Abby's story—and your

conclusions! Your despicable 'deductions,' as I suppose
you call them! I've had enough of the 'celebrated
detective'! Quite enough of Fleming Stone—and his
work!"

She stepped back and gazed at him with utter scorn
beautiful as a sculptured Medea, haughty as a tragedy
queen.

"Independent as a pig on ice!" Fibsy communicated
with himself, and he stared at her with undisguised
admiration.

"Eunice," and the pain in Mason Elliott's voice was
noticeable; "Eunice, dear, don't do yourself such
injustice."

"Why not? When everybody is unjust to me! You,
Mason, you and this—this infallible detective sit here and
deliberately build up what you call a 'case' against me—
me, Eunice Embury! Oh—I hate you all!"

A veritable figure of hate incarnate, she stood, her
white hands clasping each other tightly, as they hung
against her black gown. Her head held high, her whole
attitude fiercely defiant, she flung out her words with a
bitterness that betokened the end of her endurance—the
limit of her patience.

Then her hands fell apart, her whole body drooped,
and sinking down on the wide sofa, she sat, hopelessly
facing them, but with head erect and the air of one
vanquished but very much unsubdued.

"Take that back, Eunice," Elliott spoke passionately,
and quite as if there were no others present; "you do not
hate me—I am here to help you!"

"You can't, Mason; no one can help me. No one can
protect me from Fleming Stone!"

The name was uttered with such scorn as to seem an
invective of itself!

Stone betrayed no annoyance at her attitude toward
him, but rather seemed impressed with her personality.
He gave her a glance that was not untinged with
admiration, but he made no defence.

"I can," cried Fibsy, who was utterly routed by Eunice's imperious beauty. "You go ahead with Mr. F. Stone, ma'am, and I'll see to it that they ain't no injustice done to you!"

Stone looked at his excited young assistant with surprise, and then good-naturedly contented himself with a shake of his head, and a

"Careful, Terence."

"Yes, sir—but, oh, Mr. Stone—" and then, at a gesture from the great detective the boy paused, abashed, and remained silent.

"Now, Miss Ames," Stone began, "in Mrs. Embury's presence, I'll ask you—"

"You won't ask me anything, sir," she returned crisply. "I'm going out. I've a very important errand to do."

"Oh, I don't know about that," Elliott said; "it's almost six o'clock, Aunt Abby. Where are you going?"

"I've got an errand—a very important errand—an appointment, in fact. I must go—don't you dare oppose me, Mason. You'll be sorry if you do!"

Even as she spoke, the old lady was scurrying to her room, from which she returned shortly, garbed for the street.

"All right," Stone said, in reply to a whisper from Fibsy, and the boy offered, respectfully:

"Let me go with you, Miss Ames. It ain't fittin' you should go alone. It's 'most dark."

"Come on, boy," Aunt Abby regarded him kindly; "I'd be glad of your company."

At the street door, the old lady asked for a taxicab, and the strangely assorted pair were soon on their way.

"You're a bright lad, Fibsy," she said; "by the way, what's your real name—I forget."

"Terence, ma'am; Terence McGuire. I wish't I was old enough to be called McGuire! I'd like that."

"I'll call you that, if you wish. You're old for your age, I'm sure. How old are you?"

"Goin' on about fifteen or sixteen—I think. I sort'a forget."

"Nonsense! You can't forget your age! Why do they call you Fibsy?"

"'Cause I'm a born liar—'scuse me—a congenital prevaricator, I meant to say. You see, ma'am, it's necessary in my business not always to employ the plain unvarnished. But don't be alarmed, ma'am; when I take a fancy to anybuddy, as I have to you, ma'am, I don't never lie to 'em. Not that I s'pose you'd care, eh, ma'am?"

Aunt Abby laughed. "You are a queer lad! Why, I'm not sure I'd care, if it didn't affect me in any way. I'm not responsible for your truthfulness—though I don't mind advising you that you ought to be a truthful boy."

"Land, ma'am! Don't you s'pose I know that? But, honest now, are you always just exactly, abserlutely truthful, yourself?"

"Certainly I am! What do you mean by speaking to me like that?"

"Well, don't you ever touch up a yarn a little jest sort'a to make it more interestin' like? Most ladies do—that is, most ladies of intelligence and brains—which you sure have got in plenty!"

"There, there, boy; I'm afraid I've humored you too much you're presuming."

"I presume I am. But one question more, while we're on this absorbin' subject. Didn't you, now, just add a jot or a tittle to that ghost story you put over? Was it every bit on the dead level?"

"Yes, child," Aunt Abby took his question seriously; "it was every word true. I didn't make up the least word of it!"

"I believe you, ma'am, and I congratulate you on your clarviant powers. Now, about that raspberry jam, ma'am. That's a mighty unmistakable taste—ain't it, now."

"It is, McGuire. It certainly is. And I tasted it, just as surely as I'm here telling you about it."

"Have you had it for supper lately, ma'am?"

"No; Eunice hasn't had it on her table since I've been visiting her."

"Is that so, ma'am?"

CHAPTER 15: MARIGNY THE MEDIUM

The journey ended at the rooms of Marigny, the psychic recommended by Willy Hanlon.

As Fibsy, his bright eyes wide with wonder, found himself in the unmistakable surroundings of dingy draperies, a curtained cabinet and an odor of burning incense, he exclaimed to himself, "Gee! a clairviant! Now for some fun!"

Aunt Abby, apparently aware of the proprieties of the occasion, seated herself, and waited patiently.

At a gesture from her, Fibsy obediently took a seat near her, and waited quietly, too.

Soon the psychic entered. He was robed in a long, black garment, and wore a heavy, white turban, swathed in folds. His face was olive-colored—what was visible of it for his beard was white and flowing, and a heavy drooping moustache fell over his lips. Locks of white hair showed from the turban's edge, and a pair of big, rubber-rimmed glasses of an amber tint partially hid his eyes.

The whole make-up was false, it was clear to be seen, but a psychic has a right to disguise himself, if he choose.

Fibsy gave Marigny one quick glance and then the boy assumed an expression of face quite different from his usual one. He managed to look positively vacant-minded. His eyes became lack-luster, his mouth, slightly open, looked almost imbecile, and his roving glance betokened no interest whatever in the proceedings.

"Mr. Marigny?" said Miss Ames, eagerly anxious for the seance to begin.

"Yes, madam. You are three minutes late!"

"I couldn't help it—the traffic is very heavy at this hour."

"And you should have come alone. I cannot concentrate with an alien influence in the room."

"Oh, the boy isn't an alien influence. He's a little friend of mine—he'll do no harm."

"I'll go out, if you say, mister," Fibsy turned his indifferent gaze on the clairvoyant.

"You'll do nothing of the sort," spoke up Miss Ames. "I'm accustomed to seances, Mr. Marigny, and if you're all right—as I was told you were—a child's presence won't interfere."

Evidently the psychic saw he had no novice to deal with, and he accepted the situation.

"What do you want to know? "he asked his client.

"Who killed Sanford Embury—or, did he kill himself." I want you to get into communication with his spirit and find out from him. But I don't want any make-believe. If you can't succeed, that's all right—I'll pay your fee just the same. But no poppycock."

"That's the way to look at it, madam. I will go into the silence, and I will give you only such information as I get myself."

The man leaned back in his chair, and gradually seemed to enter a hypnotic state. His muscles relaxed, his face became still and set, and his breathing was slow and a little labored.

Fibsy retained his vacuous look he even fidgeted a little, in a bored way—and rarely glanced toward the man of "clear sight."

Miss Ames, though anxious for results, was alert and quite on her guard against fraud. Experienced in fake mediums, she believed Willy Hanlon's assertion that this man was one of the few genuine mystics, but she proposed to judge for herself.

At last Marigny spoke. His voice was low, his tones monotonous and uninflected.

"Aunt Abby—Aunt Westminster Abbey" the words came slowly.

Miss Ames gave a startled jump. Her face blanched and she trembled as she clutched Fibsy's arm.

"That's what Sanford used to call me!" she whispered. "Can it really be his spirit talking to me through the medium!"

"Don't worry," the voice went on, "don't grieve for me—it's all right—let it go that I took my own life—"

"But did you, Sanford—did you? "Miss Ames implored.

"It would be better you should never know."

"I must know. I've got to know! Tell me, Sanford. It wasn't Eunice?

"No—it wasn't Eunice."

"Was it—oh, San—was it—I?"

"Yes, Aunt Abby—it was. But you were entirely irresponsible —you were asleep—hypnotized, perhaps—perhaps merely asleep."

"Where did I get the stuff?"

"I think somebody hypnotized you and gave it to you—"

"When? Where?"

"I don't know—it is vague—uncertain—But you put it in my ear —remember, Aunt Abby, I don't blame you at all. And you must not tell this. You must let it go as suicide. That is the only way to save yourself—"

"But they suspect Eunice—"

"They'll never convict her—nor would they convict you. Tell them you got into communication with my spirit and I said it was suicide."

"Ask him about the raspberry jam," put in Fibsy, in a stage whisper.

"What!" the medium came out of his trance suddenly and glared at the boy.

"I told you I could do nothing if the child stayed here," Marigny cried, evidently in a towering passion. "Put him out. Who is he? What is he talking about?"

"Nothing of importance. Keep still, McGuire. Can you get Mr. Embury's spirit back, sir?"

"No, the communion is too greatly disturbed. Boy, what do you mean by raspberry jam?"

"Oh, nothin'," and Fibsy wriggled bashfully. "You tell him, Miss Ames."

It needed little encouragement to launch Aunt Abby on the story of her "vision" and she told it in full detail.

Marigny seemed interested, though a little impatient, and tried to hurry the recital.

"It was, without doubt, Embury's spirit," he said, as Aunt Abby finished; "but your imagination has exaggerated and elaborated the facts. For instance, I think the jam and the gasoline are added by your fancy, in order to fill out the full tale of your five senses."

"That's what I thought," and Fibsy nodded his head. "Raspberry jam! Oh, gee!" he exploded in a burst of silly laughter.

Marigny looked at him with a new interest. The amber-colored glasses, turned toward the boy seemed to frighten him, and he began to whimper.

"I didn't mean any harm," he said, "but raspberry jam was so funny for a ghost to have on him!"

"It would have been," assented Marigny, "but that, I feel sure, existed only in Miss Ames' fancy. Her mind, upset by the vision, had strange hallucinations, and the jam was one—you know we often have grotesque dreams."

"So we do," agreed Fibsy; "why once I drempt that—"

"Excuse me, young sir, but I've no time to listen to your dreams. The seance is at an end, madam. Your companion probably cut it off prematurely—but perhaps not. Perhaps the communication was about over, anyway. Are you satisfied, Miss Ames?"

"Yes, Mr. Marigny. I know the appearance of Mr. Embury was a genuine visitation, for he called me by a peculiar name which no one else ever used, and which you could not possibly know about."

"That is indeed a positive test. I am glad you received what you wished for. The fee is ten dollars, madam."

Aunt Abby paid it willingly enough, and with Fibsy, took her departure.

On reaching home they found Alvord Hendricks there. Mason Elliott had tarried and Fleming Stone, too, was still there. Eunice was awaiting Aunt Abby's return to have dinner served.

"I thought you'd never come, Auntie," said Eunice, greeting her warmly. Eunice was in a most pleasant mood, and seemed to have become entirely reconciled to the presence of Stone.

"You will dine here, too, Terence," she said kindly to the boy, who replied, "Yes, ma'am," very respectfully.

"Well, Eunice," Aunt Abby announced, after they were seated at the table, "I'm the criminal, after all."

"You seem pretty cheerful about it," said Hendricks, looking at her in astonishment.

"Well, I wasn't responsible. I did it under compulsory hypnotism."

"You owned up to it before, Aunt Abby," said Eunice, humoring her; "you said—"

"I know, Eunice, but that time it was to shield you. Now, I know for certain that I did do it, and how it came about."

"Dear Aunt Abby," and Elliott spoke very gently, "don't you talk about it any more. Your vagaries are tolerated by us, who love you, but Mr. Stone is bored by them—"

"Not at all," said Fleming Stone; "on the contrary, I'm deeply interested. Tell me all about it, Miss Ames. Where have you been?"

Thus encouraged, Aunt Abby told all.

She described the seance truthfully, Fibsy's bright eyes—not lack-luster now—darting glances at her and at Stone as the tale proceeded.

"He was the real thing—wasn't he, McGuire?" Miss Ames appealed to him, at last.

"You bet! Why, if the side wire of his beard hadn't fetched loose and if his walnut juice complexion hadn't stopped a mite short of his collar, I'd a took him for a sure-fire Oriental!"

"Don't be so impertinent, Terence," reproved Stone; "Miss Ames knows better than you do."

"It doesn't matter that he was made up that way," Aunt Abby said, serenely; "they often do that. But he was genuine, I know, because—why, Eunice, what did Sanford use to call me—for fun —Aunt what?"

"Aunt Westminter Abbey," said Eunice, smiling at the recollection.

"Yes!" triumphantly; "and that's what Sanford called me to-day when speaking to me through the medium. Isn't that a proof? How could that man know that?"

"I can't explain that," declared Elliott, a little shortly, "but it's all rubbish, and I don't think you ought to be allowed to go to such places! It's disgraceful—"

"You hush up, Mason," Miss Ames cried; "I'll go where I like! I'm not a child. And, too, I wasn't alone—I had an escort—a very nice one." She looked kindly at Fibsy.

"Thank you, ma'am," he returned, bobbing his funny red head. "I sure enjoyed myself."

"You didn't look so; you looked half asleep."

"I always enjoy myself when I'm asleep—and half a loaf is better'n no bed," the boy grinned at her.

"Well, it may all be rubbish," Alvord Hendricks said, musingly; "and it probably is—but there are people, Mason, who don't think so. Anyway, here's my idea. If Aunt Abby thinks she poisoned Sanford, under hypnotism—or any other way—for the love of heaven, let it go at that! If you don't—suspicion will turn back to Eunice again—and that's what we want to prevent. Now, no jury would ever convict an old lady—"

"Nor any woman," said Elliott. "But that isn't the whole thing. I say, Alvord, since Mr. Stone is on the job, suppose we give him full swing—and let him find the real murderer. It wasn't Eunice!"

His words rang out so vibrantly that Stone gave him a quick glance. "You're sure?" he asked, as it seemed, involuntarily.

"I am," responded Elliott, with a satisfied nod of his handsome head.

"But your being sure doesn't help much, Mason," Eunice said, a despondent look coming into her eyes. "Are you sure, Mr. Stone?"

"I can't quite answer that question yet, Mrs. Embury," the courteous voice replied. "Remember, I've only just begun to look into the matter."

"But you know all about it—from Mr. Shane and Mr. Driscoll."

"I know what they think about it—but that's a different story."

"You don't agree with their deductions, then?" asked Hendricks.

"I don't agree with their premises—therefore—" Stone smiled cryptically, and left the sentence unfinished and ambiguous, which was his deliberate intention.

"We will have coffee in the living-room," said Eunice, as she rose from the table. Always a charming hostess, she was at her best to-night. Her thin black gown was becoming and made her fair throat and arms seem even whiter by contrast.

She stood back, as the others left the room, and Hendricks, tarrying, too, came close to her.

"Brace up, dear," he said; "it will all come out right. I'm sorry Elliott dragged in this Stone, but—it will be all right, somehow."

"But it's all so mysterious, Alvord. I don't know what to do—or say—"

"Don't lose your temper, Eunice. Let me advise you strongly as to that. It never does any good—it militates against you. And here's another thing—Are you afraid of the little Desternay?"

"Afraid—how?" but Eunice paled.

"Afraid—she knows something—oh, something injurious to—"

"To me? She knows heaps!" The haughty head tossed, and Eunice looked defiant.

"You beauty!" and Hendricks took a step nearer. "Oh, you splendid thing! How I adore you. Eunice—you are a goddess to-night! And you are for me! Some day—oh, I'm not going to say it now—-don't look so alarmed—but, you know—oh, Sweet, you know! And you yes, you, too, my splendid Tiger—'"

"Hush, Alvord! Never call me that!"

"No, I beg pardon. And I don't want to. That was San's own name for you. I shall call you my Queen! My glorious Queen-woman!"

"Oh, stop! Don't you dare make love to me!

"And don't you dare say 'dare' to me! I dare all—"

Ferdinand's entrance cut short this dialogue, and Eunice and Hendricks went into the other room.

Almost immediately a visitor was announced,, and Hanlon came in.

"Why, Mr. Hanlon," Eunice said, greeting him cordially, "I'm glad to see you again."

"So am I," cried Aunt Abby, hastening to welcome the newcomer. "Oh, Mr. Hanlon, I went to see your man—Mr. Marigny, you know—"

"Yes? I called to see if you had found him all right."

The necessary introductions were made, and Hanlon took his place in the group.

He was a little ill at ease, for he was by no means a member of "society," and though he had been at the Embury house before, he seemed a trifle in awe of his surroundings.

"And I called, too," Hanlon said, "to offer you my respectful sympathy, Mrs. Embury, and ask if there's anything I can do for you."

"Why, you're very kind," said Eunice, touched by his thoughtfulness, "but I'm afraid there's nothing you— anybody can do for me."

"F. Stone can," declared Fibsy; "he can do a lot for you, Mrs. Embury." The red head nodded vigorously, as was the boy's habit, when much in earnest.

Hanlon regarded him closely, and Fibsy returned the scrutiny.

"Say," the boy broke out, suddenly. "I've seen you before. You're the man who found the hidden jackknife, in Newark!"

"The same," and Hanlon smiled at him. "Were you present?"

"I sure was! Gee! You're a wonder!"

"I was a wonder, but I don't do wonderful things any more."

"What do you do now?"

"Yes," chimed in Eunice, "what are you doing, Mr. Hanlon? You told me you were going to take up a different line of work."

"I did, Mrs. Embury; I'm a prosaic and uninteresting painter man nowadays."

"An artist?"

"In a way," and Hanlon smiled; "I paint signs—and I try to do them artistically."

"Signs! How dull for you—after your exciting performances!"

"Not so very dull," interrupted Aunt Abby. "I know about the signs Mr. Hanlon paints! They're bigger'n a house! They're —why, they're scenery—don't you know?—like you see along the railroad—I mean along the meadows when you're riding in the cars."

"Oh, scenic advertising," observed Fleming Stone. "And signs on the Palisades—"

"Not on the natural scenery," laughed Hanlon. "Though I've been tempted by high rocks or smooth-sided crags."

"Are you a steeple-jack?" asked Fibsy, his eyes sparkling; "can you paint spires and things?"

"No;" and Hanlon looked at the boy, regretfully. "I can't do that. I'm no climber. I make the signs and then they're put where they belong by other workmen."

"Oh," and Fibsy looked disappointed at not finding the daring hero he sought for.

"I must not presume further on your kindness, Mrs. Embury," Hanlon said, with an attempt at society jargon, "I merely called in for a minute. Mr. Hendricks, are you going my way? I want to see you about that sign-"

"No, Hanlon—sorry, but I'm not going now," and Hendricks shook his head. "I'm here for the evening."

"All right see you later, then. Where can I find you? I'm something of an owl, myself."

"I'll call you up after I get home—if it isn't too late," Hendricks suggested.

"Never too late for me. See that you remember."

Hanlon looked at Hendricks with more seriousness than the subject appeared to call for, then he went away.

"You got the earache?" asked Fibsy suddenly, of Hendricks, as that gentleman half absently rubbed his ear.

"Bless my soul, no! What do you mean by such a question? Mr. Stone, this boy of yours is too fresh!"

"Be quiet, Terence," said Stone, paying but slight attention to the matter.

"Oh, all right, no offense meant," and the boy grinned at Hendricks. "But didn't you ever have an earache? If not, you don't know what real sufferin' is!"

"No, I never had it, that I remember. Perhaps as a child—"

"Why, Alvord," said Aunt Abby, "you had it fearfully about a month ago. Don't you recollect? You were afraid of mastoiditis."

"Oh, that. Well, that was a serious illness. I was thinking of an ordinary earache, when I said I never had one. But I beg of you drop the subject of my ailments! What a thing to discuss!"

"True enough," agreed Stone, "I propose we keep to the theme under consideration. I've been engaged to look into this murder mystery. I'm here for that purpose. I must insist that I conduct my investigation in my own way."

"That's the right talk," approved Elliott. "Now, Mr. Stone, let's get right down to it."

"Very well, the case stands thus: Shane says—and it's perfectly true—there are five possible suspects. But only one of these had both motive and opportunity. Now, the whole five are here present, and, absurd though it my seem, I'm going to ask each one of you the definite question. Ferdinand," he raised his voice and the butler came in from the dining-room, "did you kill your master?"

"No, God hearing me—I didn't, sir." The man was quiet and composed, though his face was agonized.

"That will do, you may go," said Stone. "Mr. Elliott, did you kill your friend—your partner in business?"

"I did not," said Elliott, curtly. He was evidently ill-pleased at the question.

"Mr. Hendricks, did you?"

"As I have repeatedly proved, I was in Boston that night. It would be impossible for me to be the criminal—but I will answer your ridiculous query—I did not."

"Mrs. Embury, did you?"

"N—no—but I would rather be suspected, than to have—"

"You said no, I believe," Stone interrupted her. "Miss Ames, do you really think you killed your niece's husband?"

"Oh, sir—I don't know! I can't think I did—"

"Of course, you didn't, Aunt Abby!" Mason Elliott rose from his seat and paced up and down the room. "I must say, Mr. Stone, this is a childish performance! What makes you think any of us would say so, if we had killed Embury? It is utterly absurd!"

"You're absurd, Elliott," cut in Hendricks. "Mr. Stone is a psychologist. He learns what he wants to know not from what we say—but the way we say it. Right, Mr. Stone?"

"Right, Mr. Hendricks." Stone looked grave. "Anything more to say, Mr. Elliott?"

"Yes, I have! And it's this: I asked you to come here. I asked you to take this case—as you've already surmised—to free Mrs. Embury from wrongful suspicion. Wrongful, mind you! I do not want you to clear her if she is guilty. But she isn't. Therefore, I want you to find the real criminal. That's what I want!"

"And that's what I'm doing."

"Of course he is," Eunice defended him. "I wish you'd keep still, Mason! You talk too much—and you interfere with Mr. Stone's methods."

"Perhaps I'd better go home, Eunice." Elliott was clearly offended. "If you don't want me here, I'll go."

"Oh, no—" Eunice began, but Hendricks said, "Go on, Elliott, do. There are too many of us here, and as Eunice's counsel, I can look after her interests."

Mason Elliott rose, and turned to Eunice.

"Shall I go?" he said, and he gave her a look of entreaty—a look of yearning, pleading love.

"Go," she said, coldly. "Alvord will take care of me."

And Elliott went.

CHAPTER 16: FIBSY'S BUSY DAY

"It's this way, F. Stone," said Fibsy, earnestly, "the crooks of the situation—"

"The what?"

"The crooks—that's what they call it—"

"Oh, the crux." Stone did not laugh.

"Yessir—if that's how you pronounce it. Guess I'll stick to plain English. Well, to my way of thinkin', the little joker in the case is that there raspberry jam. I'm a strong believer in raspberry jam on general principles, but in pertikler, I should say in this present case, raspberry jam will win the war! Don't eat it!"

"Thought you were going to talk plain English. You're cryptic, my son."

"All right—here goes. That jam business is straight goods. The old lady says she tasted jam—and she did taste jam. That's all there is about that. And that sweet, pleasant, innercent raspberry jam will yet send the moiderer of Mr. Embury to the chair!"

"I think myself there's something to be looked into there, but how are you going about it?"

"Dunno yet—but here's another thing, Mr. Stone, that I ain't had time to tell you yet, that—"

"Suppose you begin at the beginning and tell me your story in order."

"Supposin' I do!" Fibsy thought a moment before he began. It was the morning after the two had dined at the Embury home, and they were breakfasting together in Stone's hotel apartment.

"Well, Mr. Stone, as you know, I left Mrs. Embury's last night d'eckly after Mr. Hendricks took his deeparture. As I s'pected, there was trouble a-waitin' for him just outside the street doorway, that Hanlon chap

was standing and he met up with Mr. Hendricks—much
to the dismay of the latter!"

"Your English is fine this morning—go ahead."

"Well—Hanlon fell into step like with Mr. Henricks,
and they walked along, Hanlon doing the talking. I didn't
dare get close enough to overhear them, for they're both
live wires, and I don't fool either of 'em into thinking
meself a ninkypoop! So I trailed, but well out'a sight—
and, hold on, Mr. Stone, while I tell you this. The fake
mejum that Miss Ames went to see yesterday afternoon,
was none other than friend Hanlon himself!"

"What? Fibs, are you sure?"

"Sure as shootin'! I spotted him the minute he came
up to Mrs. Embury's. I didn't reckernize him at first as
the whiskered Moses, but I did later. You know, Mr.
Stone, I saw him do stunts for newspapers in two towns,
and I wonder I didn't tumble to him in the spookshop.
But I didn't—I dessay because when I saw him doing his
mind-readin' tricks outdoors he was blindfolded, which
some concealed his natural scenery. Well, he hadn't
more'n tripped over the Embury 'Welcome' mat, than I
was onto him. Me thinker woiked light lightnin' and I
had him ticketed and pigeonholed in no time."

"Is he mixed up in the Embury case?"

"He's mixed up with Mr. Hendricks in some way, and
he learned from Miss Ames that Hendricks was to be
among those present, so he made up foolish excuses and
betook himself to the vicinity of said Hendricks."

"Why?"

"Wanted to converse with him, and couldn't get hold
of him otherwise. Hendricks, it would seem, didn't
hanker for said conversation."

"I remember Hanlon asked Mr. Hendricks if he were
going his way, and Hendricks said he was going to spend
the evening where he was."

"Egg-zackly. And did. But all the same, Hanlon
waited. And a wait of an hour and a half registers
patience and perseverance —to my mind."

"Right you are! And you trailed the pair?"

"Did I?" Fibsy fell back in his chair, as if exhausted. "I followed them to Mr. Hendricks' home, they chatterin' glibly all the way—and then after a few minutes' further remarks on the doorstep Hendricks, he went in—and Hanlon—! You know, Mr. Stone, Hanlon's nobody's fool, and he knew I was follerin' him as well as he knew his name! I don't know how he knew it—for I was most careful to keep out'a sight, but all the same, he did know it—and what do you think he did? He led me a chase of miles —and miles—and miles! That's what he did!"

"On purpose?"

"On purpose! Laughin' in his silly sleeve! I was game. I trotted along—but bullieve me! I was mad! And the galoot was so slick about it! Why, he walked up Broadway first—as if he had a business appointment in a desprit hurry. Then, having reached Hunderd an' Twenty-fi'th Street, he pauses a minute—to be sure I'm trailin', the vilyun and then, he swings East, and across town, and turns South again—oh, well, Mr. Stone, he simpully makes me foller him till I'm that dog-tired, I near drops in my tracks. And, to top the heap, he leads me straight to this hotel, where we're stayin'—yes, sir! right here—and makin' a sharp turn, he says, 'Good-night!' pleasant like, and scoots off. Can you beat it?"

"Poor old Fibs, that was an experience! Looks like the Hanlon person is one to be reckoned with. But it doesn't prove him mixed up in the murder mystery in any way."

"No, sir, it don't. It's only made me sore on him—and sore on my own account, too!" Fibsy grinned ruefully. "Me feet's that blistered—and I'm lame all over!"

"Poor boy! You see, he's a sprinter from 'way back. His stunts on that newspaper work prove he can take long walks without turning a hair."

"Yes, but its croolty to animiles to drag a young feller like me along, too. I've got his number. Just you wait,

Cele! Remember, Mr. Stone, he played spook-catcher to Miss Ames. That means something, sir."

"It does, indeed. This is a great old case, Fibsy. Are you getting a line on it?"

"I think so, sir," and the lad looked very earnest. "Are you?"

"A strange one. But, yet, a line. To-day, Fibs, I want you to interview that Mrs. Desternay. You can do it better than I, jolly her along, and find out if she's fried or foe of Mrs. Embury."

"Yessir. An' kin I do a little sleuthin' on my own?"

"What sort?"

"Legitermit—I do assure you, sir."

When Fibsy assumed this deeply earnest air, Stone knew some clever dodge was in his mind, and he found it usually turned out well, so he said, "Go ahead, my boy; I trust you."

"Thank yer," and Fibsy devoted himself to the remainder of his breakfast, while Stone read the morning paper.

An hour later Terence McGuire presented himself at the Embury home and asked for Miss Ames.

"Good morning, ma'am," he said, as he smiled brightly at her. "Howlja like to join me in a bit of investergation that'll proberly end up in a s'lution of the mystery?"

"I'd like it first rate," replied Miss Ames, with enthusiasm. "When do we begin?"

"Immejitly. Where's Mis' Embury?"

"In her room."

"No use a-disturbin' her, but I want'a see the jersey— the gymnasium jersey your ghost wore."

Aunt Abby looked disappointed. She had hoped for something more exciting.

But she said, "I'll get it," and went at once to Sanford Embury's room.

"Thank you," said Fibsy, as he took it. But his eager scrutiny failed to disclose any trace of jam on its sleeves.

"Which arm did you bite?" he asked, briefly.

"I didn't really bite at all," Miss Ames returned. "I sort of made a snap at him—it was more a nervous gesture than an intelligent action. And I just caught a bit of the worsted sleeve between my lips for an instant—it was, let me see—it must have been the left arm—"

"Well, we'll examine both sleeves—and I regret to state, ma'am, there's no sign of sticky stuff. This is a fine specimen of a jersey—I never saw a handsomer one—but there's no stain on it, and never has been."

"Nor has it ever been cleaned with gasoline," mused Miss Ames, "and yet, McGuire, nothing, to my dying day, can ever convince me that I am mistaken on those two subjects. I'm just as sure as I can be."

"I'm sure, too. Listen here, Miss Ames. There's a great little old revelation due in about a: day or so, and I wish you'd lay low. Will you?"

"What do you mean?"

"Why, don't do or say much about the affair. Let it simmer. I'm on the warpath, and so's Mr. Stone, and we're comin' out on top, if we don't have no drawbacks. So, don't trot round to clarviants or harp on that there 'vision' of yours, will you?"

"My boy, I'm only too glad to keep away from the subject. I'm worried to death with it all. And if I can't do any good by my efforts, I'll willingly 'lay low' as you ask."

"All right, ma'am. Now, I'm off, and I'll be back here when I come again. So long."

Fibsy went down in the service elevator and forthwith proceeded to interview the rubbish man of the house and some other functionaries.

By dint of much prodding of memory, assisted by judicious silver offerings, he finally learned that there was an apartment occupied by a couple with four children, who, it appeared, consumed large quantities of jam of all flavors. At least, their rubbish was bristling with empty jam pots, and the deduction was logical.

Seemingly unimpressed, Fibsy declared it was pickle-fiends he was searching for, and departed, outwardly crestfallen, but inwardly elated.

Going out of doors, he walked to the corner of Park Avenue, and turned into the side street.

Crossing that street to get a better view, he looked up the side of the big apartment house, and his gaze paused at the window in the tenth story which was in Miss Ames' sleeping-room. Two floors below this was the apartment of the family who were reputed jam eaters.

Fibsy looked intently at all the windows. The one next Miss Ames' was, he knew, in the Embury's pantry. Hence, the one two stories below was in the Patterson's pantry the Patterson being the aforesaid family.

And to the boy's astonished and delighted eyes, there on the pantry window-sill sat what was unmistakably a jam jar!

So far, so good. But what did it mean? Fibsy had learned that Mr. Patterson was a member of the Metropolitan Athletic Club and was greatly interested in its presidential election—which election, owing to the death of one of the candidates had been indefinitely postponed.

But further investigation of Mr. Patterson was too serious a matter for the boy to undertake. It must be referred to Fleming Stone.

So Fibsy glued his eyes once more to that fascinating jam jar up on the eighth-story window-sill, and slowly walked away.

Under his breath he was singing, "Raz Berry Jam! Raz Berry Jam!'—" to the tune of a certain march from Lohengrin, which somehow represented to his idea the high note of triumph.

He proceeded along the cross street, and at Fifth Avenue he entered a bus.

His next errand took him to the home of Fifi Desternay.

By some ingenious method of wheedling, he persuaded the doorman to acquaint the lady with the fact of his presence, and when she came into the room where he awaited her he banked on his nerve to induce her to grant him an interview.

"You know me," he said, with his most ingratiating smile, and he even went so far as to take her beringed little hand in his own boyish paw.

"I do not!" she declared, staring at him, and then, his grin proving infectious, she added, not unkindly, "Who are you, child?"

"I wish I was a society reporter or a photographer, or anybody who could do justice to your wonderful charms!"

His gaze of admiration was so sincere that Fifi couldn't resent it.

She often looked her best in the morning, and her dainty negligee and bewitching French cap made her a lovely picture.

She tucked herself into a big, cushioned chair, and drawing a smoking-stand nearer, fussed with its silver appointments.

"Lemme, ma'am," said Fibsy, eagerly, and, though it was his first attempt, he held a lighted match to her cigarette with real grace.

Then, drawing a long breath of relief at his success, he took a cigarette himself, and sat near her.

"Well," she began, "what's it all about? And, do tell me how you got in! I'm glad you did, though it was against orders. I've not seen anything so amusing as you for a long time!"

"This is my amusin' day," returned the boy, imperturbably. "I came to talk over things in general—"

"And what in particular?"

Fifi was enjoying herself. She felt almost sure the boy was a reporter of a new sort, but she was frankly curious.

"Well, ma'am," and here Fibsy changed his demeanor to a stern, scowling fierceness, "I'm a special

investigator." He rose now, and strode about the room.
"I'm engaged on the Embury murder case, and I'm here to
ask you a few pointed questions about it."

"My heavens!" cried Fifi, "what are you talking
about?"

"Don't scoff at me, ma'am; I'm in authority."

"Oh, well, go ahead. Why are you questioning me?"

"It's this way, ma'am." Fibsy sat down astride a chair,
looking over the back of it at his hostess. "You and Mrs.
Embury are bosom friends, I understand."

"From whom do you understand it?" was the tart
response; "from Mrs. Embury?"

"In a manner o' speakin', yes; and then again, no. But
aren't you?"

"We were. We were school friends, and have been
intimates for years. But since her—trouble, Mrs. Embury
has thrown me over —has discarded me utterly—I'm so
sorry!"

Fifi daintily touched her eyes with a tiny square of
monogrammed linen, and Fibsy said, gravely,

"Careful, there; don't dab your eyelashes too hard!"

"What!" Mrs. Desternay could scarcely believe her
ears.

"Honest, you'd better look out. It's coming off now."

"Nothing of the sort," and Fifi whipped out a vanity
case, and readjusted her cosmetic adornment.

"Then I take it you two are not friends?"

"We most certainly are not. I wouldn't do anything in
the world to injure Eunice Embury—in fact, I'd help her,
even now—though she scorned my assistance—but we're
not friends—no!"

"All right, I just wanted to know. Ask right out—
that's my motto."

"It seems to be! Anything else you are thirsting to
learn?"

"Yes'm. You know that 'Hamlet' performance—you
and Mis' Embury went to?"

"Yes," said Fifi, cautiously.

"You know you accused her of talkin' it over with you—"

"She did!"

"Yes'm—I know you say she did—I got that from Mr. Shane—but, lemme tell you, ma'am, friendly like, you want to be careful how you tell that yarn—'cause they's chance fer a perfectly good slander case against you!"

"What nonsense!" but Fifi paled a little under her delicate rouge.

"No nonsense whatsomever. But here's the point. Was there a witness to that conversation?"

"Why, let me see. We talked it over at the matinee— we were alone then—but, yes, of course—I recollect now—that same evening Eunice was here and Mr. Hendricks was, too, and Mr. Patterson—he lives in their apartment house—the Embury's, I mean-and we all talked about it! There! I guess that's witnesses enough!"

"I guess it is. But take it from me, lady, you're too pretty to get into a bothersome lawsuit—and I advise you to keep on the sunny side of the street, and let these shady matters alone."

"I'll gladly do so—honest, I don't want to get Eunice in bad—"

"Oh, no! we all know you don't want to get her in bad—unless it can be done with abserlute safety to your own precious self. Well—it can't, ma'am. You keep on like you've begun—and your middle name'll soon be trouble! Good morning, ma'am."

Fibsy rose, bowed and left the room so suddenly that Fifi hadn't time to stop him if she had wanted to. And he left behind him a decidedly scared little woman.

Fibsy then went straight to the offices of Mason Elliott.

He was admitted and given an audience at once.

"What is it, McGuire?" asked the broker.

"A lot of things, Mr. Elliott. First of all—I suppose the police are quite satisfied with the alibis of you and Mr. Hendricks?"

"Yes," and Elliott looked curiously into the grave, earnest little face. He had resented, at first, the work of this boy, but after Fleming Stone had explained his worth, Elliott soon began to see it for himself.

"They are unimpeachable," he went on; "I was at home, and Mr. Hendricks was in Boston. This has been proved over and over by many witnesses, both authentic and credible."

"Yes," Fibsy nodded. "I'm sure of it, too. And, of course, that lets you two out. Now, Mr. Elliott, the butler didn't do it F. Stone says that's a self-evident fact. Bringin' us back—as per usual to the two ladies. But, Mr. Elliott, neither of those ladies did it."

"Bless you, my boy, that's my own opinion, of course, but how can we prove it?"

Fibsy deeply appreciated the "we" and gave the speaker a grateful smile.

"There you are, Mr. Elliott, how can we? Mr. Stone, as you know, is the cleverest detective in the world, but he's no magician. He can't find the truth, if the truth is hidden in a place he can't get at."

"Have you any idea, McGuire, who the murderer was?"

"No, sir, I haven't. But I've an idea where to get an idea. And I want you to help me."

"Surely—that goes without saying."

"You'd do anything for Mrs. Embury, wouldn't you?"

"Anything." The simple assertion told the whole story, and Fibsy nodded with satisfaction.

"Then tell me truly, sir, please, wasn't Mr. Embury a—a—a—"

"Careful there—he's dead, you know."

"Yes, I know—but it's necessary, sir. Wasn't he a—I don't know the right term, but wasn't he a money-grabber?"

"In what way?" Elliott spoke very gravely.

You know best, sir. He was your partner—had been for some years. But—on the side, now—didn't he do this? Lend money-sorta personally, you know—on security."

"And if he did?"

"Didn't he demand big security—didn't he get men— his friends even—in his power—and then come down on 'em—oh, wasn't he a sort of a loan shark?"

"Where did you get all this?"

"I put together odds and ends of talk I've heard—and it must be so. That Mr. Patterson, now—"

"Patterson! What do you know of him?"

"Nothing, but that he owed Mr. Embury a lot, and his household stuff was the collateral—and—"

"Were did you learn that? I insist on knowing!"

"Servants' gossip, sir. I picked it up in the apartment house. He and the Emburys live in the same one, you know."

"McGuire, you are on a wrong trail. Mr. Embury may have lent money to his friends—may have had collateral security from them —probably did—but that's nothing to do with his being killed. And as it is a blot on his memory, I do not want the matter made public."

"I understand that, Mr. Elliott—neither do I. But sposin' the discovery of the murderer hinges on that very thing—that very branch of Mr. Embury's business—then mustn't it be looked into?"

"Perhaps it—must—but not by you."

"No, sir, By F. Stone."

CHAPTER 17: HANLON'S AMBITION

An important feature of Fleming Stone's efficiency was his ability to make use of the services of others. In the present case, he skilfully utilized both Shane and Driscoll's energies, and received their reports— diplomatically concealing the fact that he was making tools of them, and letting them infer that he was merely their co-worker.

Also, he depended greatly on Fibsy's assistance. The boy was indefatigable, and he did errands intelligently, and made investigations with a minute attention to details, that delighted the heart of his master.

Young McGuire had all the natural attributes of a detective, and under the tuition of Fleming Stone was advancing rapidly.

When assisting Stone on a case, the two usually lived together at some hotel, Stone going back and forth between there and his own home, which was now in a Westchester suburb.

It was part of the routine that the two should breakfast together and plan the day's work. These breakfasts were carefully arranged meals, with correct appointments, for Stone had the boy's good at heart, and was glad to train him in deportment for his own sake; but also, he desired that Fibsy should be presentable in any society, as the pursuit of the detective calling made it often necessary that the boy should visit in well-conducted homes.

Fibsy was, therefore, eating his breakfast after the most approved formula, when Stone said, "Well, Fibs, how about Sykes and Barton? Now for the tale of your call on Willy Hanlon yesterday."

"I went down there, Mr. Stone, but I didn't see Hanlon. He was out. But I did a lot better. I saw Mr. Barton, of Sykes and Barton, and I got an earful! It seems friend Willy has ambitions."

"In what line?"

"Upward! Like the gentleman in the poetry-book, he wants to go higher, higher, ever higher—"

"Aeroplane?"

"No, not that way—steeplejack."

"Painting spires?"

"Not only spires, but signs in high places—dangerous places-and, you know, Mr. Stone, he told us—that day at the Embury house —that he didn't climb—that he painted signs, and let other people put them up."

"Yes; well? What of it?"

"Only this: why did he try to deceive us? Why, Mr. Barton says he's a most daring climber—he's practicing to be a human fly."

"A human fly? Is that a new circus stunt?"

"You know what I mean. You've seen a human fly perform, haven't you?"

"Oh, that chap who stood on his head on the coping of the Woolworth Building to get contributions for the Red Cross work? Yes, I remember. He wasn't Hanlon, was he?"

"No, sir; he was the original—or one of the first ones. There are lots of human flies, now. They cut up tricks all over the country. And Willy Hanlon is practicing for that but he doesn't want it known."

"All right, I won't tell. His guilty secret is safe with me!"

"Now, you're laughing at me, Mr. Stone! All right just you wait —and Hanlon goes around on a motor-cycle, too!"

"He does! Then we are undone! What a revelation! And, now, Fibs, if you'll explain to me the significance of Hanlon's aspiring ambitions and his weird taste for motor-cycles, I'll be obliged."

Fibsy was extremely, even absurdly, sensitive to irony. Sometimes it didn't affect him seriously, and then, again, he would be so hurt and embarrassed by it, that it fairly made him unable to talk.

In this instance, it overcame him utterly, and his funny little freckled face turned red, and his eyes lost their eagerness and showed only chagrin.

"Come, come," said Stone, regretting his teasing, but determined to help the boy overcome his sensitiveness to it, "brace up, Fibs; you know I meant no harm. Forgive a chap, can't you—and begin all over again. I know you have something in your noddle —and doubtless, something jolly well worth while."

"Well—I—oh, wait a minute, Mr. Stone—I'm a fool, but I can't help it. When you come at me like that, I lose all faith in my notions. For it's only a notion—and a crazy one at that, and —well, sir, you wait till I've worked it up a little further —and if there's anything to it—I'll expound. Now, what's my orders for to-day?"

Fibsy had an obstinate streak in his make-up, and Fleming Stone was too wise to insist on the boy's "expounding" just then.

Instead, he said, pleasantly: "To-day, Fibs, I want you to make a round of the drug stores. It's not a hopeful job—indeed, I can't think it can amount to anything—but have a try at it. You remember, Mr. Hendricks had the earache—"

"I do, indeed! He had it a month ago—and what's more, he denied it—at first."

"Yes; well, use your discretion for all it's worth—but get a line on the doctor that prescribed for him—it was a bad case, you know—and find out what he got to relieve him and where he got it."

"Yessir. Say, Mr. Stone, is Mr. Hendricks implicated, do you think?"

"In the murder? Why, he was in Boston at the time— a man can't be in two places at once, can he?"

"He cannot! He has a perfect alibi—hasn't he, Mr. Stone?"

"He sure has, Fibsy. And yet—he was in the party that discussed the possibilities of killing people by the henbane route."

"Yessir—but so was Mr. Patterson—Mis' Desternay said so."

"The Patterson business must be looked into. I'll attend to that to-day—I'll also see Mr. Elliott about that matter of personal loans that Mr. Embury seemed to be conducting as a side business."

"Yes, do, please. Mr. Stone, it would be a first-class motive, if Mr. Embury had a strangle-hold on somebody who owed him a whole lot and couldn't pay, and—"

"Fine motive, my boy—but how about opportunity? You forget those bolted doors."

"And Mr. Patterson had borrowed money of Mr. Embury—"

"How do you know that?"

"I heard it—oh, well, I got it from one of the footmen of the apartment house—"

"Footmen! What do you mean?"

"You know there's a lot of employees—porters, rubbish men, doormen, hallmen, pages and Lord knows what! I lump 'em all under the title of footmen. Anyway, one of those persons told me—for a consideration—a lot about the private affairs of the tenants. You know, Mr. Stone, those footmen pick up a lot of information— overhearing here and there—and from the private servants kept by the tenants."

"That's true, Fibs; there must be a mine of information available in that way."

"There is, sir. And I caught onto a good deal—and specially, I learned that Mr. Patterson is in the faction— or whatever you call it—that didn't want Mr. Embury to be president of that club."

"And so you think Mr. Patterson had a hand in the murder?"

Stone's face was grave, and there was no hint of banter in his tone, so Fibsy replied, earnestly, "Well, he is the man who has lots of empty jam jars go down in the garbage pails."

"But he has lots of children."

"Yes, sir—four. Oh, well, I suppose a good many people like raspberry jam."

"Go on, Fibsy; don't be discouraged. As I've often told you, one scrap of evidence is worth considering. A second, against the same man—is important—and a third, is decidedly valuable."

"Yessir, that's what I'm bankin' on. You see, Mr. Patterson, now—he's over head and ears in debt to Embury. He was against Embury for club president. He was present at the henbane discussion. And—he's an habitual buyer of raspberry jam."

"Some counts," and Fleming Stone looked thoughtful. "But not entirely convincing. How'd he get in?"

"You know his apartment is directly beneath the Embury apartment —but two floors below."

"Might as well be ten floors below. How could he get in?"

"Somebody got in, Mr. Stone. You know as well as I do, that neither Mrs. Embury nor Miss Ames committed that murder. We must face that."

"Nor did Ferdinand do it. I'll go you all those assumptions."

"All right, sir; then somebody got in from the outside."

"How?"

"Mr. Stone, haven't you ever read detective stories where a murder was committed in a room that was locked and double-locked and yet somebody did get in—and the fun of the story is guessing how he got in."

"Fiction, my boy, is one thing—fact is another."

"No, sir; they're one and the same thing!"

"All right, son; have it your own way. Now, if you're ready to get ready, skittle off to your chain of drug stores,

and run down a henbane purchase by any citizen of this
little old town, or adjacent boroughs."

Fibsy went off. He had recovered from the sense of
annoyance at being chaffed by Stone, but it made him
more resolved than ever to prove the strange theory he
had formed. He didn't dignify his idea by the name of
theory, but he was doggedly sticking to a notion which, he
hoped, would bring forth some strange developments and
speedily.

Laying aside his own plans for the moment, he went
about Stone's business, and had little difficulty in finding
the nearby druggist whom Hendricks frequently
patronized.

"Alvord Hendricks? Sure he trades here," said the
dapper young clerk. "He buys mostly shaving-cream and
tooth-paste, but here's where he buys it."

"Righto! And, say, a month or so ago, he bought some
hyoscine—"

"Oh, no, excuse me, he did not! That's not sold hit or
miss. But maybe you mean hyoscyamine. That's another
thing."

"Why, maybe I do. Look up the sale, can't you, and
make sure."

"Why should I?"

Fibsy explained that in the interests of a police
investigation it might be better to acquiesce than to
question why, and the young man proved obliging.

So Terence McGuire learned that Alvord Hendricks
bought some hyoscyamine, on a doctor's prescription,
about a month ago—the same to be used to relieve a
serious case of earache.

But there was no record of his having bought
hyoscyarnus, which was the deadly henbane used in the
medicine dropper-nor was there any other record of
hyoscyamine against him.

Satisfied that he had learned all he could, Fibsy
continued his round of drug-store visits, in an ever-

widening circle, but got no information on any henbane sales whatever.

"Nothin' doin'," he told himself. "Whoever squirted that henbane from that squirter into that ear—brought said henbane from a distance, which, to my mind, indicates a far-seeing and intelligent reasoning power."

His present duty done, he started forth on his own tour of investigation. He went to a small boarding house, in an inconspicuous street, the address of which had been given him by Mr. Barton, and asked for Mr. Hanlon.

"He ain't home," declared the frowning landlady who opened the door.

"I know it," returned Fibsy, nonchalantly, "but I gotta go up to his room a minute. He sent me."

"How do I know that?"

"That's so, how do you?" Fibsy's grin was sociable. "Well, look here, I guess this'll fix it. I'm errand boy to— you know who—" he winked mysteriously, "to the man he takes his acrobat lessons off of."

"Oh," the woman looked frightened. "Hush up—it's all right. Only don't mention no names. Go on upstairs— third floor front."

"Yep," and Fibsy went quietly up the stairs.

Hanlon's room was not locked, but a big wardrobe inside was—and nothing else was of interest to the visitor. He picked at the lock with his knife, but to no avail.

As he stood looking wistfully at the wardrobe door, a cheerful voice sounded behind him:

"I'll open it for you—what do you want out of it?"

Fibsy looked up quickly, to see Hanlon himself, smiling at him. Quick to take a cue, the boy didn't show any embarrassment, but putting out his hand said, "How do you do, Mr. Hanlon?"

"Fine. How's yourself? And why the sneak visit, my boy?"

Fibsy looked his questioner square in the eye, and then said, "Oh, well, I s'pose I may as well speak right out."

"You sure may. Either tell the truth, or put up such a convincing lie that I'll think it's the truth. Go ahead."

"Here goes, then," Fibsy made a quick decision, that Hanlon was too keen to stand for any lie. "I'm engaged on the Embury murder case."

"I know that's true—though it's hard to believe."

Fibsy chose to ignore this dig, and went on. "I'm here because I want to see how you're mixed up in it."

"Oh, you do! Why not ask me?"

"All right, I ask you. How are you connected with the murder of Sanford Embury?"

"Will anything I say be used against me?" Hanlon's tone was jocular, but he was staring hard at Fibsy's face.

"If it's usable," was the nonchalant reply.

"Well, use it if you can. I'm mixed up in the matter, as you put it, because I'm trying to find the murderer on my own account."

"Why do you want the murderer on your own account?"

"I didn't agree to answer more than one question. But I will. I don't want the murderer particularly—but I'm interested in the case. I've the detective instinct myself—and I thought if I could track down the villain—I might get a reward—"

"Is there one offered?"

"Not that I know of—but I daresay either Mr. Elliott or Mr. Hendricks would willingly pay to have the murderer found."

"Why those two? Why not Mrs. Embury?"

"Innocent child! Those two are deeply, desperately, darkly in love with the—the widow."

"Let's leave her out of this!"

"Ha, ha! a squire of dames, eh? and at your age! All right —leave the lady's name out. But I've confessed my hidden purpose. Now tell me what brings you to my domicile, on false pretenses, and why do I find you on the point of breaking into my wardrobe?"

"Truth does it! I wanted to see if I could find a false beard and a white turban."

"Oh, you did! And what good would that do you? You have cleverly discerned that I assumed an innocent disguise, in order to give aid and comfort to a most worthy dame of advanced years."

"You did but why?"

"Are you Paul Pry? You'll drive me crazy with your eternal 'why?'"

"All right, go crazy, then—but, why?"

"The same old reason," and Hanlon spoke seriously. "I'm trying, as I said, to find the Embury murderer, and I contrived that session with the old lady in hopes of learning something to help me in finding him."

"And did you?"

"I learned that she is a harmless, but none the less, positively demented woman. I learned that she deceives herself—in a way, hypnotizes herself, and she believes she sees and hears things that she does not see and hear."

"And tastes them? and smells them?"

"There, too, she deceives herself. Surely, you don't take in that story of her 'vision'?"

"I believe she believes it."

"Yes, so do I. Now, look here, McGuire; I'm a good-natured sort, and I'm willing to overlook this raid of yours, if you'll join forces. I can help you, but only if you're frank and honest in whacking up with whatever info you have. I know something—you know something—will you go in cahoots?"

"I would, Mr. Hanlon," and Fibsy looked regretful, "if I was my own boss. But, you see, I'm under orders. I'm F. Stone's helper—and I'll tell you what he says I may—and that's all."

"That goes. I don't want any more than your boss lets you spill. And now, honest, what did you come here for?"

"To look in that wardrobe, as I said."

"Why, bless your heart, child, you're welcome to do that."

Hanlon drew a key from his pocket, and flung the wardrobe door wide.

"There you are—go to it!"

Swiftly, but methodically, Fibsy took down every article of wearing apparel the wardrobe contained, glanced at it and returned it, Hanlon looking on with an amused expression on his face.

"Any incriminating evidence?" he said at last, as Fibsy hung up the final piece of clothing.

"Not a scrap," was the hearty reply. "If I don't get more evidence offen somebody else than I do from you, I'll go home empty-handed!"

"Let me help you," and Hanlon spoke kindly; "I'll hunt evidence with you."

"Some day, maybe. I've got to-day all dated up. And, say, why did you tell me you wasn't a steeplejack painter, when you are?"

"You're right, I am. But I don't want it known, because I'm going to branch out in a new field soon, and I don't want that advertised at present."

"I know, Mr. Barton told me. You're going to be a human fly, and cut up pranks on the edges of roofs of skyscrapers—"

"Hush, not so loud. Yes, I am, but the goal is far distant. But I'm going to have a whack at it—and I know I can succeed, in time."

Hanlon's eyes had a faraway, hopeful look, as if gazing into a future of marvelous achievement in his chosen field. "Oh, I say, boy, it's glorious, this becoming expert in something difficult. It pays for all the work and training and practice!"

The true artist ambition rang in his voice, and Fibsy gazed at him fascinated, for the boy was a hero-worshipper, and adored proficiency in any art.

"When you going to exhibit?" he asked eagerly.

"A little try at it next week. Want'a come?"

"Don't I. Where?"

"Hush! I'll whisper. Philadelphia."

"I'll be there! Lemme 'no the date and all."

"Yes, I will. Must you go? Here's your hat."

Fibsy laughed, took the hint and departed.

"What a feller!" he marveled to himself, as he went on his way. "Oh, gee! what a feller!"

Chapter 18: The Guilty One

"Alvord, you shock me—you amaze me! How dare you talk to me of love, when my husband hasn't been dead a fortnight?"

"What matter, Eunice? You never really loved Sanford—"

"I did—I did!"

"Not lately, anyhow. Perhaps just at first—and then, not deeply. He carried you originally by storm—it was an even toss-up whether he or Elliott or I won out. He was the most forceful of the three, and he made you marry him—didn't he now?"

"Don't talk nonsense. I married Sanford of my own free will—"

"Yes, and in haste, and repented at leisure. Now, don't be hypocritical, and pretend to grieve for him. His death was shocking—fearful—but you're really relieved that he is gone. Why not admit it?"

"Alvord, stop such talk! I command you! I won't listen!"

"Very well, dearest, I'll stop it. I beg your pardon—I forgot myself, I confess. Now, let me atone. I love you, Eunice, and I'll promise not to tell you so, or to talk about it now, if you'll just give me a ray of hope—a glimmer of anticipation. Will you—sometime—darling, let me tell you of my love? After such an interval as you judge proper? Will you, Eunice?"

"No, I will not! I don't love you—I never did and never can love you! How did you ever get such an idea into your head?"

The beautiful face expressed surprise and incredulity, rather than anger, and Eunice's voice was gentle. In such a mood, she was even more attractive than in her more vivacious moments.

Unable to control himself, Hendricks took a step toward her, and folded her in his arms.

She made no effort to disengage herself, but said, in a tone of utter disdain, "Let me go, Alvord; you bore me."

As she had well known, this angered him far more than angry words would have done.

He released her instantly, but his face was blazing with indignation.

"Oh, I do—do I? And who can make love to you, and not bore you? Elliott?"

"You are still forgetting yourself."

"I am not! I am thinking of myself only. Oh, Eunice— dear Eunice, I have loved you so long and I have been good. All the time you were Sanford's wife, I never so much as called you 'dear'—never gave you even a look that wasn't one of respect for my friend's wife. But now— now, that you are free—I have a right to woo you. It is too soon—yes, I know that—but I will wait—wait as long as you command, if you'll only promise me that I may— sometime—"

"Never! I told you that before—I do not want to be obliged to repeat it! Please understand, once for all, I have no love to give you—"

"Because it is another's! Eunice—tell me you do not care for Elliott—and I won't say another word—now. I'll wait patiently —for a year—two years—as long as you wish—only give me the assurance that you will not marry Mason Elliott."

"You are impossible! How dare you speak to me of my marriage with anybody, when my husband is only just dead? One word more, Alvord, on the subject, and I shall forbid you my house!"

"All right, my lady! Put on your high and mighty air, if you choose—but before you marry that man—make sure that he did not himself prepare the way for the wedding!"

"What do you mean? Are you accusing Mason of—"

"I make no accusations. But—who did kill Sanford? I know you didn't do it—and Elliott has engaged Stone to prove that you didn't. It is absurd, we all know, to suspect Aunt Abby—I was out of town—who is left but Mason?"

"Hush! I won't listen to, such a suggestion! Mason was at his home that night."

"Are you sure?"

"Of course, I'm sure! And I don't have to have it proved by a detective either! And now, Alvord Hendricks, you may go! I don't care to talk to anyone who can make such a contemptible accusation against a lifelong friend!"

But before Hendricks left, Elliott himself came in.

He was grave and preoccupied. He bowed a little curtly to Hendricks, and, as he took Eunice's hand, he said, "May I see you alone? I want to talk over some business matters—and I'm pressed for time."

"Oh, all right," Hendricks said, "I can take a hint. I'm going. How's your sleuth progressing, Elliott? Has Mr. Stone unearthed the murderer yet?"

"Not yet—but soon," and Elliott essayed to pass the subject off lightly.

"Very soon?" Hendricks looked at him in a curious manner.

"Very soon, I think."

"That's interesting. Would it be indiscreet to ask in what direction one must look for the criminal?"

"It would very." Elliott smiled a little. "Now run along, Hendricks, that's a good chap. I've important business matters to talk over with Eunice."

Hendricks went, and Elliott turned to Eunice, with a grave face,

"I've been going over Sanford's private papers," he said, "and, Eunice, there's a lot that we want to keep quiet."

"Was Sanford a bad man?" she asked, her quiet, white face imploring a negative answer.

"Not so very, but, as you know, he had a love of money—a sort of acquisitiveness, that led him into questionable dealings. He loaned money to any one who would give him security—"

"That isn't wrong!"

"Not in itself—but, oh, Eunice, I can't explain it to you—or, at least, I don't want to—but Sanford lent money to men—to his friends—who were in great exigency—who gave their choicest belongings, their treasures as security—and then—he had no leniency—no compassion for them—"

"Why should he have?"

"Because—well, there is a justice, that is almost criminal. Sanford was a—a Shylock! There, can you understand now?"

"Who were his debtors? Alvord?"

"Yes; Hendricks was one who owed him enormous sums—and he was going to make lots of trouble—I mean Sanford was—why, Eunice, in Sanford's private safe are practically all of Hendricks' stocks and bonds, put up as collateral. Sanford holds mortgages on all Hendricks' belongings—real estate, furniture—everything. Now, just at the time Sanford died these notes were due—this indebtedness of Hendricks to Sanford had to be paid, and merely the fact of San's death occurring just when it did saved Alvord from financial ruin."

"Do you mean Sanford would have insisted on the payment?"

"Yes."

"Then—oh, Mason I can't say it—I wouldn't breathe it to any one but you but could Alvord have killed Sanford?"

"Of course not, Eunice. He was in Boston, you know."

"Yes, I know. But—Mason, he hinted to me just now, that that maybe you killed San."

"Did he, dear? Then he was angry or—or crazy! He doesn't think so. Perhaps he was—very jealous."

"Yes, he was! How did you know?"

"I have eyes. You don't care for him—particularly—
do you —Eunice?"

Their eyes met and in one long look, the truth was
told. A great love existed between these two, and both
had been honest and honorable so long as Eunice was
Sanford's wife. And even now, though Embury was gone,
Elliott made no protestation of love to his widow—said no
word that might not have been heard by the whole world,
but they both knew—no word was necessary.

A beautiful expression came over Eunice's face—she
smiled a little and the love-light in her eyes was
unmistakable.

"I shall never lose my temper again," she said, softly,
and Mason Elliott believed her.

"Another big debtor to Sanford is Mr. Patterson," he
went on, forcing himself to calm his riotous pulses, and
continue his business talk.

"How is that man mixed into our affars?"

"He's very much mixed up in San's affairs. But,
Eunice, I don't want to burden you with all these details.
Only, you see, Alvord is your lawyer, and—it's
confoundedly awkward—"

"Look here, Mason, do this—can't you? Forgive
Alvord all Sanford's claims on him. I mean, wipe the
slate clean, as far as he is concerned. I don't want his
money—I mean I don't want to keep his stocks and
things. Give them all back to him, and hush the matter
up. You know, we four, Sanford and Alvord and you and
I, are the old quartet—the 'three boys and a girl' who
used to play together. Now one of us is gone—don't let's
make any trouble for another of the group. I've enough
money without realizing on Alvord's securities. Give
them all back to him—and forget it. Can't we?"

"Why, yes, I suppose so—if you so decree. What about
Patterson?"

"Oh, those things you and Alvord must look after. I've no head for business. And anyway—must it be attended to at once?"

"Not immediately. Sanford's estate is so large, and his debtors so numerous, it will take months to get it adjusted."

"Very well, let anything unpleasant wait for a while, then."

Now, on this very day, and at this very hour, Fibsy was in Philadelphia, watching the initial performance of a new "human fly."

A crowd was gathered about the tall skyscraper, where the event was to take place, and when Hanlon appeared he was greeted by a roar, of cheering that warmed his applause-loving heart.

Bowing and smiling at his audience, he started on his perilous climb up the side of the building.

The sight was thrilling—nerve-racking. Breathlessly the people watched as he climbed up the straight, sheer facade, catching now at a window ledge—now at a bit of stone ornamentation—and again, seeming to hold on by nothing at all—almost as a real fly does.

When he negotiated a particularly difficult place, the crowd forebore to cheer, instinctively feeling it might disturb him.

He went on—higher and higher—now pausing to look down and smile at the sea of upturned faces below—and, in a moment of bravado, even daring to pause, and hanging on by one hand and one foot, "scissor out" his other limbs and wave a tiny flag which he carried.

On he went, and on, at last reaching the very top. Over the coping he climbed, and gaily waved his flag as he bowed to the applauding crowds below.

Then, for Hanlon was a daring soul, the return journey was begun.

Even more fascinating than the ascent was this hazardous task.

Fibsy watched him, noted every step, every motion, and was fairly beside himself with the excitement of the moment.

And, then, when half a dozen stories from the ground—when success was almost within his grasp something happened. Nobody knew what—a misstep—a miscalculation of distance—a slipping stone—whatever the cause, Hanlon fell. Fell from the sixth story to the ground.

Those nearest the catastrophe stepped back—others pushed forward—and an ambulance, ready for such a possible occasion, hurried the wounded man to the hospital.

For Hanlon was not killed, but so crushed and broken that his life was but a matter of hours—perhaps moments.

"Let me in—I must see him!" Fibsy fought the doormen, the attendants, the nurses.

"I tell you I must! In the name of the law, let me in!"

And then a more coherent insistence brought him permission, and he was immediately admitted to Hanlon's presence.

A priest was there, administering extreme unction, and saying such words of comfort as he could command, but at sight of Fibsy, Hanlon's dull eyes brightened and he partially revived.

"Yes—him!" he cried out, with a sudden flicker of energy, "I must talk to him!"

The doctor fell back, and made way for the boy. "Let him talk, if he likes," he said; "nothing matters now. Poor chap, he can't live ten minutes."

Awed, but very determined, Fibsy approached the bedside.

He looked at Hanlon—strangely still and white, yet his eyes burning with a desperate desire to communicate something.

"Come here," he whispered, and Fibsy drew nearer to him.

"You know?" he said.

"Yes," and Fibsy glanced around as if f to be sure of his witnesses to this strange confession, "you killed Sanford Embury."

"I did. I—I—oh, I can't—talk. You talk—"

"This is his confession," Fibsy turned to the priest and the doctor; "listen to it." Then addressing himself again to Hanlon, he resumed: "You climbed up the side of the apartment house—on the cross street—not on Park Avenue—and you got in at Miss Ames' window."

"Yes," said Hanlon, his white lips barely moving, but his eyes showing acquiescence.

"You went straight through those two rooms—softly, not awakening either of the ladies—and you killed Mr. Embury, and then—you returned through the bedrooms—" " Again the eyes said yes.

"And, passing through Miss Ames' room, she stirred, and thinking she might be awake, you stopped and leaned over her to see. There you accidentally let fall—perhaps from your breast pocket- -the little glass dropper you had used—and as you bent over the old lady, she grabbed at you, and felt your jersey sleeve—even bit at it—and tasted raspberry jam. That jam got on that sleeve as you climbed up past the Patterson's window, where a jar of it was on the window-sill—"

"Yes—that's right," Hanlon breathed, and on his face was a distinct look of admiration for the boy's perception.

"You wore a faintly-ticking wrist-watch—the same one you're wearing now—and the odor of gasoline about you was from your motor-cycle. You, then, were the 'vision' Miss Ames has so often described, and you glided silently away from her bedside, and out at the window by which you entered. Gee! it was some stunt!"

This tribute of praise was wrung from Fibsy by the sudden realization that what he had for some time surmised was really true!

"I guess it was that jam that did for you," he went on, "but, say, we ain't got no time for talkin'."

Hanlon's eyes were already glazing, his breath; came shorter and it was plain to be seen the end was very near.

"Who hired you?" Fibsy flung the question at him with such force that it seemed to rouse a last effort of the ebbing life in the dying man and he answered, faintly but clearly:

"Alvord Hendricks—ten thousand dollars—" and then Hanlon was gone.

Reminding the priest and the doctor that they were witnesses to this dying confession, Fibsy rushed from the room and back to New York as fast as he could get there.

He learned by telephone that Fleming Stone was at Mrs. Embury's, and, pausing only to telephone for Shane to go at once to the same house, Fibsy jumped into a taxicab and hurried up there himself.

"It's all over," he burst forth, as he dashed into the room where Stone sat, talking to Eunice. Mason Elliott was there, too—indeed, he was a frequent visitor—and Aunt Abby sat by with her knitting.

"What is?" asked Stone, looking at the boy in concern. For Fibsy was greatly excited, his fingers worked nervously and his voice shook.

"The whole thing, Mr. Stone! Hanlon's dead—and he killed Mr. Embury."

"Yes—I know—" Fleming Stone showed no surprise. "Did he fall?"

"Yessir. Got up the climb all right, and 'most down again, and fell from the sixth floor. Killed him—but not instantly. I went to the hospital, and he confessed."

"Who did?" said Shane, coming in at the door as the last words were spoken.

"Willy Hanlon—a human fly."

And then Fleming Stone told the whole story—Fibsy adding here and there his bits of information.

"But I don't understand," said Shane, at last, "why would that chap kill Mr. Embury?"

"Hired," said Fibsy, as Stone hesitated to speak; "hired by a man who paid him ten thousand dollars."

"Hanlon a gunman!" said Shane, amazed.

"Not a professional one," Fibsy said, "but he acted as one in this case. The man who hired him knew he was privately learning to be a 'human fly,' and he had the diabolical thought of hiring him to climb up this house, and get in at the only available window, and kill Mr. Embury with that henbane stuff."

"And the man's name?" shouted Shane, "the name of the real criminal?"

Fibsy sat silent, looking at Stone.

"His name is Alvord E. Hendricks," was Stone's quiet reply.

An instant commotion arose. Eunice, her great eyes full of horror, ran to Aunt Abby, who seemed about to collapse from sheer dismay.

Mason Elliott started up with a sudden "Where is he?" and Shane echoed, with a roar: "Yes, where is he? Can he get away?"

"No," said Stone; "he can't. I have him covered day and night by my men. At present, Mr. Shane, he is—I am quite sure—in his office—if you want to go there—"

"If I want to go there! I should say I do! He'll get his!"

And in less than half an hour, Shane had taken Alvord Hendricks into custody, and in due time that arch criminal received the retribution of justice.

Shane gone, Fibsy went over the whole story once again.

"You see, it was Mr. Stone's keeping at it what did it. He connected up Hanlon and the jam—he connected up Mr. Hendricks and the Hamlet business—we connected up Hanlon and the gasoline- -and Hanlon and the jersey and the motor-cycle and all!" Fibsy grew excited; "then we connected up Hendricks and his 'perfect alibi.' Always distrust the perfect alibi—that's one of Mr. Stone's first maxims. Well, this Hendricks—he had a pluperfect alibi—couldn't be shaken—so Mr. Stone, he says, the more perfect the alibi, the more we must distrust it. So he went for that alibi—and he found that Mr. Hendricks was sure in Boston that night, but he didn't have any real reason, not any imperative reason for going—it was a sorta trumped up trip. Well—that's the way it was. He had to get Mr. Embury out of the way just then, or be shown up—a ruined man—and, too, he was afraid Mr. Embury'd be president of the club—and, too—he wanted to—"

Fibsy gave one eloquent glance at Eunice, and paused abruptly in his speech. Every one knew—every one realized that love of Sanford Embury's wife was one reason, at least, for the fatal deed. Everybody realized that Alvord Hendricks was a villain through and through—that he had killed his friend—though not by his own hand.

Eunice never saw Hendricks again. She and Aunt Abby went away for a year's stay. They traveled in lovely lands, where the scenery and climate brought rest and peace to Eunice's troubled heart, and where she learned, by honest effort, to control her quick temper.

And then, after two of the one-time friendly quartet had become only a past memory, the remaining two, Eunice and Mason Elliott, found happiness and joy.

"One of our biggest cases, F. Stone," said Fibsy, one day, reminiscently.

"It was, indeed, Fibs; and you did yourself proud."

"Great old scheme! Perfect alibi—unknown human fly—bolted doors—all the elements of a successful crime—if he hadn't slipped up on that Raspberry jam!"

THE END

Resurrected Press Mysteries From Louis Tracy

The Albert Gate Mystery
Four men murdered and a fortune in diamonds belonging to the Turkish Sultan stolen, while the Foreign Office official in charge has gone missing. Was it a common jewelry theft or was it a case of international intrigue? This is the question that barrister detective Reginald Brett must solve.

The Bartlett Mystery
When Ronald Tower is murdered on his way to a bridge game on the yacht Sans Souci it at first appears a common crime. But as Rex Carshaw finds, a tragic case of mistaken identity leads to political scandal among the rich and powerful of New York.

The Strange Case of Mortimer Fenley
When the wealthy Mortimer Fenley is struck down by a shot from an express rifle on the steps of his mansion, detectives Winter and Furneaux of Scotland Yard must find the culprit. Was it the artist who claimed he was painting a picture at the time of the shot? The disaffected younger son? Or is there another suspect?

The Stowmarket Mystery
For five generations the Fergus-Hume family has been cursed. Each of the baronets has met a violent end. When the fifth baronet is found slain by a ceremonial Japanese dagger, suspicion falls on his cousin David. It falls to barrister detective Reginald Brett to prove his innocence and find the real murder in a case that spans two continents and as many centuries.

Visit www.resurrectedpress.com

Resurrected Press Mysteries by J. S. Fletcher

The Orange-Yellow Diamond
When an elderly pawnbroker is murdered in the London parish of Paddington, a young, down on his luck writer is accused of the crime. But then it's found the pawnbroker had had in his possession an extraordinary South African diamond worth over eighty-thousand pounds — a diamond that's now missing. It falls to Melky Rubenstein to unravel the mystery and prove the young man's innocence.

The Middle Temple Murder
When an elderly man's body is found on the steps of chambers in the Midde Temple, one of the Inns of Court, it falls to newspaperman Frank Spargo and Detective-Sergeant Rathbury to solve the crime. The murdered man, for indeed it was murder, was found with no money or identification on his person except for a piece of paper with the name and address of a young barrister. Who is the victim? Why was he killed? Who is the murderer?

Scarhaven Keep
Bassett Oliver, the famed actor, has gone missing. When Oliver fails to show for a rehearsal, aspiring playwright Richard Copplestone finds himself sent to the small village of Scarhaven on the northern coast of England to track down the actors movements. What he finds is mystery. Find the answers as Copplestone unravels the mystery of Scarhaven Keep.

Visit www.resurrectedpress.com

Resurrected Press Mysteries by Fergus Hume

The Green Mummy

Professor Braddock hoped to compare the burial practices of the Egyptians with those of the ancient Peruvians with his latest acquisition, the mummy of the last Inca, Caxas. But on arrival, the packing case proved to hold not the mummy, but the body of his assistant Sidney Bolton. It falls to Archie Hope to discover the murderer if he is to marry the professors step-daughter, Lucy Kendal. Who killed Bolton and where is the mummy? Was it the sea captain Hervey? The mysterious Don Pedro? Cockatoo the Polynesian servant? The professor, himself? And what has become of the emeralds? These are the questions that Hope must answer amongst the secrets of the past in The Green Mummy.

The Mystery of a Hansom Cab

"Truth is said to be stranger than fiction, and certainly the extraordinary murder which took place in Melbourne Friday morning goes a long way towards verifying that saying." Thus opens The Mystery of a Hansom Cab, the best selling mystery of the nineteenth century. When a man is found dead in a hansom cab one of Melbourne's leading citizens is accused of the murder. He pleads his innocence, yet refuses to give an alibi. It falls to a determined lawyer and an intrepid detective to find the truth, revealing long kept secrets along the way. Fergus Hume's first and perhaps most famous mystery... The Mystery Of A Hansom Cab.

Visit www.resurrectedpress.com

Resurrected Press Mysteries from the Dr. John Thorndyke Series

Dr. John Thorndyke - Lecturer on Medical Jurisprudence and Forensic Medicine. Before Bones, before CSI, before Quincy, M.E– there was Dr. John Thorndyke solving the most baffling cases of Edwardian London using the latest tools of medical science. Read about his cases in:

The Eye of Osiris
John Bellingham, noted Egyptologist has vanished not once but twice in the same day. Now Dr, Thorndyke must unravel the tangled claims on his estate, solve the riddle of the missing man and find the "Eye of Osiris".

The Mystery of 31 New Inn
When Dr. Jervis is whisked away in a coach with no windows to an unknown location to treat a man in a coma from undivulged causes it is Dr. Thorndyke who must come up with the solution.

The Red Thumb Mark
The first of Dr. Thorndyke's cases finds him trying to prove the innocence of a young man accused of being a diamond thief despite the fact that his finger print was found at the scene of the crime.

John Thorndyke's Cases
More cases of medical mysteries as told by his trusted assistant Jervis, M.D. Eight stories of crime and deduction in Edwardian London.

Visit www.resurrectedpress.com

Resurrected Press Mysteries by John R. Watson & Arthur J. Rees

The Hampstead Mystery

High Court Justice Sir Horace Fewbanks found shot dead in his Hampstead home, a butler with a criminal past, a scorned lover and a hint of scandal. These are the elements of the Hampstead Mystery that Detective Inspector Chippenfield of Scotland Yard must unravel with the assistance of the ambitious Detective Rolfe. But will he be able to sort out the tangled threads of this case and arrest the culprit before he is upstaged by the celebrated gentleman detective Crewe. Follow the details of this amazing case at it plays out across Hampstead, London and Scotland until it reaches a stunning conclusion in the courts of the Old Bailey.

The Mystery of the Downs

When Harry Marsland was caught in a sudden down pour he sought shelter at Cliff Farm. Met at the door by a young woman clearly expecting someone else he is only too glad to get inside to wait out the storm. When they hear a noise upstairs in the deserted house they investigate only to discover the body of the farm's owner, Frank Lumsden, dead of a gunshot wound. Who then, killed Lumsden, and why? Who was the woman expecting and did she have any roll in the murder? These are the questions that private detective Crewe must answer in The Mystery of the Downs.

Visit www.resurrectedpress.com

Other Resurrected Press Mysteries

Mysteries on a Train

Before the Orient Express there was:

The Rome Express by Arthur Griffiths
A man is found dead in his first class sleeping compartment on the express from Rome to Paris. Who was his murderer? The Countess? The English General? His brother the clergy man? The maid who has disappeared? Is the French justice system up to solving the crime? Read about it in The Rome Express.

The Passenger from Calais by Arthur Griffiths
Colonel Basil Annesley finds he is the only passenger on the train from Calais to Lucerne. That is until a mysterious woman shows up at the last minute to book a compartment. Who is after her? What is her secret? Is she a criminal or a victim? Read about it in The Passenger from Calais

Visit us at www.resurrectedpress.com

About Resurrected Press

A division of Intrepid Ink, LLC, Resurrected Press is dedicated to bringing high quality, vintage books back into publication. See our entire catalogue and find out more at www.ResurrectedPress.com.

About Intrepid Ink, LLC

Intrepid Ink, LLC provides full publishing services to authors of fiction and non-fiction books, eBooks and websites. From editing to formatting, from publishing to marketing, Intrepid Ink gets your creative works into the hands of the people who want to read them. Find out more at www.IntrepidInk.com.